BLINDSIDED

BLINDSIDED

NATALIE WHIPPLE

HOT
KEY
BOOKS

First published in Great Britain in 2014 by Hot Key Books
Northburgh House, 10 Northburgh Street, London EC1V 0AT

A CIP catalogue record for this book is available from the British Library.

ISBN: 978-1-4714-0215-9

1

This book is typeset in 10.5 Berling LT Std using Atomik ePublisher

Printed and bound by Clays Ltd, St Ives Plc

FSC

Hot Key Books supports the Forest Stewardship Council (FSC),
the leading international forest certification organisation, and is
committed to printing only on Greenpeace-approved FSC-certified paper.

www.hotkeybooks.com

Hot Key Books is part of the Bonnier Publishing Group
www.bonnierpublishing.com

To Ginger Clark, for believing in me, and to everyone at Hot Key Books, for believing in Fiona.

Chapter 1

The goalie always tenses when I approach, which makes me smile because I know I'll score before I've even kicked the ball. She can't see my eyes, can't anticipate my moves, and it turns out this makes me an excellent soccer player. I aim for the low right corner—the ball *zings* by her before she can lunge for it.

"Curse you, Fiona!" She bites back a smile. "If you weren't on my team, I'd hate you so much."

"Guess it's good I am then," I say as she kicks the ball back to me. Stopping it, I tap it back and forth between my feet like Seth taught me.

One of our defenders joins in the conversation. "We might have a chance at winning this year. It's so hard to compete when we don't have enough gifted players to make a whole team."

"It'll still be fun, though. All the schools we're playing have just as few." I roll the ball onto my foot and pop it into the air, trying to juggle it from knee to knee. It doesn't work so well. Since I haven't been playing long, I'm still struggling to visualize where my knees would be between my shorts and shin guards.

A midfielder laughs as she calls, "For someone with a

killer instinct on the field, you sure are relaxed about the competition!"

I laugh. "Maybe I'm just that good."

Or I'm enjoying the fact that all I have to worry about is my grades and soccer. That's nothing in comparison to my old life, where every day I had to stress about what my syndicate-boss father would make me steal next. The three months since I made that deal—Dad leaves us alone, and Miles, who managed to imitate Dad's mind-controlling scent, won't share it with the world—have been the best of my whole life.

The goalie snatches the ball from me, a mock glare on her face. "It's annoying that I can't argue with that, seeing as you've only been playing for a few months and you rock."

"I have a good teacher." I grin like an idiot at the thought of all the hours I've spent with Seth because of soccer.

"True." The defender sighs, looking over to the adjacent field where the boys practice. Seth and Hector pass the ball back and forth as they run across the field. Their timing is perfect, since Hector's sensitive hearing means he can hear any whispered directions. "Sometimes I can't believe Seth isn't gifted with perfect aim, because I swear he never misses."

"He's just an obsessive practicer." I'm glad none of them can see my face, because I must look like I'm lying. Seth may not have perfect aim, but he does have perfect vision—more than perfect, since it's so sharp he can see through things. Even my invisibility. And nobody knows about it.

"Girls! Ten laps and you're done!" Coach Ford's low, booming voice spreads over the field before she moves on to the boys. The other girls groan, but I happily jog with them. I'm not sure I'll ever get enough of running.

About five laps in, someone whistles long and sharp on the boys' team. Carlos. Ever since practices started, he's gloated about being starting goalie as a sophomore. Like this is supposed to impress me enough to break up with Seth and "realize the error of my ways," as he always tells me. He cups his hands around his mouth. "Looking good, Fiona!"

Hector and Seth both kick soccer balls at him, which causes the rest of the team to join in. Seth looks right at me, his eyes seeing all my post-practice grime. He says he thinks it's hot that I'm athletic, but I'm still not sure I *look* hot. He'll never give me a straight answer, like any good boyfriend, though it drives me crazy.

As I pack up my things to go, I notice some of my team members huddled together, whispering. Not in a gossipy way— they all seem nervous, maybe even scared. I follow their glances and see a man standing in the bleachers. And he's watching me. For how long, I don't know.

He's too far away to see clearly. All I can make out is long hair, a ridiculously thin frame, and black marks on his arms that I'm pretty sure are tattoos. I try not to jump to conclusions, but the way my team is freaking out puts me on edge.

I head over to them to ask, "Who's that guy in the bleachers?"

They stare at me like I'm suddenly visible. The other striker clears her throat. "Uh, we gotta go, Fi. You probably should, too, okay?"

They run off before I can ask more questions. Clearly everyone's afraid of that guy, so I'm guessing those tattoos are probably jaguars.

Which means he's from Juan's syndicate.

A chill runs down my spine. So far Juan Torres hasn't stirred up any trouble with my mom and me, but I've always wondered how long that would last.

I look back up to the bleachers to see if I can get a better visual, and the guy is gone. I stare at the spot he was standing in, wondering how I didn't catch him leaving. I only looked away for a moment. He can't have just disappeared—I should know. But he must have an ability dangerous enough to clear a field in seconds.

Hands come down on my shoulders, and I let out a little scream. Could that guy be a teleporter?

Seth laughs. "Jumpy today, are we?"

I turn around and smack his arm. "Don't do that! I thought you were…never mind."

His brow furrows. Sometimes I hate that he can see my expressions—especially because I can't. There's no hiding from him. He says in a low voice, "You look seriously scared. Did something happen?"

I look into his blue eyes, knowing it's pointless to lie. "There was a guy in the bleachers. He had big black tattoos, and the other girls freaked out and left without telling me who it was. Then when I looked back he was gone."

"Shit. Definitely one of Juan's guys—they show up every now and then." Seth goes into full worry mode. "So he saw you?"

"Pretty sure he was looking right at me."

Seth chews on his fingernail, thinking. "Hector, wrap it up, we gotta go."

Even though Hector is a field away, he calls the boys' team

4

in and they start packing up their stuff. He and Carlos are by our sides in under a minute.

"What's up?" Hector asks as he puts his earplugs back in. His ears hurt if he doesn't wear them most of the time, but he always takes them out for soccer. "We haven't done laps yet."

"One of Juan's guys was here," Seth says.

Carlos cringes. "Back on the rounds again, huh? Better tell Dad to get the money ready."

"You think he was here for that? Not me?" I ask.

Hector shrugs. "They show up every six months or so, bleed the gifted families dry, make threats. Not saying you're safe, but whoever it was probably didn't come here *for* you, you know?"

I take a deep breath, but it doesn't quite calm my nerves. "It'll take *a lot* of money for Juan to ignore me."

"Let's not think about this right now. We should get out of here." Seth puts his hand on my shoulder and follows my arm until his fingers are laced with mine. Little things like that remind me how careful we need to be about keeping his real ability secret—it can be hard to remember when I'm so used to him seeing me.

We walk towards his beat up black truck. Hector and Carlos climb into the bed, and I take the passenger side.

Seth's knuckles are white as he grips the steering wheel, and when I put my hand on his knee he's the one jumping. "Sorry, Fi, but I'm freaking out here."

"We knew this could happen." I try to sound calm. Mom and I might be out of my dad's control, but being safe from every syndicate is impossible. "My mom's been saving—we're prepared."

5

He nods. "It'll probably be fine. But we'll do whatever we have to in order to keep you safe. I promise."

I should be saying that to him. If Juan doesn't think our money is enough, there's no way I'm dragging him, Brady, or the Navarros into it. But I don't push the topic, because he'll fight me on it and I'm too tired for that. "You coming over later?"

"Of course." He smiles, his eyes flashing with mischief. "Doing homework with you is my favorite."

I laugh. So many of our study sessions have devolved into making out instead. "Yes, *homework*, because my mom is home tonight."

He frowns as he parks in front of my place. "I guess I'll take what I can get."

"You better." I hop out and wave to him as I head inside. The house is quiet and cool. I stand there for a moment to listen and wait, just in case something is off and I'm walking into a trap. Seeing that guy today brought everything back. My criminal senses are in overdrive—it feels like this is only the beginning.

Instead of showering, I sit on the couch and pull out my phone. My thumb hovers over number two, my speed dial for Miles. Maybe I'm overreacting. It certainly wouldn't be the first time. I did ruin Graham's plans to keep us safe because I didn't dare trust him. But then it doesn't hurt to be careful, to make sure Miles knows we might have trouble on the horizon.

I press the button and wait for him to answer.

Chapter 2

"Hello?" The voice is not Miles, but familiar all the same. It still weirds me out that my brothers live together after so many years of fighting, but Graham didn't exactly have a lot of places to go when he left Dad's syndicate. Miles took him in with surprisingly little convincing by Mom, I think because he wanted to spare me the pain of living with Graham.

"Where's Miles?" I ask.

"In the bathroom. You want me to hand him the phone?" I can almost picture Graham's evil grin.

"Ew, no."

He laughs. "What's up? Miles seems to get all the calls—did you lose my number?"

I wince, not really wanting to talk to Graham. He tries to be nice and does his best to make up for all he did, but it's still difficult. No matter how hard I try to forget, part of me is still scared of him. "No, I didn't lose it."

He sighs, and I think it sounds regretful. "Yeah, I figured."

"Can you tell him to call me when he gets out?"

"Actually, we're already running late. We have to pick up Allie before the movie, and she hates missing previews."

"Ugh." Allie is Graham's girlfriend. It's hard to accept that reality. Because seriously, who'd want to date an infamous syndicate lapdog? This Allie chick must have a hardcore bad boy complex, which is surprising because apparently she's *really* smart. She's twenty-one and already in a doctorate program for chemistry.

"Is it so hard to give me a message to pass on?"

Yes, yes it is. Especially when it showcases my paranoia all too well. "It's not really a message-type conversation. I'll just call—"

"Is something wrong? Is Mom okay?"

To his credit, he really does sound worried. And he did put his life on the line to get us out of the syndicate before Dad turned me into his deadliest assassin. I should probably stop throwing up walls. Well, *some* walls, at least. "She's fine, but there was a guy watching me at soccer practice…"

"What kind of guy?" There's a pause. "Don't tell me this is some kind of love triangle drama, because you can leave that to Miles."

"No!" I bite back my annoyance. "He had tattoos, Graham. And The Pack says Juan's guys come here to collect money from the gifted families every six months. Pretty sure he's with them."

He swears. There's shuffling noises, as if he's searching for something. "What'd he look like? I'll look him up in the Registry."

I roll my eyes. The government made up this Registry for people with "potentially dangerous abilities" ages ago, but it's horribly inaccurate even if a person does show up in there. Under my name it claims I may or may not be able to possess

8

other peoples' bodies, which is ridiculous. "That thing is a joke, and I didn't get a good look at him anyway."

"Hmm...you can't give me anything? I am pretty familiar with Juan's guys—maybe I'll recognize him."

It isn't likely. Juan's syndicate is bigger than Dad's, at least in numbers. When your henchmen are so recognizable, I guess there needs to be a lot more of them. The chance of Graham recognizing one guy on extortion duties in a tiny town like Madison is low. But I decide I'll humor him anyway, otherwise he might come here and check for himself. "He was in the bleachers so I couldn't see much more than his long black hair and big tattoos, but he seemed really skinny if that helps."

"How skinny?" Graham asks rather seriously.

"Uh...I don't know."

"On the verge of starving to death? Or is he gangly like your boyfriend?"

"Hey!" Seth is perfect just the way he is. He has way more muscle than people give him credit for. "Don't be a jerk or I'll hang up."

He sighs. "Well?"

I purse my lips, trying to remember the brief moment I saw him. "Maybe more on the starving to death side?"

"I was hoping you wouldn't say that."

"Why?" My heart speeds up a bit. If Graham does recognize this guy, then he's a lot worse than your average lackey.

"It's just...Juan's right-hand man fits that description. He can walk through walls, but if he eats it doesn't work. So he starves himself as much as he can. If he pops some Radiasure he can even take other people through walls with him." There's a pause, and I fill it with my own worry. "No one knows much about him, not even his name. He just goes by The Phantom."

I gulp, thinking about the way he disappeared. If it was this wall walker, he could have sunk through the bleachers to look like he was gone. "Way to freak me out, Graham."

"Sorry, he's just the first person I thought of! It probably isn't him. He'd be on big missions—not somewhere like Madison." I hear a voice in the background. "Hey, Miles is done so we gotta go. We'll talk later, okay? Tell me if you find out more."

"Sure. Bye." I hang up, determined to only talk with Miles for the rest of my life. Instead of feeling comforted, I am more on edge than ever.

I rush for the shower, hoping that'll distract me from my overactive imagination. But even with the warm water pounding my skin, I can't shake the feeling I'm being watched. Even if that guy wasn't a wall walker—maybe he jumped down or has super speed or I'm just blind—the *idea* that someone could enter any place they want is scary.

What if he walked right into my house? Is he standing on the other side of the shower curtain?

Okay, no more of that. Turning off the water, I dry myself and dress in minimal clothing. I'm invisible, so no matter where a wall walker went they still couldn't see me. Graham probably wanted to freak me out. I wish he'd grow up and stop with the teasing.

A loud knock echoes through the quiet house, and all my attempts to calm myself are ruined. I'm not sure whether I should answer or not, but I creep down the hall and check the peephole anyway.

When I see who's there, I let out a relieved sigh and unlock it. "Hey! What's with the surprise visit?"

"You didn't answer your phone. Figured you were in the shower since everyone was home from practice." Bea steps in, looking worried. She runs both hands through her wild hair. "So my brothers told me and Brady about Juan's guy. You okay?"

I purse my lips, not wanting to talk or think about him anymore. "I'm fine, but thanks for checking on me."

"You're welcome." She plops on the couch. "I'm giving up precious boyfriend time to make sure my best friend is safe, you know."

I laugh as I sit next to her. After Brady declared his love for Bea when she was under my dad's control, they finally got together after being friends since childhood. Though Brady is still worried about hurting her with his overwhelming strength, Bea is slowly bringing him around. "I'm sorry—I know how hard it is to get alone time."

Her lips stretch into a wide grin. "No kidding. Stupid brothers. They're everywhere."

"Has he kissed you yet?"

"I wish." She leans her head back. "I'm trying to be patient, but if we could move past hand holding that'd be awesome."

"He's so paranoid."

"Tell me about it. He hasn't hurt me by accident since he was like eight, but still."

I nod, feeling oddly sad the more we talk about this. Truth is, sometimes I get jealous of Bea and Brady. They might have the strength problem to deal with, but at least they're both visible. I get this pang in my gut every time she asks me to take a picture of them together—I'll never know what I look like next to Seth or anyone. "You want some ice cream? I need ice cream."

"Sure." She points at the blank TV. "And a movie."

"Okay, twist my arm." I hand her the remote and go to the kitchen. Bea likes the most chocolatey ice cream possible, so I pull out the brownie fudge and top it with more chocolate syrup.

Bea has already picked a romantic comedy from the DVR by the time I get back, and we settle in. Being constantly surrounded by guys, it's nice when we can sneak in some girl time. If we try to watch these at her house, Carlos spends the whole movie cracking lame jokes. Plus Hector tells us how stupid and unrealistic the romances are.

Just when we get to a good make-out scene, I hear the garage door open. My brow creases as I check my phone's clock. Mom isn't supposed to be home for an hour, but the door slams and she yells, "Fiona? Are you here?"

"Yeah! Did you not see Sexy Blue outside?"

Mom practically falls into the room, panting and eyes wide. When she sees me, she looks a little less panicked. "Thank goodness."

I'm not sure I want to ask, but I do anyway. "What's wrong?"

"Juan's men." She puts her hand to her heart. "A whole group of them came into the bowling alley. I left the second I saw them."

"Oh no." I could write off one guy, but a whole squad? And both of us saw them less than a few hours apart. There's no denying it now—he's come for us.

Chapter 3

Bea pauses the movie, seeming just as panicked as I feel. She grabs my hand and pulls me off the couch. "You guys should come to my house, just in case they show up here tonight."

I pull back. "No way."

"Why not?" Her voice has an edge to it, and I imagine I'm about to piss her off.

"Because the last time you guys helped me, you almost killed us with your voice, two people got shot, and your mother had to reveal things she shouldn't have." We haven't spoken of Rosa's healing ability since that day, but I'll never forget how those wounds closed up right before my eyes. "It's a miracle that I managed to keep you safe from my dad, Bea. I won't put your family in the path of Juan, especially after all you've done to avoid him."

"But—"

"I'm sorry, sweetie." Mom's initial shock seems to have faded, morphing into determination. "Fiona's right. This isn't your fight, and it's pointless to get you involved when resolving it could be as easy as striking a deal."

Bea shakes her head. "But he usually never sends more than

a couple guys! I don't think money will work."

"Don't underestimate us." Mom gives her a flat look as she opens the door telekinetically. "Do you honestly think this is the first time I've been in trouble? I wouldn't forget who you're dealing with."

I can't help but smile at my mother's show of strength. It seems like the longer we're free, the more confident she gets. I can finally see who she used to be before Dad controlled her. "You should go."

Bea clenches her jaw. "Fine, but if you're in a bind you better come to us for help."

"We will." I shuffle her towards the door. "Don't tell Seth, okay? He's already worried enough."

She stops on the porch, hands on hips. "I won't lie about your safety to him or anyone."

"I'm not asking you to. Just don't mention it if you don't have to." I sigh, feeling bad for pushing her away. The truth is, I *am* scared, and I want to let Seth and The Pack protect me. But I already brought them too close to syndicate life once—I swore to myself I wouldn't do that again. "I'll call you when I find out more. I promise."

Her eyes narrow. "You better."

"See ya!" I try to keep it light. I even watch her get back in Sexy Blue and drive away. But the second I close the door, the smile is gone. "How much money have you saved, Mom?"

She paces the living room, thinking. "Almost twenty thousand."

My heart sinks. That's chump change in syndicate money. There's no way that would buy us more than a month. "I should have gotten a job."

"No. I wanted you to enjoy life." She stops at one of her long, thin pots that frame the television. When she's not working, she spends most of her time telekinetically sculpting. "If only I could sell a few more big pieces like this. I'm just starting to get more orders, thanks to that showcase in Phoenix."

I let out a long sigh. "Why is it so hard to make money honestly?"

She chuckles. "I don't know, hon."

Silence overcomes us as we stare at each other. Mom isn't as afraid to look at me or touch me as she used to be, but it still feels like there's a gap we can never breach. It's because she can't see my eyes—she can't really understand what it means to be the way I am. Lately I hate that feeling. I want her to see me like Seth does. I'd even settle for telling her that Seth says I have her nose and eyes. But I can't betray his secret.

Sometimes that really bothers me.

"So…" I say. "What if they don't accept the money?"

Mom purses her lips, as if she was hoping I wouldn't ask. "Fight our way out and head for Tucson to meet up with Graham and Miles?"

"That might be interesting. You take their weapons, I sneak up on them from behind." I sit on the couch, oddly at ease with this conversation. "But Tucson is nowhere near outside of Juan's territory."

She sits next to me. "Well, if we go west we have Val to deal with."

Valerie Sutton's syndicate may not have a lot of territory, but Southern California still has a lot of media sway. The fact that she can read minds—literally see what people want—only helps her rake in money through every entertainment business possible. If you watch a movie, hear a song, see an ad, chances are Val has something to do with it.

And that means you pad her syndicate's pockets, pay for their Radiasure, keep her in power. But how can anyone avoid all media? Val will always bank on people's boredom.

"Something tells me Val won't be happy with us about the kidnapping incident," I say.

Mom nods. "Probably not, and if she got her hands on us she could pick our brains for all the secrets she wants."

The idea makes me sick. Not because she'd know everything about me, but because she'd know my friends' secrets—that Seth can see me, that Rosa has healing blood, and that Miles holds the key to taking out my dad. "Yeah, going west is bad."

"East isn't much better."

"Nope." The Midwest is no-man's-land, filled with roving gangs trying to build enough following to grow into a real syndicate. The Northeast belongs to Walter Barrington, who can erase memories. And the South is home to Maude Thomas, who some say is immortal but no one really knows.

"We'd have to start over and over. Forever." Mom's voice is sad, and I wonder if she just wants a home like I do. Why is that so much to ask? "There's no way we could get overseas with our abilities and no syndicate help. Not that international syndicates are any better."

"There's nowhere to run," I whisper. Maybe we got away from Dad, but that doesn't change the reality for all ultra-gifted people—everyone's looking to use you, and tools like me and

Mom are priceless. "We don't have anything else we can strike a deal with?"

"Oh, sure we do. We could trade contract jobs, or there's always selling out Miles' scent-replicating ability to take down your father. You know how much your dad and Juan hate each other. Juan would definitely go for that." Her eyes get that glint in them. "Or wait, did you mean non-horrible options?"

I roll my eyes. "Yes, preferably."

"No, we don't have any of those."

"Awesome." I pull out my phone and start typing.

Mom tries to look at the screen, but I angle it away from her. "Who're you texting?"

"Seth. He was gonna come over tonight, but I figure he shouldn't if a bunch of thugs might show up." I hit send, bummed that I can't see him at least one more time before all this goes down.

"You blamed it on me, didn't you?"

"No!" I scoff, though she's totally right. I said she wanted "mother daughter time," which is kind of what we're doing anyway. We wait in the quiet, my ears straining to hear anything that might signal an ambush.

Chapter 4

Three days go by, and no one comes to force us to work for Juan. But that doesn't stop me from worrying, because his men are everywhere. They stand outside the school and eat at the diner and loiter in the parks. All they do is watch, while everyone in town squirms and tries to pretend they're not there.

As The Pack and I take our usual courtyard table at lunch, the warm air feels heavy with fear. The sun might be shining, but it may as well be gray and cloudy with how everyone acts. People don't chat and laugh, but instead look over their shoulders while they whisper conversations.

"This is weird," I say as I sit by Seth.

"It really is." Brady claims the seat opposite me, eyeing the crowd of students. "Have you noticed that with every day Juan's people stick around, everyone seems to sit closer and closer to us? Or is that just me?"

"Not just you, bro," Carlos says. "Pretty sure they think it'll be safer to be next to the gifted kids if a fight starts."

"Talk about tables turning." Bea slides in next to Brady, glancing at the other tables with annoyance. "Hate on us for years, label us as The Pack because our abilities are stronger, but

18

when things go bad we're suddenly the coolest people around?"

"It's kind of suffocating," Seth admits. He's always been a loner, and even needs his space from me sometimes.

"At least my ears aren't killing me," Hector says through a mouthful of hamburger. "I might even be able to take out my plugs if people keep being so quiet."

"Well, as long as *you're* happy," Bea says. "So what if the town is crawling with thugs and no one knows why? Hector's ears don't hurt!"

Hector blinks a few times. "Sorry for finding a silver lining."

"That's one thin silver lining, dude," Carlos adds. "Especially when my Fiona could be in serious danger."

I groan. "If you keep talking like that I hope I do get kidnapped."

Carlos pouts. "Why are you so mean to me?"

"Because..." Seth grabs me by the waist. "She's taken."

"And it's fun," I add.

Seth laughs and kisses my cheek, to which Carlos makes a gagging sound as usual. I wish he'd stop, because I can't help being invisible. It probably wouldn't look half as weird if Seth wasn't "kissing air." What I'd give to be visible in moments like this.

Someone clears their throat behind me, and I turn to find a few students I don't know. I think they might be freshmen. "Hey, Fiona. What's up?"

"Um, nothing?" I look around our table, wondering if the rest of The Pack is weirded out by this. Seems they are. "Do you need something?"

"We just...wanted to ask you a question," one of the girls

says, looking from side to side like her backup might flee at any second.

"About what?"

The teal-haired girl practically shakes, and I can't tell if it's because of me or not. "Do you maybe know what's going on with all the guys in town?"

I bite my lip, unsure of what to say. She's asking because I'm syndicate-born, as if that makes me the expert on all criminal activity. "Why are you asking me?"

Her teal eyebrows pop up. "I…um…"

"Chill, Fi." Bea nudges my shoulder, her expression seeming to beg me to be nice to the little freshman. "She's not blaming you—we're all looking for someone who might have answers, you know?"

"We know you're cool," another girl with an abnormally small nose says. "But my parents are freaking out, and…well, they told me to ask if you recognized this kind of behavior. It's like they're standing guard, but why?"

Bea sighs, seeming to take pity on these normal girls despite her complaining a second ago. "No one's even come to take our money," she says. "We wait every night, but then nothing."

"Same here," I say, the weight of waiting feeling heavier each day. From the little I've dared to watch Juan's men, it does seem like they're staking out Madison. I wouldn't be surprised if they set up a border soon, there's so many thugs. It doesn't make sense. "I wish I knew, but I don't."

A scrawny boy steps forward. "My parents are this close to pooling money for a vigilante group. It sounds like they should."

I barely restrain my groan. "Seriously?"

"Mine were thinking The Triumvirate," the teal-haired girl says. "Or The Freedom Squad."

"Huh, we thought maybe Fighters For Peace." The boy's face is way too serious, and for the first time in my life I realize less gifted people might actually take those idiots seriously.

The girl claps her hands together. "Oh, yeah! I've heard good things—"

"Guys, stop," I say, unable to let this continue. "I may not know why Juan's people are here, but I do know you shouldn't waste your money on vigilante protection."

The girl frowns. "Why not?"

"Because they way overcharge for their services, and they use Radiasure just as much as the syndicates."

The boy's eyes bug out. "No way! They fight for good."

I shake my head. "And how can they compete with syndicates who use enhancement drugs constantly? They might have different motives, but every group in power gets what they want the same way. Vigilantes follow their own rules, kill people, take Radiasure—they justify it because they see themselves as saviors. They're con artists at best, gangs at worst. And do you know what Radiasure does to you when you use it like that?"

They shake their heads.

"It exaggerates your ability, right? Well, you get addicted to that feeling—of being more powerful—and when your body doesn't have Radiasure it *hurts*. The worst addicts go crazy from messing with their genes so much. Then they die. You want those kinds of 'vigilantes' taking your money?"

Only after I finish do I realize I shouldn't have said that. Hope has officially left the building.

"So you're saying our only option is to stay out of Juan's way," the tiny-nosed girl says quietly.

Yes, that's exactly their only option, but I can't seem to get myself to say it. They're scared enough. "No, I just meant... never mind."

The freshmen leave, and I feel slightly guilty for scaring them when they were looking for reassurance.

I barely noticed the sound of a helicopter before, but suddenly the propeller beats are loud. Looking up, I see three large helicopters zoom across the sky at disturbingly low altitude. Just when those are gone, two more come. Then one more.

"Ugh!" Hector says with his hands over his ears. "Make it stop!"

Carlos makes a face. "That was weird. Those looked like military choppers."

"What?" I say. This idea had not even crossed my mind, but now that it has my heart races. "How do you know that?"

"They had American flags on them, duh," he says.

I look at Seth, who seems to have picked up on my concern. He opens his mouth, but before he gets anything out his eyes lock on something behind me. Turning, I gasp at the sight of men in Army uniforms filing into the courtyard.

The government's here.

And I'm the infamous daughter of a major criminal.

Who knows why they've come, but if they see me...Before I can finish the thought, Seth grabs my arm. He pushes me toward the bushes on the outskirts of the courtyard, and we crouch down. He puts his lips to my ear. "Don't move."

Like I even can. My eyes are plastered to the scene unfolding before my eyes. Students huddle together, shaking, as dozens of men and women line the open halls. Principal Long appears from around the corner, and she's with an imposing man who has a shaved head and wears a crisp uniform.

"Students," she says, straightening her suit jacket nervously. "I'm sure you've noticed what's going on in town. But never fear, the U.S. Army has come to our aid."

The man steps forward. His smile seems forced. "Everyone! I'm Major Norton, and your cooperation today would be most appreciated. We're here for your safety—please follow directions and don't worry. We just need to ask a few security questions."

He whispers something to Principal Long, and she offers a clumsy salute before walking off.

"Students, please form a single file line and follow me!" Major Norton calls. "Soldiers, make sure everyone complies."

I've never felt so trapped in my life. Soldiers inside my school. Juan's men outside. What the hell is going on? At least I can definitely say they're not all here for me, but then again, I'm not sure that's a good thing anymore.

Chapter 5

My legs won't move as I watch everyone slowly form a line. Just what, exactly, are they planning to do to each of us? Maybe there was a time when the government was good, but right now it feels like they're just another syndicate doing what they want, how they want.

"You should run," Seth whispers to me. "It wouldn't be hard to sneak past the guards. I don't know what I'd do if you got arrested."

I look him in the eye and see intense fear. "But they have me on the school records. Even if I got out today, pretty sure they'd check up on absent students. Wouldn't it look bad if I disappeared? That says guilty all over it. Maybe I can explain why my mom and I are here."

He puts his head to mine. "Why do you have to be right constantly?"

"You know I'm not." I put my arms around him, trying to be strong. "But I have nothing to hide. If they're asking security questions, I shouldn't have a problem, right? But what about you?"

He bites his lip. "I hadn't thought of that."

"Well, you need to!" I smack his arm. "What if they catch you lying about your ability?"

"You there!" a woman in uniform calls from the other side of the bushes. She's seen us. "Line up!"

We shoot to our feet. I guess the time for strategizing is over. Seth and I are the last ones in the long line. I'm not sure where it leads from where I stand, and I'm not looking forward to getting there. No one dares to speak, what with the armed soldiers everywhere, but it feels like people are looking at me as if they know I could be in trouble.

I'm more worried about my boyfriend. It'll be easy for me to say I'm not affiliated with a syndicate now, and there's no hiding my ability. But Seth? It all depends on the questions asked. I don't want to think about what they'd do to him if they found him withholding information, but I picture a holding cell and starvation tactics.

I squeeze his hand tighter, but he doesn't look my way. Now more than ever, we have to make it look like he can't see me. If anyone got too observant…

The bell rings to signal the end of lunch, and still the line slugs along at a miserably slow pace. At this rate it'll take the rest of school to get this over with. Which gives me plenty of time to imagine all the possible questions they could ask.

People go into the office one by one, and I count the seconds it takes for each person to leave. There doesn't seem to be a pattern in time length. I spot the teal-haired freshman girl I talked with going in, and she's out in less than a minute. Bea is next—it takes her much longer to be freed. She glances our way, and then I hear her voice in my ear, "Be careful, Fi. He asked a lot of questions about Radiasure."

My eyes go wide. Is that what this is about? There is an old, blown up Radiasure factory outside of town. And just a few months ago Miles, with the help of his super-hacker girlfriend, Spud, found rumors about the real Radiasure formula being discovered in China. Does the Army think they'll be able to find something here in Madison? They must.

Now Juan's men make sense—he's heard about the formula, too.

Finally, it's only Seth and me in line. He glances at my square geek frames. "You should go before me."

"No, you," I say.

"You need to go first." The finality in his voice makes me wonder if he's more nervous than he lets on.

"Okay." I let go of his hand, and a soldier ushers me into the office. We pass the secretary counter, where three guards browse through papers the printer spits out. When I step into the principal's office, Major Norton's eyes narrow. "Fiona McClean, I presume?"

I gulp. "Yes, sir."

He stares like I'll suddenly be visible if he glares hard enough. "Never thought I'd stand face to face with one of Jonas' daughters."

My lip curls at the word 'daughters,' because I try so hard to forget that Dad has other women, other children. Blood or not, they aren't *my* family. But I don't doubt he's never seen Dad's women. The government doesn't dare touch Las Vegas these days—that place is my dad's personal fortress.

Major Norton gestures for me to take a seat, so I do. I have to put my hands on my knees to keep them from bouncing nervously. He holds up a plaque covered in fancy calligraphy. "This is my certification from the Army as a legally binding lie detector, just in case you don't believe me. Are you familiar with this ability?"

I gulp as I look over the document. Questions are one thing, but he's a human lie detector on top of it? Seth and I could both be screwed now. "Yes, I've heard of it."

He smirks. "I figured you had, but I have to explain the process by law. My ability allows me to hear the lies in your voice—I can pick up the changes in tone and what they mean—so I'll know immediately if you answer any of my questions untruthfully. Do you understand?"

I force myself to look right at him, his steely eyes not expressing one wisp of emotion. "Yes, sir."

"Good. Now, please don't be too alarmed—we're doing this as a security precaution. Since this school is the largest usable facility in Madison, we'll have to share it with you students until we resolve the current syndicate issues. If you pass, you'll be cleared to continue attending school as normal, okay?"

"Okay..." With what Bea said about their interest in Radiasure, I can't help wondering if there's more to it.

"All right." Major Norton looks at a paper in front of him. "First question: Are you working for your father?"

"No," I say quickly.

Major Norton raises his dark eyebrows, seeming surprised that I wasn't lying. "Okay. Have you ever worked for your father?"

I pull at the hem of my dress, ashamed. "Yes."

"When did you stop?"

"Six months ago, me and my mother escaped." It seems like longer than that sometimes, but right now it doesn't feel long enough.

The Major makes a note on the paper. "Interesting. And you've lived in Madison for the entire six months?"

"Yes."

More note scratching. "Do you know why your mother chose this town?"

I glare at him, angry over his implication that my mother is suspicious. She was the biggest victim in all this. "My older brother Graham, not my mother, chose it because it was a good decoy location. He lied to my father about looking into Radiasure while he helped us get settled. Besides, it's also small and remote and deep within Juan's territory, who's my father's biggest rival."

"I see." He purses his lips, as if that wasn't the answer he wanted. "Since you've lived here, have you used your ability to commit crimes?"

My heart about jumps up my throat as I search through the past several months. "I don't think so, unless eavesdropping on my friends while they think I'm sleeping counts. Because I've done that a few times."

He smirks. "No, it doesn't count. I'm assuming you did use your ability to commit crimes prior to living here?"

"Yes…" Maybe I will get in trouble after all. I've stolen enough to keep me in jail for the rest of my life. "But I was under my dad's control—I wouldn't have done it if I had a choice."

"We are aware of your father's ability." He seems surprisingly sympathetic. "I won't hold those actions against you. Next question: Have you ever seen Radiasure?"

"Yes." I can't seem to escape that drug no matter what I do.

"Have you ever consumed Radiasure?"

"No."

Again, he looks surprised that's my honest answer. I find that particularly insulting, as if all syndicate-born people live and breathe the drug. Sure, a lot of them do, but they're also not stupid enough to waste a power boost on an ability that can't be boosted. "Are you aware of Madison's history?"

"Yes."

He raises an eyebrow. "What do you know?"

"That it's the remnants of an old town called Radison, where they used to manufacture Radiasure. The factory was destroyed during the drug riots, when the FDA officially outlawed the substance."

Major Norton is quiet for a long time, and I get the sense that other students didn't know this information. What if he asks me where I got it? I'd rather not have to tell him about Miles and Spud. That's too close to secrets I'd like to keep.

"Do you know anything else about Radison?" he finally asks.

"No, not really. I mean, I've seen the ruins out in the desert, but that's about it."

"What were you doing out there?"

"Running." This time I stare the Major down, wondering if he'll pick up on the half truth. He doesn't seem to. Maybe I won't have to expound on the time I also *hid* out there. "I like to run in the desert sometimes with my friends. There isn't exactly a lot to do here, you know?"

"I see." He scribbles more on his paper. "And do you go to

these ruins often?"

I gulp. "Not really."

"Is there anywhere else you like to go in the desert? Other... interesting landmarks?"

The caves come to mind immediately, but I really don't want to tell him about those. They are a Pack secret. So I pick another common running location and hope for the best. "We visit this waterfall in a valley south of the ruins. It's not much, but there's a pretty creek and tiny pond, a few trees."

"Sounds like a nice place." The Major smiles at me. "Well, to my surprise, it seems like I'll be able to clear you, Miss McClean."

I let out a long breath. "Oh good. So I can go?"

"Yes." He stands and extends his hand to me. I take it, and his shake is on the verge of painful. "You'll be eighteen next year. We could use someone with your talents and knowledge."

"Oh, um..." *Yeah, no, never.* "Thanks. I'll think about it."

"Please do. I'd draft you if I could."

I cringe as I head for the door, words escaping me. Always a tool. I guess that's one thing the government doesn't have in common with syndicates—they can't force me to work for them.

"Oh, Miss McClean?" Major Norton says just as I'm about to open the door.

I turn. "Yes, sir?"

His eyes lose all of the feigned friendliness. I know this look—Graham does it just before he makes a threat. "I wouldn't go running out in the desert anymore if I were you."

"Yes, sir." I leave, his command only making me want to go out there more than ever.

Chapter 6

The soldiers at the secretary counter give me a clearance card and shuffle me out the door. Seth is right there, looking at me with what I'm pretty sure is relief. I have a feeling he made the effort to watch the whole thing, and will now get a killer headache because of it. They take Seth in before I can say anything to him, and I stand there in a fit of nerves.

"Excuse me, ma'am," a soldier says after a couple minutes. "School has been canceled for the rest of the day. You can go."

"Oh, I was just waiting for my boyfriend." I feel stupid telling this man about my relationship, but I don't want to leave Seth here. "Is that okay?"

He doesn't seem impressed with my loyalty. "I guess, but I'm gonna have to ask you to stay at least fifty feet away from the office."

"Sure." I do as he says, though it seems stupid. Fifty feet is the average distance for people with sensitive hearing—it should be obvious that's not my ability. I settle in a small patch of shade offered by one of the courtyard's trees. Pulling out my dreaded math book, I wait.

And wait.

31

And wait.

I thought I was in there a long time, but my phone says Seth's been answering questions for over thirty minutes now. Or *not* answering. My guess is he was totally blindsided by the human lie detector thing like I was.

As the time pushes forty-five minutes, I start to panic. He's so stubborn he probably isn't speaking at all, and now he looks suspicious so Major Norton is asking even more questions. How will he get around telling the Major his real ability? He'll find out somehow. Maybe he already has. And Seth is eighteen—are they trying to sell him on enlistment, too?

Just after an hour passes, the office door opens, and I rush over. Seth looks pale, and though he does a good job hiding it I can tell he's spooked.

"Are you ok—?"

"Let's go. Now." Seth hooks his arm with mine, his long, fast strides hard to keep up with. The guards watch us as we walk down the quiet walkways. Everyone else has already cleared out, and I feel like an intruder in my own school.

When we get to the parking lot, there's a large military vehicle surrounded by a ton of soldiers. And for good reason, because Juan's men are on the other side of the school gate, clearly livid about the government's intrusion. Their yelling is in Spanish, and I can only catch bits and pieces. Mostly the swear words, since Senorita Gonzalez gets mad when people say them in class.

The soldiers wheel out big boxes, while a blond woman in a lab coat points and whispers commands. The Army taking over the school makes even more sense now: they need the science labs. This only gives me further proof that this invasion has something to do with the old factory. The government is after the exact same thing as any syndicate—the Radiasure formula.

Seth's old, black truck is parked by the fence, and as we approach, one of Juan's thugs breaks off from the crowd. My grip on Seth's arm doubles as I recognize this man as the one watching me at soccer practice: pale skin, long hair parted down the middle, and so thin even the jaguar tattoos on his arms look malnourished. But for all his seeming fragility, there is a confidence in his eyes that tells me not to underestimate him.

He stops on the opposite side of the chain-link fence, staring at me with a smug grin. "Hello, Fiona," he says with a strong accent I can't place. "I wondered if they would let you leave."

"Why wouldn't they?" I say while Seth unlocks the car.

His grin grows wider. "Only the government would throw away the chance to use someone like you. This is why they will never get this country back in order."

Seth tugs at my arm. "C'mon. Don't talk to him."

I'm not stupid—this is an obvious threat. My answer needs to be equally clear. "I'm not working for Juan."

"We'll see." His eyes seem hungry, and I get the sense that he'd love to make me. "But for now, I—"

"You there!" A soldier calls. He's on the other side of the gate with creepy guy, gun at ready. "Back away from the students. You are trespassing on federal property. Leave now."

The guy turns his head, not at all impressed with the soldier. "Or what?"

"Sir, please vacate the premises before I have to shoot you."

He puts his hand to the fence. "I don't feel like it."

The gunshot cracks through the air, and I scream. Not because Juan's guy is dead, but because the bullet went right through him. I can't seem to stop staring at his arm, which is now on our side of the fence. He steps completely through, laughing at the soldier's shocked expression. "That tickled."

"The Phantom," I whisper. Maybe Graham was trying to scare me—but he was right. Juan's second-in-command is here in Madison.

He turns. "Yes, Fiona. Are you scared?"

I can't speak, can't think. Seth opens the car door and says, "Get. In. Now."

But I'm frozen in shock. What does it matter if I leave? He probably knows where I live, and he can walk in any time he feels like it. "What do you want?"

"We'll talk later." He walks toward the Army truck. The soldier talks frantically into his comm unit about the intruder. "Unfortunately, I have other things to deal with right now."

"Guess I'll see you later, then." I get in Seth's car, glad I can act strong even when I'm sure I don't look it. Seth revs the engine and peels out of the parking lot. He doesn't say anything, but by the way his breaths heave I know he's pissed. "Go ahead and yell," I say.

"Are you crazy?" His voice explodes out of him. "You didn't have to talk to him! What the hell were you thinking?"

I sigh, my mind racing over the giant amount of information I've gained today. It's funny how a few clues can open up so many horrible possibilities. "You can't cower to people like that—it only makes them feel more powerful. I don't want him thinking he has me running already."

He shakes his head. "You should run. We should all get out of here."

I glare at him. "Seth, stop."

He parks in front of my house and leans back in the seat. "This isn't supposed to be happening. We already did this shit."

"I know." Since we started dating, I've always worried what might happen if syndicate life caught up to me again, what it might do to the people I care more about now than ever, what I might have to sacrifice to keep them safe. "But I also think you know we can't run."

His look is desperate. "Why not?"

"Because life on the run is a life of crime anyway," I say. "What did they ask you about that took so long to answer?"

He goes still, and the fear drains from his perfect eyes. He turns off the car, opens his door, and I follow him up my path without another word. Out here it's not safe. Inside is barely better. We climb the stairs to my room, and I turn on music while he shuts the door. We sit on the floor in front of my bed.

"It was close, Fi. Way too close," he whispers.

"How so?"

"It says in my school files that I'm a math savant, so the Major asked me if it was true and I had to say no." He lets out a long sigh. "Then he asked what my real ability was and I said my vision was really sharp."

My eyes go wide. "Did he call you on it?"

He shakes his head. "But he seemed to think it was pretty suspicious that I hid my real ability, asked me a lot of questions about why. All my reasons kept flagging as lies."

"What'd he do?"

35

"He got pissed." Seth squeezes his eyes shut and lies on the floor. I've come to recognize this as the I-used-my-ability-too-much-and-now-have-a-splitting-headache pose. "I finally passed by saying I wanted to major in mathematics in college, and they look down on you if you aren't a savant, which is true."

I lie down on my stomach, put my fingers to his temples, and rub in little circles. "Did they ask you about Radiasure?"

"Ugh, yeah. That's where it got even worse." His voice is grouchy, but there's a smile on his lips so the head massage must be helping. "He'd made notes of Brady going running in the desert, and then you, so he asked me about our relationship and if we went any specific places."

I stop. "Seriously? He asked me about places, too."

"Yeah?" He grabs my hands and makes them do the circles again. "Mmm, better. But anyway, I felt like I shouldn't tell him about going to the factory, you know? So that flagged as a lie, and he got worked up about what I was hiding in the desert. I finally said I take you to that little waterfall in the valley and was embarrassed to talk about my personal life. He bought that one, and that's when he let me go."

"Funny, I also used the waterfall. At least our stories matched." Hearing Seth's account confirms too many of my suspicions. "This is about that 'real' Radiasure formula rumor floating around the syndicate channels, the one not disclosed to the public."

"I hate to admit you're right, but there's no other reason for all these people to show up here. Which means if they find what they're looking for…" Seth pinches the bridge of his nose, the pain clear on his face.

"Rest." I kiss his forehead. "You shouldn't have spied on my interview."

"I was—"

"Worried, I know. You need to stop. It's annoying." I rub his head until he dozes off. He'll feel better after a break from seeing. Then I pull out my phone and call Miles.

He picks up immediately this time. "Fiona! What's up?"

"Nothing good, I'm afraid." I sneak out of my room so I don't wake Seth, and tiptoe down to the kitchen to grab some Pop Tarts. "Juan's right-hand man is in town, plus the Army just set up camp at my school and interrogated every student."

There's a pause. "I'm waiting for the punch line."

"There isn't one. Didn't Graham tell you I called the other day?"

"Yeah, but I thought you were just being paranoid. Did you actually see The Phantom this time?"

I roll my eyes. "I saw a bullet pass right through him, and then he walked through a fence and threatened me. Oh, and the Army Major asked me about the factory and Radiasure, which I'm pretty sure means they're all here in the quest to make it again."

"Well crap," he says too matter-of-factly.

"It can't happen, Miles. You know that as well as I do." This world is bad enough with a limited supply of Radiasure—people overdose, they die from their mutations, they kill to get more. The idea of unlimited access to the drug is more terrifying than anything I can think of.

"What are you saying? You're gonna stop them from finding it?"

"I don't know…" Part of me wants to say I'll stop them no matter what. But it's a huge risk, and I'm not sure I have to jump in that far. I'm finally *out* of that crime mess—do I really want to risk going back? "Right now I'm more concerned about how much they suspect us of knowing things. They grilled the whole Pack today, which puts all my friends at risk. I want to cover my tracks so they'll leave us alone."

"Fair enough. What do you need me to do?" Miles says.

My smile is so big my cheeks hurt. I can always count on him. "I need you to get in contact with Spud. She can tell us for sure how much the Army or Juan suspect us."

He's so quiet I wonder if the line went dead, but then he says, "Yeah, uh, that might be hard to do."

Chapter 7

There's no way I could have heard him right. Spud is the best hacker in the world—she even hacked into my dad's iron-clad network to find the real Radiasure formula rumors in the first place. Plus, Miles has made it pretty clear he's dating her. It's not like it'd be difficult to ask her. "What's so hard about it? I bet she could find out in less than a day."

Miles clears his throat. "It's not that she couldn't do it. She just happens to be busy with a really important job right now is all. I don't think she has time."

"What kind of job?"

"You know I can't tell you that."

I frown. It was worth a shot. "Couldn't you just ask?"

There's a long pause, and I get the sense he doesn't want to. "Look, I'll ask, okay? But don't get your hopes up too high. She's under a ton of stress as it is, and I hate burdening her more than necessary. She's already in so much danger."

It's hard to believe what I'm hearing, and yet I know the kind of pain in Miles' voice. You only sound like that when you're worried about someone you care about. I thought his relationship with Spud was like all his others: casual, physical, for fun. Now I'm pretty sure I was wrong. "You're in love with her."

"Fi…"

He doesn't need to say more. I sit on a kitchen stool, an unexpected flood of emotions hitting me. My brother is in a real relationship. With the most infamous hacker alive. He knows enough about her to be in love. Miles has always been mine—in a big brother way, but still. Now he has someone else to think about, to worry over, to care for. Tears prick at my eyes. "So she's more important than me now?"

"Hey, you know that's not true," Miles says softly. "She just… yeah, you're right, she means the world to me. I stress about her safety all the time, especially because I have no way to protect her."

I'm not stupid—Spud is on everyone's list. If she ever got caught, she'd be locked up or tortured or dead, probably all three. "This is weird."

Miles laughs. "It is, isn't it? Never saw it coming, and yet here I am in a long-term, long-distance relationship. And I wouldn't trade her for anything."

"Oh, gag me," I say, though I think I can accept this once I get used to it. "Well, I guess all I can do is be glad you can put in a good word for me. Tell me if you hear anything from her?"

"Sure. And, Fiona?"

"What?"

"Please don't do anything impulsive until I *do* hear back from her. I can tell you're freaking out—you don't think things through when you panic."

I let out an indignant squeak. "That's not true!"

40

"Do I need to remind you of how you just *had* to go to the factory to see if Graham was telling the truth despite Spud saying he was?"

I pout, the guilt over that still strong. "Shut up."

"Whatever. Just promise me."

"Sure. I won't do anything stupid. Bye." I hang up before I can hear his answer, because I have a feeling he can pick up on my plans even over the phone. If I have to wait forever to hear from Spud, I have to do *something* in the meantime. It's not like the Army or Juan's men will pause their plans while Spud is busy.

"What's with the nasty glare?" Seth stands in the doorway, looking groggy and therefore adorable. "And what are you doing that's not stupid?"

Crap, how much did he hear? "Nothing."

His eyes narrow as he comes closer. "You'd be horrible at lying if people could see you."

"Whatever." Someday I'll learn to trick him, but today is not that day. So I smile as I walk over to him, and then I kiss him in a way I hope will make him drop it. He pulls me closer, and before I know it we're fooling around on the couch. We haven't gone all the way yet, though it's times like this I think it would be easy.

Then I open my eyes.

Minus the places my dress still covers, Seth appears to be floating a few inches off the couch. He kisses me just above my bra. It feels amazing, but to my eyes it looks like he's making out with air. And there's something extremely odd about watching him enjoy skin I can't see.

41

"We better stop." I push him back and do my best to hide my discomfort.

He still seems to pick up on it, though we've never talked about why I always stop him right before things get too intense. "Yeah, you're right."

Seth sits next to me, but there's a distance I can't explain. It makes me wonder if I've hurt his feelings, or if he thinks he hurt mine. I turn on the TV to drown out the silence.

"Don't think I've forgotten about what you said on the phone," he says after we've both cooled off.

I cringe. "You'll just get mad at me."

"Psh." He puts his arm around me, and all seems well again. "Of course I'll get mad at you—that's what we *do*, Fi."

I try not to smile, but it's true. We still argue about plenty of things. It doesn't seem to stop us from being crazy about each other. "How about we make a deal? If I'm going to get yelled at, I want something in return."

He rolls his eyes. "Fine, what do you want?"

Since I'd rather not tell him, I pick the one thing he hates more than anything. "You have to draw me."

"Fionaaaa," he whines.

"Deal or not?" I'm pretty sure he won't take it. Every time I convince him to draw it ends up with me complaining about how bad he is at it. Why couldn't the one person who can see me be an artist instead of a math freak?

"Why do you make me do this all the time?"

"Because…" My body wilts, and I lean into him for support. I always thought being seen would be enough, but now I want more. *I* want to see. *I* want to know. I feel so close to having

42

details about myself I never dreamed of having—and yet so far away because I will *never* see myself. "I need to see what you see, so I can imagine what we look like together."

The bump in Seth's throat bobs, and he squeezes my shoulder. "Fine, it's a deal."

"I'll get paper!" Jumping up, I grab a notebook and pencils from my backpack and am back in seconds. I shove them into Seth's lap and sit facing him. "I was talking with Miles about all the people showing up here to make Radiasure and then suspecting us of knowing too much. I think we should cover our tracks."

Seth makes a big scratch across the paper, and then he looks me right in the eye. Angry, of course. "You can't avoid trouble for more than a few months, can you?"

I frown. "C'mon, look how close it was for you today. What if they find our trails out there in places they don't think we should be? What if they find our prints at the factory or something we left by accident? They'll keep coming at us until they get what they think we have."

"Maybe…" He starts on a fresh page, making a clumsy attempt at a head. I almost want to ask if my skull is really that lumpy, but he'll just glare at me. He looks at my face again, then back to the page. "I mean, we don't have any real information for them, do we? I've never seen anything at the factory but twisted metal…though maybe some of that metal had traces of Radiasure. Who knows?"

I nod, thinking. "When Miles told me about the real formula, he said the public version was missing a top secret element. Whatever that is, any evidence would be at the factory, and if we saw it…even by accident…these people don't strike me as the type who'd let witnesses go."

Seth works on my eyes, which already seem too big for the head he drew. "I hate that you're probably right, but it'd be seriously dangerous even to hide our tracks."

"I know. Major Norton told me not to go out there anymore, like that wasn't gonna make me curious."

He snorts. "He told me that, too. I don't think he's the smartest guy around."

"Clearly."

"Let's talk to The Pack about it. If they're in, we'll have enough people to cover our butts."

I purse my lips, thinking. "I'd rather not put them at risk, though."

"We're all at—" Seth drops the pencil, and his eyes fill with terror. I turn to see what has him so freaked out and gasp. It's like a nightmare, but this is all too real. The Phantom stands in my living room, seeming pleased with our surprise.

Chapter 8

The Phantom looks around before his eyes fall on me. "Is your mother not home yet?"

As scared as I am, I somehow find the strength to stand. "Why do you want to know?"

His laugh is quiet as he pulls a glowing blue pill from his pocket. He swallows the Radiasure dry, and I wonder if he took it just to intimidate me. "You didn't answer my question."

"How about you go back out and knock like a decent human being?" I put my hands on my hips. "Then I'll answer my door and your question."

"Fiona," Seth hisses.

"Your boyfriend seems properly afraid of me." The Phantom comes closer, his chin tipped up in a challenging gesture. "Why not you?"

I don't have an answer that is more sophisticated than "instinct kicking in." Every day of my life I've lived with fear—if I always gave into it I'd be nothing but a puddle of whimpering and shaking. "It's not exactly the first time I've met someone with a terrifying ability who pops Radiasure like it's nothing, is it?"

"This is true." Another step closer, to the point that he's

almost in my personal bubble. "Speaking of extraordinary abilities, I'll only ask one more time: Where's your mother?"

"I'm not telling."

"We'll see about that." Before I can react, The Phantom charges for me. I brace myself to be tackled, but instead am met with a cold sensation that makes my whole body shudder. That's when I realize he's walking right through me, and I let out an involuntary scream.

By the time I recover and turn around, The Phantom has a knife to Seth's throat. I can't breathe, can't think, knowing how easy it would be for him to slice my boyfriend's neck right open. "This boy seems to hang out with you a lot. I could get rid of him if you want."

I force down the lump in my throat. There's no other choice now. "Let him go. I'll take you to her."

"That's better." The Phantom lowers his knife and points toward the door. "Shall we?"

"Yes." I hold out my hand to Seth. "Can I borrow your keys?"

Seth gives me the "you're crazy" look, but he gives them to me anyway. "You'll be back, right?"

"As long as she listens well," The Phantom says. We go outside and get in Seth's black truck. My skin crawls being so close to Juan's most prized henchman, the feeling of him walking through me still too fresh in my mind.

I try to focus on driving, on the heat rippling the horizon and the deep blue of the late afternoon sky. Madison is still as small and boring as ever, but the stucco houses and rocky yards we pass have become a sign of home. As we hit Main Street, where the old diner, dry cleaners, bar, and other stores seem to be stuck in the seventies, a strange sense of responsibility comes over me.

This is *my* town.

No one touches *my* town.

My eyes go wide as I realize I sound just like my dad. Is this how it starts? People threaten the stuff you care about, and you go to whatever lengths necessary to keep it safe. As I pull into the bowling alley parking lot, I shake it off. It's not the same thing—I'm only trying to stay out of harm's way. And kind of failing so far.

The Superbowl looks like a disco inside, with nonstop flashing lights and loud, party music. I suppose the owners think this will make bowling seem less lame, but everyone knows it doesn't work. Lucky for them, it's the only entertaining place in town minus the pool. I'd go more often if The Pack wasn't banned.

"She should be around here somewhere," I say, scanning the shoe rental, snack bar, and small arcade section. Really hope she didn't ditch out like a few days ago.

"Lauren McClean, working here…" The Phantom clucks his tongue. I can't disagree with him. Mom, even as a non-criminal, is talented and smart and not exactly bowling alley material. "Such a shame."

"Better honest money than illegal." I walk down the main pathway, looking at each group of people in hope of finding her. People gape back at us, seeming horrified to see me with one of Juan's tattooed men. I can hear the rumors now. Just when people were starting to be nice to me.

"Are you having trouble finding her?" The Phantom says when we reach the middle lanes. "Please don't tell me this is a diversion—she hides now, you disappear at the first chance.

This would make me very unhappy."

I gulp, thinking of how quickly he went for his knife before. "No, that's not it at all."

"Better convince me." The Phantom's voice has lost all playfulness. He's getting tired of batting at his prey, and I don't want to know what happens then.

There's only one place left to check. "She's probably in the break room."

I head that way as everyone else packs up and starts to leave. No one told them to get out of here, and yet it's like they know not to be anywhere near Juan's people if they can help it. When I open the door, Mom's sitting at a round table with her phone in hand. She smiles when she sees me.

"Fiona! I didn't know you'd be vi—" The moment Mom sees The Phantom come in, shock hits her face. Once it washes off, she pulls me behind her and glares at him. "How dare you use her to get to me."

He raises an eyebrow. "I just want to discuss certain matters with you and your daughter. It's not my fault you made it so difficult to locate you. I had to follow your little girl instead."

My face goes red. "That's why you were at the school?"

"Of course." He sits at the flimsy card table and motions for us to do the same. "Let's talk, ladies. That's all I'm asking."

Mom takes her seat again, looking like she has no idea what's going on. I sit next to her, nervous and curious myself. "You wanna talk?" Mom says. "Fine. Talk."

"I will make this very simple, Lauren," The Phantom says. "Juan's been watching you for a couple months now, so don't think he doesn't know why you're here."

"And why is that?" Mom asks without a hint of anything but indifference. I, on the other hand, am kind of disturbed about the idea of Juan keeping tabs on us for that long. But maybe I should consider us lucky that he didn't pick up on it sooner.

The Phantom's eyes narrow. "You know why."

Mom shrugs. "Do I?"

I don't think he can tell, but it's clear to me that Mom's baiting for information. Because obviously *we* don't know what he's thinking about us living here, but I get the sense it's different from the truth.

"Let's not play games. Every syndicate has this information, thanks to an assassination in China that has you O'Connells written all over it."

I stifle a gasp. So Dad really went through with his mission to find the real Radiasure formula. Who did he send instead? Maybe I don't want to know, because they're probably dead. I hope they are, because it'd be worse if they were captured by another syndicate.

Mom raises an eyebrow, seeming just as surprised by this information as I am. "Looks like you do know everything."

"Yup," I add, because this works in our favor—obviously Juan doesn't know we're not working for Dad anymore. They must think we're here to make Radiasure just like they are.

"So here's how it'll work." The Phantom reaches into his back pocket and pulls out a slick black card. When the lights hit it, an image of a jaguar gleams back. "The Torres syndicate is willing to overlook your trespassing under one condition. If you agree—I get to give you three million dollars."

Mom purses her lips. "Must be one hell of a condition."

"All Juan asks is that you do nothing." The Phantom puts the card on the table and slides it over. "You can do that, right?"

"You want us to ignore our orders? That's it?" she asks.

He nods.

There has to be some kind of catch, though at the same time it does make sense. Juan wants to produce Radiasure first. Whoever does will clearly have the advantage. If we do nothing, that's one less syndicate to worry about meddling. Except we're not actually working for Dad…I frown, realizing there's a bigger issue here.

"We do nothing, and you can promise our safety as long as we're in your territory?" Mom asks.

"Of course." The Phantom's dark eyes gleam with anticipation. "What's your answer?"

"We'll do nothing, but you can have this back." To my surprise, Mom slides the card to him. "Safety is enough. I don't want to owe Juan anything."

The Phantom takes it in his spindly hands. "You're smarter than you look."

"Don't forget it." Mom stands, and I follow her outside. I'm about to head back to Seth's car when she bursts out laughing. Then she leans in to say, "Well, that was easy enough—we don't even have orders to ignore! Looks like as long as we lie low we can sail past this mess scot-free."

"Yeah," I whisper, my mind reeling. Maybe we're safer from Juan than I thought we could be, but I can't escape one thought: Dad hasn't sent a crew here to search the area. What could he be doing that is more important to him than reproducing Radiasure?

Chapter 9

At least Movie Night hasn't changed much. Bea's dad still makes amazing burgers. Her mom still prepares a spread of toppings. And of course there's always fighting over which movie to watch. But her older brothers Joey and Tony haven't come for a month because of demanding college classes. Plus, Bea and Brady are usually so distracted with each other they forget to protect me from Carlos.

"So, Fiona," Carlos says as he sits next to me at the picnic table. I glare at Bea, who is giggling and flirting with Brady by the condiments. So much for backup. "How do you feel about polyamorous relationships?"

"I didn't realize you knew such big words," I reply.

Hector makes a sizzling sound. "Nice burn, Fi."

"She's avoiding the question," Carlos says.

Seth pulls me closer. "Stop asking my girlfriend inappropriate stuff. We're together, and that's not about to change."

"Plus I'm not interested in you." I bite into my burger, which is filled with peppers and avocado and cheese.

The guys laugh, though Carlos does look a little hurt by the news. I almost feel bad, but I've learned the boy can't take a hint or even a direct statement. Why he's decided to fixate on me of all people I'll never know.

"You need to move on, dude," Hector says through a huge bite of burger, complete with barbecue sauce on his face. "There are tons more invisible girls out there for you to terrorize."

I snort. "If only."

After dinner, we spread blankets on the grass, set up the projector, and pick a movie. By the time we get everything ready it's dark, thanks to the short winter days. Though it's not freezing, it's definitely cold enough that we huddle under blankets and drink cocoa.

Bea hops up as the opening credits begin, pulling out the one device I hate more than anything—a camera. "Smile, everyone!"

The camera flashes. I didn't smile or even look at it, not like anyone will be able to tell. She takes a few more, and I have to restrain myself from yelling at her to stop. I know this is what normal people do, but I hate looking at my missing face next to everyone else.

Seth nudges me. "Is it really so bad?"

I'm not sure how to answer that when we're surrounded by people who don't know he can see me. It's not like I can get into a lengthy discussion about how hollow and stupid those pictures make me feel. "Yeah, it is."

"I'm sorry, Fi." He puts his arm around me, and I try to concentrate on the movie. But Bea and Brady are laughing while they take pictures together, and envy flares inside me like a hot coal. I know they aren't, and yet it feels like they're rubbing their visibility in my face. Seth squeezes my shoulder. "Should I ask for the camera next? Seems like you're distracted by it."

"Why bother?" It sounds harsher than I intended. "It'll just be you and some floating clothes."

He frowns. "What's wrong with that?"

"*Everything.*" Sometimes I hate that there are things I will never experience like other people. They are often tiny. They probably shouldn't matter. But times like these make me feel inhuman.

"Fi." He leans in so he can whisper right in my ear. I still worry Hector could hear. "There is *nothing* wrong with being invisible."

He's trying to comfort me, but I can't help but be a little angry. "Easy for you to say, being visible and all."

Seth sighs. "You're determined to let this bother you. Even after everything."

By "everything" I assume he means the fact that he's told me what I look like, but he can't say that with Hector so near. "I don't want it to bother me—sorry I can't figure out how to stop wanting to see myself."

He opens his mouth to say something, but a loud *whooping* sound cuts him off. I look up to the open sky, searching for whatever made the noise. That's when I see the dark mass in the air. My first thought is that either the Army or The Phantom brought a flier to Madison, but then I catch the distinct scent of blueberries.

"Miles! Graham!" I'm immediately on my feet and running to them as they touch down in the grass. Miles scoops me into a bear hug. Graham stands there awkwardly. We don't do hugs—we barely do friendly nods. "What're you doing here?"

Miles sets me down. "Oh, you know, just seeing what our

little sister is up to."

"And by that he means making sure you don't do anything stupid," Graham says with a glare. "Mom told us about The Phantom and your deal."

Bea's jaw drops. "You made a *deal* with Juan's guy?"

That one sentence gets everyone up and surrounding us. Hector, Carlos, and Brady pummel me with questions about if I'm working for Juan or if I paid them off and what the hell is going on in Madison.

"Whoa!" I hold my hands out, pushing them back. "Give me some space and time to answer."

Hector folds his arms, in full defensive mode. "You better answer quick, because I don't want to think of you as a traitor."

"Keep your pants on." I look from side to side, figuring now is as good a time as any to tell them what Seth and I discussed. I lower my voice. "Hector, do you hear anyone in the area that shouldn't be here?"

"Hold your breath." Hector pulls his plugs out. I've never asked how far he can hear, but I figure he'll pick up on any breathing around the house. After The Phantom telling me Juan's been watching us, better safe than sorry. He shakes his head. "Just Mom and Dad inside."

"Okay, in the living room." We shuffle inside, and that's when I notice something. "Miles, you're limping. What happened?"

He looks down at his leg, as if he didn't even notice. "Oh that? Just had a run in with some stairs. Twisted my ankle. It's not that bad."

I'm not sure I buy it. "Since when did you get clumsy?"

"I was late to class and miscalculated some steps." He shrugs as he claims the single recliner for himself. "Should I report all my injuries to you from now on?"

"Only ones that immobilize you," I say.

Everyone crams onto the couches except for Graham, who floats on his permanent pillow of air. I stand before them, but it feels odd. Like I'm the leader. Since when? "Juan thinks Mom and I are still working for my dad, so The Phantom wanted us to ignore our orders in exchange for money. My mom told him we'd ignore our orders—because, of course, we don't have any—and we didn't take the money."

The Pack lets out a collective sigh.

"Still doesn't explain why they're all here, though," Hector points out. "And from the grilling we got from the Army at school, seems like it has to do with Radiasure."

I nod. "You remember what I told you that night we went to the factory?"

"You mean when you ruined my brilliant plan?" Graham says.

I wish he could see my glare. "Yes, that night. If only you'd explained you had a decoy store of Radiasure here to throw Dad off the trail sooner."

Graham rolls his eyes, but says nothing more. I don't like him being here—and I'm sure my friends are still wary of him—but he knows about Rosa's ability, the Navarro's greatest secret, so he's in the group whether we want it or not.

I clear my throat. "The Phantom implied that the real Radiasure formula has been leaked to all the syndicates. So basically it's a race to find something out in the desert that will allow them to produce the pills again."

They nod, as if they were expecting as much. Maybe I don't

give The Pack as much credit as I should. Even if they've never been part of a syndicate, it almost seems like their efforts to avoid Juan have taught them all they need to know.

Seth puts his elbows to his knees, his face serious. "The Army held me for an hour because I knew stuff about the desert. Fiona and I were talking about whether or not we should cover our tracks out there."

"It wouldn't be good to have the Army poking around," Carlos says, more concerned than I expected. "Who knows what they'll do if they know we not only know about the factory, but that we've spent time exploring it?"

"They'll detain us until we give them answers, that's what." Hector puts his hand over his mouth, like he just caught himself talking too loudly. We definitely don't want their parents knowing about this. "Then we'd get attention from Juan *and* the Army. Not good."

"We just got out of trouble—I don't want to get back in," Brady says. "Once they start sweeping the area they'll figure out those are my footprints all over the place."

Bea bites her lip. "What if we've been other places they don't want us to know about? We don't know how big the original factory site was."

"Exactly." I put my hands on my hips, this conversation only proving what we need to do. "If we don't want them digging into our business, we need to make sure nothing can be traced to us."

Graham sits up from his relaxed floating position. "Just what, exactly, do you know about that desert anyway?"

We all look back and forth at each other, no one seeming

particularly interested in answering him. This piques Miles' interest. "Are you implying you know the location of what they're looking for?"

"No!" I blurt out, though it feels like a half truth. "I mean, we don't even know *what* they're looking for except that it has to do with Radiasure."

"But it's possible that you've come across it." Graham is practically salivating over the idea. "You could have actually seen what they're looking for and not known it."

Miles swears. "That's not good. Is there any particular place you're worried about?"

"Besides the factory? Maybe." Seth tips his chin up. "Not sure I trust someone in here enough to talk about it."

"Who could you be referring to?" Graham asks sarcastically.

Seth stares him down. "You."

Graham flies right up to Seth's face, and I immediately get flashbacks of him grabbing my neck and squeezing so hard I thought I might die. "I'd start trusting me, because you're stuck with me."

"That's enough." I shove myself between them. "Look, Graham, we could have made you leave and we didn't. You made us trust your plan without explanations—guess you get to see how that feels now."

Graham's nostrils flare, but it's the first time I don't shake in front of him. The Pack would never let him get away with hurting me. After what seems like an eternity, he finally relaxes. "I'm only going along with this because I don't want you to get hurt. These soldiers and thugs could jeopardize everything we made here."

The sincerity in his expression takes me off guard. Part of me still doesn't want to believe it, but Graham's changing. Being free from Dad has done the same thing for him as it has for Mom and me. For the smallest moment, it feels like we're family again. "Thank you."

"Of course." He looks down, seeming embarrassed.

"So we all agree on this?" I ask. Everyone nods. "Good, this is what we're gonna do."

Chapter 10

We split up into two teams—one to destroy any possible evidence around the factory, and another to obscure the trails we run south of town. I purposely put Graham on the factory team so he doesn't get near the pools, along with Carlos to guide them in the dark with his night vision. Miles insisted on going with Graham, though I didn't think he should with his twisted ankle. I couldn't argue when he said he'd keep an eye out for anything suspicious from our older brother.

Which means Seth, Brady, Bea, Hector, and I stand at the edge of town nearest the cave, where our secret pools lie deep underground. Surveying the land under an almost-full moon, I breathe in the cool air. The desert is quiet tonight, with barely a breeze to call wind. A coyote howls in the distance. There's no sign that anyone's been out here to search yet.

The paths we use most are barely visible among the desert brush and pot holes left by Brady, but the faint footprints are enough. Surely any good tracker could find them, and the Army has to have brought at least one, if not many.

"Hector," I say. "Take the southern path with Bea and cover up any tracks or worn parts in the trail. Make sure we haven't

59

left anything under the interstate bridge. Seth and I will take the path to the little waterfall, while Brady tears up everything between here and the cave to hide his pot holes."

"Got it." Hector holds up the shovel he brought. "C'mon, sis. Let's get this done."

"Hell yeah. And don't worry, Fi, you'll be able to hear my scream no matter how far away we get." Bea smiles at me reassuringly. How she knows I'm nervous is beyond me.

"It's not like I'll miss anyone sneaking up on us," Hector says.

"I know." I gulp, almost considering calling off the whole thing. This is the exact opposite of what Major Norton told me to do, and if he finds out...I can't even think about how The Phantom might react. This is definitely not "doing nothing." "Just be careful. If there's any sign of someone following you, get out."

"Yup." Hector heads south, Bea trailing right behind him.

"Better get to destroying stuff." Brady smiles with a disturbing amount of excitement. "It's not every day I'm *allowed* to do this, you know."

"Try to be quiet?" I say.

He laughs. "Yeah, right."

We head off down the biggest path, which is really just a thin snaking line. Right now it seems more dangerous than that, like a fuse leading to a bomb. I'll sleep much better once I know the line has been cut.

After about five minutes' running, we stop at a big cactus surrounded by bunches of dry brush. This is where we turn to the right when we run to the cave, and I figure it's a good place to break the trail. "Brady, start here. Seth and I will head left towards the waterfall now."

"Sounds good." He motions for us to move away. "Watch out."

Seth grabs my hand and we step back several yards. Brady's pale skin practically glows in the moonlight where it's not covered by dark fabric. His muscles flex, and then he slams his fist into the ground. The earth cracks and groans beneath his powerful arm, and the cactus threatens to fall over. The trail beneath Brady is gone. "That felt good. Meet you back at the house."

He's off with a big leap. When he lands, the ground cracks again. Sure hope there's no one around to hear, because that's so not quiet.

"Our turn." Seth shuffles along the ground in the opposite direction of Brady, brushing the dirt to hide footprints and obscure the path. I can't help but laugh because we must look ridiculous. "Shh, we're supposed to be discreet," he says.

"But you look like a penguin!" I snort at that, and then he's laughing, too.

"Only you could laugh when we're directly ignoring orders from a syndicate *and* the Army."

"Hey, you all seemed plenty eager to make sure no one suspected us more." I jump off the path when I spot a crinkled water bottle. Picking it up, I come back and stuff it in Seth's backpack.

"You have a way of rallying people, Fi. You're a natural leader."

I stop, the idea more upsetting to me than anything. All the leaders I know are horrible people. I don't want to be like that. "No, I just want to protect what I have here."

"Lots of people *don't* protect what they should, nor do they convince others to do the same." He keeps sliding his feet along. "Let's keep going—you'll leave prints standing there like that."

"Oh, right." I follow right behind him and try to ignore the growing pit in my stomach. No more thinking of who I could become if I keep leading. "So am I the only one who's noticed that none of my dad's people are here?"

"I thought that was because of your deal," Seth says.

I put my hands on my hips, still scooting forward and searching for evidence. There should be a lot more at the waterfall. "Maybe I'm not giving him enough credit, but I don't think he's the kind of person who'd honor a deal if it meant losing a chance to produce Radiasure."

"Hmm…true." Seth doesn't say anything else for awhile, but then comes back with, "Maybe he's waiting for other people to do the hard work, and he'll steal it later?"

"I guess that's possible." But it still feels like I'm missing something. If Dad was the one who got the formula from China, I'd think he'd be willing to get his hands dirty out here, too.

The closer we get to the waterfall, the easier it is to hear the little creek that only runs in the winter according to Seth. That small trickle of water tumbles off a cliff, making a pond in the valley below. At least until summer comes and dries it all up. On the warmer winter days, we take food and go there with The Pack to mess around. Mostly it's a game to see who will get caught off guard and pushed into the water first.

With our destination almost in reach, we become quiet. Maybe because we're tired, or perhaps it feels like speaking is bad luck. The way Major Norton talked, I'd have thought we'd see at least some evidence of his team searching out here.

There have been no lights, no digging sites, no tire tracks.

But as we approach the cliff that leads down to the base of the waterfall, it seems like it's brighter than it should be in the small valley. I grab Seth's arm. "I think someone's down there."

He squints at the nearby ledge, I think so he can look through it. "You're right. The Army has something set up."

"We could have just looked over the ledge." I poke him. "Now you'll get another horrible headache."

"I only looked for a second." He nods toward the path. "Let's go. They beat us to it—if there was any evidence of us there they've already found it."

"Wait." Curiosity wells up inside of me to the point that I can't contain it. "I should go down there to hear what they're saying."

Seth shakes his head. "No way. We're not out here to spy— we're trying to *avoid* trouble, remember?"

I sigh. He has a point, but there's something about this that bothers me. "You don't think it's weird that they happen to be looking in the *exact* spot you and I mentioned to the Major when he questioned us? Shouldn't they be up around the factory? That's the most logical place."

His face fills with suspicion, and I can tell he's wavering. "You're right. This spot seems like a weird place to search so early on. It's nowhere near the factory."

"What if…" A sinking feeling comes over me. "Maybe they weren't trying to clear us for school, but were actually using that as an excuse to get local intel. If they used us, we deserve to know what they're doing."

"No. That can't be it." Seth purses his lips, fighting himself.

"Okay, it could be."

"See? I have to go down there."

"I guess so." A flicker of mischief crosses his face. "Does this mean you're gonna take your clothes off in front of me?"

"No." I smack his arm. "You wouldn't be looking."

He frowns, glancing back at the cliff. "I don't like not seeing you for many reasons, but mostly because I won't be able to make sure you're okay. What if you get caught?"

"You'd only be more nervous if you could see what I was doing. Now turn off your ability so I can get invisible."

He smirks. "How will you know I've actually turned it off?"

"Do you really want to suffer the consequences for lying to me about that?" I put my hands on my hips. "Because it would be ugly."

His shoulders slump, and I realize he's not just trying to get a free view. He's honestly scared. "Just…be careful, okay?"

I hug him tightly. "Of course. You forget this isn't my first time."

"Yeah." He blinks rapidly, and then cringes. "It's off, and it's really weird not to see you."

That's how I feel all the time. I go for my shirt, but this wave of embarrassment washes over me. "Turn around."

He gives me an incredulous look. "I just said I can't see you!"

"It's still weird!" And secretly I'm afraid he's lying. I mean, what guy would miss a chance to see his girlfriend naked? He rolls his eyes, but turns around. "Thank you."

I peel off my running gear quickly and place it in a pile. My skin crawls with insecurity—this is the first time I've been completely invisible outside my bathroom since I found out

Seth could see me. It used to be so easy, but now I feel too exposed. "Watch my clothes. I'll be back soon."

"You better be." Seth turns around, his eyes flitting back and forth in a panic. I guess he really did turn it off.

"I'm hurrying." I head to the spot in the cliff where you can climb down to the valley. It's almost like a ramp, though not as smooth or safe. I have to force myself to focus on the rocks right in front of me and not the view. If I can't see how far away the bottom of the gulch is, then I'll survive my fear of heights.

When I get to the bottom, I follow the creek up to where the pond forms. There are armed guards everywhere, which seems odd against something as simple as a small pool of water. But at least it's not Juan's people—I'm more afraid of what The Phantom would do to me than the Army's punishments. I creep closer, squinting against the bright lights near the waterfall. It looks like there's a table and lab equipment there, plus that blond girl in a lab coat I saw the day the Army arrived. Major Norton stands over her, surveying everything.

I have to see what they're up to.

Adrenaline courses through me as I approach the guards. They don't seem to notice me, but I need to be careful because the ground has become soft under my feet. Even in the darkness, surely they'd see my footprints appear out of nowhere. That'd be a dead giveaway.

I step on every rock I can, stay away from the pond's edge, and creep past the closest pair of guards unnoticed. After I maneuver through another set, I'm close enough to the lights to see and hear clearly, so I settle near the cliff wall where no one should run into me.

"How long will it take to know?" Major Norton asks the blond girl. At a closer look, it's hard to believe she's a scientist because she doesn't look much older than a teen, with a sweet face and hair pulled into a long ponytail. Early twenties at most. She must be some kind of science savant.

"Now that I've added the necessary chemicals, it shouldn't be more than a few minutes," the blond girl says.

"Good." Major Norton seems excited. "Either we'll have our match, or we'll be able to rule out one place in this godforsaken desert."

"It's a good lead, sir, according to the formula." The girl picks up some papers, and my heart about leaps from my chest. "See here? The element should be in liquid form in Earth's temperature range, so there may be traces in the desert water."

My brow pinches together in confusion. I pictured some kind of metal, but if they're looking for an element that's liquid…

The pools.

No. The caves are so far away from the factory! Why would the element be so far out and hidden in a place that doesn't look manmade? Did the factory owners hide it there? It seems strange that they wouldn't keep it right under their thumb at the plant. Then something clicks. Maybe the element naturally occurs in the cave—and they built the factory in a place close but not so close to reveal its location. That makes more sense.

And dear, sweet, too-strong-for-his-own-good Brady just had to find it. That place means the world to him and Seth. If that's really what everyone's after, I can't let anyone find it. We need to know if the element really is at our secret pools, which means we need the formula.

I stare at the scientist girl, watch her talk to the Major and flip through papers that have to be the formula. My fingers tingle with the urge to steal it, and I'm afraid to listen to that impulse. As much as I want to pore over that document, I don't exactly have a place to put it. Maybe it'd fit in my mouth with some creative folding, but I'd need a significant distraction to pull it off.

No, I can't steal again. This time it wouldn't even be for my dad, but would be my own choice to break the law. I can't do that. As much as I wish I had the power, I'm not stupid enough to think I can stand up to Juan and the Army all on my own. The priority is to lie low so I can keep my quiet, perfect life, even if that means Radiasure is produced again.

My stomach turns at the thought. How can I let that happen if I have a chance to stop it? Am I that big a coward?

Major Norton nods. "Yes, this could be it. I knew that Seth Mitchell boy was suspicious—he was the only one who didn't pass the lie examination. We'll have to start pulling in parents next, see if we can get more."

My eyes go wide. I knew it. The government is just another word for syndicate, except they're under the delusion that they still have claim to the entire country. If they're playing dirty, too, then why feel bad about stealing from them? Gritting my teeth, I stand and silently close in on my prey.

That formula is mine.

Chapter 11

I sure hope Seth has kept his word about not watching me, because he'd freak over how close I am to the lab table. Even my hands shake at each step I take. The scientist is so close I could reach out and touch her. I still have no idea how I'll be able to take the papers without anyone seeing, but maybe I can get close enough to read some of it.

"Almost ready," the blond girl says as she stares at a test tube filled with what looks like pond water. "If it glows and increases in viscosity, we have it."

Glowing? This makes me worry even more.

Major Norton stares at the vial, looking oddly childish in his anticipation. I use the opportunity to tiptoe even closer to the pile of papers resting at the edge of the table. I only notice I'm holding my breath when my lungs start to burn, but out of habit I let the air out slowly and silently. With how bright the lights are, it's easy to see the bold lettering at the top of the first page.

TOP SECRET: Undisclosed Formula and Production Methods for Radiasure.

I only get a few lines in before the words make no sense.

Chemistry is almost as horrible as math for me. Seth might be able to make sense of all this gibberish if I can get it out of here.

The blond girl lets out a long sigh. "It doesn't look good, sir. This isn't it."

Major Norton nods. "If it was this easy, someone would have been able to reproduce it years ago. It's not over yet."

"I know." The girl grabs the papers, and I bite back a curse. "It's just hard not to want it right now when I've been searching for so long. This has been my whole life."

He puts his hand on her shoulder in a fatherly way. "That's why we asked you to help the Army with this mission."

I stare at the girl, wondering what her seemingly perfect façade hides. She doesn't look like she has an evil bone in her body, but I know better than most that appearances can be deceiving. What would make someone like her so bent on producing Radiasure again?

Static crackles over the comm unit at Major Norton's side. "Sir, we have intruders at the factory. Awaiting your orders."

I cover my mouth to stifle a gasp, knowing exactly who's there.

Major Norton grabs the unit and puts it to his mouth. "Do you have a visual?"

"No, sir. An alarm was tripped on the east side."

The Major swears. "Scour the area. Detain anyone you find. We're on our way." He turns to the scientist. "I'm sorry, but our work here will have to be cut short."

She nods. "It's a wash, anyway."

Major Norton yells commands like a veteran, his voice so loud I'm sure Seth can hear it up on the cliff. The soldiers gather around the large Army vehicles parked on the other side of the pond, while the scientist works to clean up her stuff. I chew my lip as I stare between her and the formula pages.

One elbow to her head…

No. I take a few steps back, horrified with my own thoughts. Since we left Dad, I've told myself over and over that I never would have done what I did on my own, and yet here I am on the verge of attacking someone. And I still kind of want to, because I *need* that formula. I have to know if the pools really are what they want. If not, then we wouldn't have to worry anymore.

The scientist slips the formula into a folder, and my heart sinks. Chances are getting slimmer. My ideas to stop her increase in violence.

A soldier comes up to her. His knuckles are sharp bone, and spikes jut out from his forearms almost like depictions of dinosaurs. "Ma'am?"

"Yes?" She turns, and I know this is the only moment I'll get. So I slip my fingers into the folder, hoping the spiked soldier doesn't notice. I get the papers out and drop under the table. My heart pounds as I wait to discover if they caught me or not.

"I'll be your personal guard on the way back," the soldier says.

"Okay. Just one moment. Let me clean this up." The scientist stands inches away from me as I try to fold the papers as quietly as possible. I have to get it small enough to stuff in my mouth, which isn't as easy as I thought it would be. The stack of pages grows thicker at every fold, but it's still too long to cover. "Are we leaving the table?"

"No, let me fold it up," the soldier replies.

I cram the paper in my mouth. It stretches out my cheeks, and I have to pinch my lips closed. The table flies up—I curl into a ball and pray they don't walk into me. There's no way they wouldn't put me in prison if I got caught.

Their footsteps scrape at the ground as they walk by me. Once they're a few yards off, I risk craning my neck to watch them leave. I don't dare get up—there's no telling how much dirt is now sticking to my butt. As the trucks drive off, I stand and brush off as much as I can.

Something rustles the bushes near the waterfall, and I whirl around in a panic. Did they leave guards? There's a figure barely lit in the moonlight, and when I recognize the broad shoulders and thin build I wish it were a soldier.

I duck behind the nearest bush, mortified, and spit out the paper. It's now semi-transparent thanks to my mutant spit. "Seth! What the hell are you doing?"

"That guy started yelling—I thought you were in trouble!" He tosses something at me, and it lands in the bush. My shirt. Then come my sweater and pants and shoes. "So sue me for wanting to come to the rescue."

"You looked?" I scramble for my clothes.

He sighs. "Is it really so bad for me to see you naked? It's not like we got together yesterday."

And there it is. I've wanted to pretend he's okay with us not going further, but he isn't. I wish I could tell him how weird it is for me, except that would probably make him feel even worse. Besides, now is not the time. "They left because of intruders at the factory, so we better hurry and make sure everyone's okay."

He cusses. "We need to find Brady. He'll get us there fast."

"Yeah." Now dressed, I grab the crumpled formula papers and stand. As I head toward Seth and the path up the cliff, I carefully pull open the sheets and hope my spit didn't mess them up too badly.

"What's that?" Seth says when I get to him.

We waste no time, climbing the slope as we talk. "Remember how Graham asked if we might have come across what they're looking for? Well, I think we have."

"What?"

"Their scientist girl said the element is a *liquid*, and it's supposed to glow or something. She was doing a test to see if the waterfall contained any of it, but it was negative."

"Shit." Seth doesn't need to say more for me to know he gets exactly what I'm trying to say.

I hold out the papers. "This is the formula, so we can test the cave water ourselves. Then we'll know just how much trouble we're in."

"Whoa." He stops just shy of the top. "You *stole* that from the Army?"

The way he says it makes me feel an inch tall, but I'm already mad at him for looking at me when he promised not to. "Yes. I stole it, just like they stole our knowledge of this place through an unnecessary interrogation. Do you have a problem with that?"

"Of course I do!" he says as we run for the booming sounds to the west. Brady must be that way. "They're gonna notice, Fi. And who do you think they'll suspect when they do?"

I don't answer for a moment, because he has a point. "They

could think it slipped out of the folder when they were rushing to pack everything up."

It may be dark, but I can feel his eye roll. "Or they'll realize you're the only one who could steal that with no one noticing."

"Well it's done, so we'll just have to deal with it." I squint into the night, hoping to see Brady or some clear sign of him. There's a dark spot on the horizon that seems to change shape like dust. "You think Brady's making that cloud?"

"Probably." Seth pulls a laser pointer from his pocket and turns it on and off. In the darkness it should stand out well enough to catch Brady's eye. "So how much trouble are they in at the factory? Are we gonna have to break them out?"

"I don't know. All I heard was that an alarm was tripped, and they didn't have a visual." My heart pounds from both the running and the fear of what could happen to Miles, Carlos, and Graham. If any of them are caught, they'd be tied to us in a heartbeat.

Maybe all of this was a horrible idea.

The ground starts to shake beneath my feet, and we both stop running. It's impossible to run when Brady gets too close. He skids to a stop, showering us with dust. "Done already? I didn't quite get to the cave yet."

Seth shakes his head. "We have a problem—the Army was at the waterfall. We gotta get to the factory fast. I'll explain on the way."

"Start talking." Brady holds out his arms, and Seth and I take a seat on his biceps. He has no problem lifting us into the air. "Hold on to my forearms if you think you might fall."

He takes off, and I have to cling to his arm as he bounds

through the desert. I've never been with Brady while he runs faster than any normal human, and it's both thrilling and horrifying how amazing he is. I'm not sure he's using his full force, but it feels like we're covering miles in just a few minutes.

Seth seems much more comfortable with Brady's speed than I do. He talks into Brady's ear—I assume to explain what I did at the waterfall—and seems to trust that his brother won't drop him. Brady slows the closer we get to the factory. By the time we reach the broken down strip mall, we're all walking again. Or rather creeping and hiding behind anything we can, just in case.

There are so many lights in the distance. It seems as if the Army has set up an entire base at the factory, complete with a wired fence and search lights scanning the desert for anyone who doesn't belong. As we huddle behind a group of rocks just south of the ruins, I catch the distinct sound of machinery and wonder if they're digging up the place.

The giant helicopters suddenly make a lot more sense.

"What do we do?" Brady whispers. "If they got caught… there's no way we're getting them out."

"Well, better make sure they're in there first," Seth says.

"No." I put my hand on his arm before I remember we're fighting. "It's too far and there are too many places to look—you'll kill your head."

Brady winces. "She's right, bro."

"So what?" His eyes are determined and maybe a little cold when they meet mine. "We already did the invisible thing once tonight, and if either of you suggest that Fi should sneak into that fortress I'll lose it."

Neither of us answer.

"Okay then." Seth's eyes narrow as he begins his search. I try not to cringe as I watch him, but as the minutes pass I worry he'll be in agony for days because of this. "I don't see them in the trucks or the tents. It looks like the Army has found something underground though…"

"Seth, stop." My voice quivers at the words. "They must have gotten out. Let's check back at Bea's house."

"Let me make sure." He grimaces as he pushes his ability, and then he gasps. "There's a whole building underground! They've unearthed stairs and some weird looking machinery. It looks like…"

He falters, and I grab him in an attempt to keep him up. Brady does most of the work though. Seth probably would have fallen on me otherwise. I try to cover his eyes to make him stop. "That's enough! They aren't there, so let's go."

"Wait!" Seth doesn't flinch at my hands because he sees right through them. "This is crazy. They're uncovering all sorts of equipment."

Panic swells as I picture just how many layers of metal and earth he might be looking through. It's probably more than he's ever done, and I don't know what that will do to him.

"Seth!" Brady says too loudly when we're supposed to be hiding. "No more!"

"Fine."

I remove my fingers from his face and wait for Seth's eyes to focus on me, but instead they fill with horror. Then he cries out in agony and collapses.

Chapter 12

Brady lays Seth gently on the ground, while I kneel down and tap his cheek. "C'mon, punk, wake up."

"What do we do?" Brady pulls at his hair, and his frightened expression reminds me too much of the time Dad shot Seth. "He's never passed out before. What if he has brain damage?"

"Don't say that." I can't think like that, not as I put my ear to his chest and listen for a heartbeat. What if he needs a doctor? When no one knows your real ability, it's kind of hard to go to the hospital and explain what happened. "He's breathing, and his heart is beating. The pain must have been too much for his body to handle."

"Let's get home." Brady carries him, but we don't run in fear that it'll hurt Seth more. The whole way back I flip between being on the verge of tears and wanting to cuss Seth out for being that reckless. It feels like he was making a point about my spying and stealing at the waterfall. Like, if I abuse my ability so will he. Or was this underground part of the factory really that interesting?

Once we're back within Madison's borders, Brady risks speaking. "It seems like you guys fought."

I look at the ground, not really wanting to talk about it. But when it comes to the topic of Seth being able to see me, Brady is literally the only person I can go to because no one else knows. "He promised not to look at me, but he did. Then he freaked over me stealing the formula. So yeah, I'm a little pissed."

Brady nods. "When he told me the story, he said he thought the commotion was because they caught you—so he had to check. You were so close to the Major that he could have shot you point blank, and everyone was running past you while you were completely vulnerable. One wrong move, and you might have been dead."

I look at Seth, placid in his brother's unwavering arms. No matter how hard I try, it's impossible to see myself like he does. He saw a naked girl walking around a bunch of armed soldiers—but I felt completely safe in my shell of invisibility. I'm not sure whether I should love him for wanting me safe or resent him for seeing me as weak. "Well, he forgets no one else sees what he does."

"It's true, but you do realize he'd fall apart if he lost you, right?"

Brady's words make the guilt rush in, leaving me defenseless. Seth's spent his entire life picking up the pieces from his mother's death. Of course he's majorly worried about my safety. "It's really annoying when you go all 'voice of reason' on me. Now I can't be mad at him."

He smirks. "You're welcome."

We take every side road through town, hoping to avoid any of Juan's people who might be out. The last thing we need is another threat right now. By the time we get back to Bea's house, it must be almost daybreak because it seems lighter than before. Everyone is standing out front, and I hear Bea yell, "There they are!"

"Tell them Seth tweaked his knee and fell asleep while I was carrying him," Brady whispers as they run toward us. "I'll take him inside. Come when you can."

"Okay," is all I get out before Miles grabs my shoulders and looks me over like he could see if I was injured.

"What took so long?" Graham says at the same time as Miles.

I glance at Brady, who is already taking Seth to their house. Bea and Hector follow him, asking all sorts of questions. I hate lying to Miles, but I don't have a choice. "Sorry we worried you. Brady didn't think we should run after Seth hurt his knee."

Miles lets out a relieved sigh. "After everything we saw at the factory, we were thinking a lot worse."

"Yeah, I bet. They were at the waterfall, too. I heard the alert when you guys tripped the alarm."

"Just how close were you to hear that?" Graham asks with a suspicious glare.

I gulp, hoping they don't freak out as much as Seth did. Pulling out the papers, I hand them to Miles. "Close enough to get this."

As he unfolds the sheets, Graham and Carlos crowd around him. Their jaws drop when they read the top line. I'm not sure if I'm seeing horror on their faces or disbelief. Miles looks up first. "Fi…"

"I know, but we needed it. After hearing their conversation I think we *might* know the location of what they want," I say

78

before he can tell me I shouldn't have done it. I don't want to hear it again right now.

He nods slowly. "I wish Spud had time to check, so you didn't have to do this. Seems I can't keep anyone I care about safe."

"We can't talk about this out here." Graham snatches the papers from Miles, folds them, and hands them back to me. "Let's get some rest—we'll decide what to do with this later."

Carlos gives him an incredulous look, eyes glowing in the dimness. "Who died and made you king?"

"I…" Graham seems sheepish.

"He's right. We should rest," I say, wanting to see Seth as soon as possible. "Meet at my place for dinner, okay? We'll fill each other in then."

Carlos doesn't seem completely satisfied with my answer, but then glances back at his home. "If our parents weren't about to wake up to an empty house, I'd fight you on that. Tell Bea and Hector to hurry back home."

"I will." I turn to Miles and Graham. "You guys can go. I'll just make sure Seth's okay. Brady will drive me home."

"Don't take too long," Miles says. "Mom won't overlook you staying out all night."

I shrug. "Sometimes I sleep over at Bea's after movie night."

"I'm guessing you call her, though," Graham points out.

Rather than admit he's right, I roll my eyes and head for Seth's house. "I can handle Mom."

No one answers me back, and when I turn around they're already a speck in the dawn sky. Carlos trudges to his house as I knock softly on Seth's door. I figure that'll be enough for Hector to hear. When it opens, I'm met with a face that surprises me.

It's Seth's dad, wearing only pajama pants and staring at me with a face that screams drunk. This is maybe the fifth time I've seen him since I met his sons. The first time he walked in while Seth and I were making out in the living room—super great first impression. Not that I feel the need to get his approval, but it makes an already awkward situation that much worse.

"Mr. Mitchell," I say, trying to suppress my discomfort. "You're up early."

"Never went to bed." He reeks of alcohol, and he scratches at the blond scruff on his face. "Seth's in his room with the others."

"Okay."

He leaves the door open for me and walks away. It still blows my mind how well he can walk though I've only seen him high and drunk. Seth told me he has perfect balance. So even when he's on a construction site it's hard for people to tell how smashed he is, because he can jump from beam to beam and land as gracefully as a cat.

"Seems like you guys had quite the party tonight," Seth's dad says as I follow him down the hall.

I gulp. "Something like that."

"Things sure have gotten interesting for my boys since you showed up." He shuts his bedroom door, leaving me to ponder what that's supposed to mean. Then again, it could just be the ramblings of a drunk man.

I open Seth's door without knocking. Hector sits at the desk, trying to look cool though I can tell he's worried about his best friend. Bea is at the edge of the bed, and Brady takes up most of the floor. They all turn to me when I enter.

"How is he?" I ask.

Brady cringes. "He's out."

I nod, knowing this means way more than Bea and Hector can understand. Hours have passed without Seth waking up. As worried as I was when it happened, that doesn't compare to now. Just how long can he sleep before we really do have to take him to a hospital?

"He better have just tweaked his knee," Hector grumbles. "If it's worse, there goes our soccer season."

Bea rolls her eyes. "Nice way to show you care, bro."

Hector holds up his hands. "What do you want me to do? Burst into tears?"

"Just don't be a—"

Seth lets out a loud groan, and his hands go straight to his head. Hector stands, his eyes filled with panic as he puts his hand on Bea's shoulder. "We better get outta here. He's gonna be pissed at you for waking him up."

Bea stands. "Okay."

Brady ushers Bea and Hector out while Seth continues to moan. Just as Brady's about to leave, he leans down to whisper, "Take care of him while I get some meds."

"Of course." I shut the door behind Brady and rush to Seth, who's curled into a ball and buried in blankets. He jumps when I touch him, as if he didn't know there was anyone here. Maybe he didn't, because when his eyes meet mine they're filled with fear and pain.

"W-who are you?" he whispers.

"It's me," I say as softly as I can.

He still winces at my voice. "I…you…you're a skeleton."

My eyes go wide. I don't want to make him talk more, but I'm pretty sure he's saying that he's seeing through layers he doesn't want to see through. If I'm a skeleton, this whole room must look crazy to him. He might not even be able to block it with his eyelids.

"It hurts so much," Seth says through gritted teeth.

"Shh." I lie next to him and put my hands on his head. My fingers make little circles over and over, but this time it doesn't seem to help. Seth keeps wincing and cringing like every move he makes hurts.

Brady finally comes back with water and two large, white pills. "Get him to take these."

I stand, taking the pills and glass from him. "What are they?"

Brady looks to the side. "You don't wanna know, Fi. But trust me, they'll help."

He doesn't have to say more—I've heard them talk plenty about their dad's love of pain meds. These must be from his stash. His illegal stash. As much as I don't want to give these to Seth, he actually does need them. "Here, Seth. Can you sit up to drink a little?"

Seth shakes his head. "I'm not taking those. Give them back to Dad."

"But…" I look to Brady, unsure of what to do. Arguing right now seems majorly counterproductive.

Seth holds out his hand. "Just…stay…with me."

I sigh, wishing he wasn't so stubborn, wanting him to feel better so I could tell him that. But I set the glass and pills on his desk and crawl into his bed. Seth wraps his arms around me tightly, his head nestled into the crook of my neck. His breaths are ragged from pain, and I hold him as close as I dare.

Brady leaves without another word, and it's just me and Seth. Even though there's no chance anything will happen, I'm still very aware that this is the first time I've been in Seth's bed like this. We've mostly kept to couches or secluded places at school, and it was hard enough to control myself there. Here under his covers, surrounded by him, he's all I can think about.

I watch him clench his jaw, listen to the sharp gasps he takes, rub his temples in hopes that it'll eventually help. If only I could take away the pain. Kissing his forehead, I wonder how I can want someone so much and yet be so chicken about going further.

If I could just see myself…that would fix everything.

Chapter 13

Next thing I know, someone is nudging me out of a deep sleep. I peek one eye open. The room is bright and I squint, but I saw enough to know that I'm still right next to Seth in his bed.

"Are you okay?" I ask as I force myself to adjust to the sun seeping through the window.

"Still hurts a little. I can control it again, though." Seth looks like he's been through hell, though he still manages a smile. "But if this is how I get to wake up after, I think it might have been worth it."

I shove him, though I bite back a laugh. "That's not funny."

"No, it's awesome." He puts his lips to my neck, but instead of kissing it he gives me a raspberry. I yelp and giggle, which makes him cringe. He puts one hand to his head. "Okay, maybe I'm not as recovered as I thought."

I frown. "Sorry."

"Don't be. This used to happen when I was a kid if I got carried away—I'd lose control pretty often." He lies back and stares at the ceiling. "There was just so much to see, and I couldn't believe I was actually able to see it. I try so hard *not* to use it…I had no idea I could go that far."

Part of me is relieved to hear it had nothing to do with my own recklessness. Of course it didn't. Seth isn't like that. "Maybe you can see more than we know, but that was scary for me and Brady. We didn't even know if you'd wake up again."

When he looks at me, I know he can see the worry on my face. As much as I want to hide my feelings from him at times, right now I'm glad he can tell how upset I am. His eyes are soft as he puts his hand on my cheek. "I'm sorry."

"I know, and I'm sorry for getting mad at you about looking." I put my hand over his, wanting to stay here all day. "Just what did you see down there?"

His eyes light up. "They were digging out this huge underground facility. I couldn't see much past the lights, but there was all sorts of machinery. I had no idea so much would still be there, but it looks like it was buried before it was ever blasted."

I sit up, surprised. "You mean it wasn't buried *in* the explosion?"

"Maybe it was, but the stuff didn't look very damaged. Old, yeah. Caked in dirt, of course. But it wasn't shards like on the surface."

"Weird." Pursing my lips, I can't help but wonder what that means. Did someone at the Radiasure factory get wind of the plan to destroy it? Were they planning to come back for it someday?

"That's not the worst part." Seth's brow furrows, and he looks away from me. "Before I pushed too hard and passed out, I saw a blue light beyond the dirt."

I gulp. "More Radiasure?"

He nods. "Most likely."

"Great. So the Army's gonna find it." For some reason this pisses me off, as if I've failed because there's more of that drug in the world.

"Fi…" Seth says my name like he knows what I'm thinking, but doesn't know how to answer. "Can I see the formula?"

I pull it from my pocket and hand it over, but my mind is elsewhere. Major Norton seems like the kind of guy who'll do whatever he must to complete a mission. He'll use that Radiasure on his soldiers. I'm sure of it. They'll get cocky and fight anyone who threatens them. And then what will Juan's men do to retaliate?

The Phantom will steal the Radiasure, that's what. Then the Army will try to arrest him, but that'll never happen. I can see it playing out in my head, each move escalating the violence. Just like during the drug riots in the seventies, this area will become more like a warzone than a town.

"This is some dense stuff," Seth says after a few minutes of reading. "I don't understand half of it, but I think this is the substance they're looking for. It's an element I've never heard of: merinite."

"Merinite," I repeat. "It doesn't say what it is?"

"It might. I'm not sure." He shakes his head, setting the papers on my lap. "This is way above me, Fi. Sorry."

"It's okay." What did I expect? Seth may be the smartest guy I know, but that doesn't mean he knows everything. If a high school student could figure it out at one glance, I'm sure Radiasure would have never gone out of production in the first place. "Maybe Miles will know. He's in college."

"Maybe, and Hector's better at chemistry than I am. He could help." Seth tugs at my arm. "But for now, how about you come back—"

My phone chirps, and I grab it from the nightstand. It's a text from Miles: *Remember how I said Mom will be pissed if you're not home?*

My phone says it's past noon, and I swear. "I didn't realize how late it is. My mom's gonna kill me."

Seth sighs. "Can't I just keep you to myself for one day?"

I smile, kissing him on the forehead. "But you get to keep more of me to yourself than any other boyfriend in the world. It's totally unfair."

He rolls his eyes.

"We're meeting at my place for dinner, The Pack and all. Rest until then, okay?" I say as I gather my hoodie and bag.

"Yes, Mom."

"Don't call me that. It's creepy."

"Yeah, I regretted it the moment it came out."

"As you should." Laughing, I head for the door and wave before I shut it again. When I turn to head down the hall, I jump because Mr. Mitchell is standing there. Two run-ins this close together? I'm not liking this trend, especially when I just came out of his son's room after a whole night. "Um…"

Mr. Mitchell waves his hand carelessly, and the expression on his face screams high as a kite. "Don't worry, I won't tell. It's about time Seth grew a pair."

Can I go die now? There's nothing I can say to this, so I scoot past him and pray he goes back to his room and stays there forever and ever. I hear the mower going, so I run outside knowing Brady will save me from the awkward.

"Everything okay with Seth?" Brady asks as he drives me home. Sometimes I feel bad that they chauffeur me everywhere, but Mom almost always needs the one car we have.

"I think so. His head still hurts some, but he seems like himself."

"That's good."

"Yeah." I tap my fingers on the windowsill, trying to remain calm, though there are way too many men with jaguar tattoos on Main Street. Brady pulls to a stop in front of my house. Miles' car is parked in the driveway, and I stare at it, confused.

"Something wrong, Fi?" Brady asks.

"No…not really." But in my gut it feels like something is off. "I thought Miles came with Graham, since they flew to Bea's house. But his car's here, so it surprised me."

Brady nods. "Maybe they're leaving at different times?"

"Probably. I hear Graham's girlfriend is pretty clingy." I shake off the paranoia. With all that's going on, I swear my brain is trying to read into everything. "See ya later."

"Yup!"

I get out and head up the front path, dreading Mom's wrath. Sure enough, she's standing in the living room, arms folded and face set to the brink of rage. Her glare immediately has me apologizing. "I'm so sorry. I fell asleep and—"

"Asleep, huh?" Her voice makes it clear she doesn't believe me for a second. "So you weren't out in the desert causing trouble?"

My stomach sinks. I thought she'd worry about me being with Seth, not that. "How'd you know?"

"Because of this." She holds out a red piece of paper, torn and ragged at the edges. I take it, and each word I read makes me regret everything I did last night more and more.

My men say they saw your little girl coming in from the desert with her friends this morning. I'm willing to chock it up to teens being stupid this time, but you've been warned. Going back on our agreement would be unwise.

—The Phantom

Chapter 14

"Do you not realize how serious our situation is? This isn't the time to be messing around," Mom says in her sternest of voices. "Please tell me you weren't doing anything dangerous out there."

I could lie. She knows how often I go running in the desert with Seth and Brady. I could easily say we were getting in one last run before the whole area was blocked off. But for the first time in my life, I actually *want* her advice. So I pull the formula out of my pocket and hold it out to her.

She snatches it from my hand, and when she realizes what it is her face goes slack with shock. "Where did you get this?"

"The Army was out there, and I went to get a closer look. They were talking about this element and…it sounded familiar. So I took it, to make sure." I stare at my feet, fear finally washing over me. Now I get why Seth was so upset—I'm getting in way over my head. "I went on instinct, from all those years of training. I know it was wrong, but I'm afraid we'll lose everything we have here."

I brace for a lecture, for Mom to yell at me, ground me, something. She is silent, looking over the paper intently. She flips through more pages, and I can't read her expression. When she looks back to me, there's no sign of anger in her brown eyes. "You know where the secret element is?"

"What?" I say, taken back by her not yelling.

She holds up her hands. "Never mind. I don't want to know the details—details are dangerous. But if you do, you know what that means, don't you?"

I gulp. "It means if anyone finds out, I'm in big trouble."

"Yes, but also something else." She leans back, seeming unsure of whether she should go on. "You might be the only one who can stop Radiasure from being made again, which means you have a big decision to make."

Mom's right. Either I protect my friends and lie low until the fight for Radiasure is over, or I put everyone in harm's way and make sure that horrible drug never gets made again. Maybe if I was only putting myself at risk, I could be okay with it. But I can't make this decision for my friends and family. This is too much for one invisible girl to handle. "What do I do, Mom?"

She puts her hands on my shoulders. "Sit down. I'll get the Pop Tarts."

I do as she says, and she's back with a big box of cheap pastry goodness. Digging in, I realize I'm starving after all that running last night. Mom watches me in silence, to the point where I have to ask, "What?"

She shakes her head. "Oh, I guess I'm not sure what to tell you, honestly."

"Awesome." I snort. "You have plenty of advice when I don't want it!"

Mom smiles, and I'm so glad she's not yelling because I

need her support. It's nice to know we're a team now, with no abusive Dad to get in the way. "Well, what do you want me to say? I know just as well as you do that stopping them would be the right thing to do, but I can't tell my baby girl to throw herself into harm's way."

Sighing, I can't say I disagree. "When I heard about this quest for Radiasure, it made me mad, but I didn't think I could do anything about it. I've been trying to tell myself it would lower the drug's value. Everyone would be able to get it, which means everyone would have an equal footing. But deep down I know…"

"Whoever got it first would keep it for themselves? Use it to expand their territory? Do whatever the hell they please with no one to stop them?" Mom rattles off.

"Yeah, pretty much." Because as horrible as syndicates are, in a weird way they also keep the country floating because they balance each other out. If one person were in charge people would suffer even more. "So would I be a terrible person if I turned a blind eye to what I might know?"

"Hmm." Mom taps her chin, thinking. "Not necessarily. People ignore bad things all the time to keep themselves safe. Think about when we first came here—sure, someone could have told the cops or Juan but ultimately their fear protected us. They didn't want to earn the wrath of your father."

This doesn't make me feel better. "I don't like the Army or Juan thinking I'm scared of them."

She smirks. "You're not afraid? Because I am. Not being protected by a syndicate is so scary I even lied to The Phantom that we were still in one."

"Well, I am scared..." I put my head in my hands, struggling to find the words. "But I don't want them to *know* that. They should be afraid of me. I'm not weak anymore. If I wanted, I could stop them."

Mom stares at me like she's not sure who I am. "Well, it sounds like you're a lot more courageous than I am."

"No." *More like crazy.* "Sometimes I worry I'm more like Dad than I should be."

She holds out her hands, and I put mine in hers. "Fiona, being a leader doesn't mean you have to be a *bad* one. Not that I'm saying you should do this, but don't be afraid of becoming your father. That will never happen—you have too strong a moral compass."

I tackle her into a hug. Maybe I still don't know what to do, but it's nice to sort it out a bit. "Thanks, Mom."

"You're welcome." She hugs me, and I savor it. There was a time when she wasn't much of a mother because of what Dad did to us—it feels like we've been making up for lost time.

"Whoa, did someone die?" Miles' voice sounds groggy, and when I look up he seems to have just rolled out of bed.

"No," I say.

"Are you begging Mom not to ground you?" he asks next. "Because I purposely slept in to avoid that blowout. Should I go back to bed so you can finish?"

"Very funny. I'm much more supportive of my kids than you give me credit for, son." Mom holds up the formula to me. "I wasn't half bad at chemistry. I'll see if I can figure some of this out for you, okay?"

My eyebrows pop up in surprise. "That would be amazing

if you could."

Miles shakes his head. "Am I still dreaming? Is our mother seriously not freaking out about this?"

"Yup." Mom stands from the couch, heading for her beloved coffee pot.

Miles takes her seat, staring me down suspiciously. It doesn't have nearly the effect he thinks, since his eyelids still sag with sleep. "Are you sure you're invisible? Or are you so good at persuading people that we only *think* you're invisible?"

I snort. "Unless I can also persuade myself into thinking I'm invisible, no."

"I'm not convinced. Never thought Mom would be so calm about what you did." He turns on the TV, flips it to a baseball game.

"This is how she is now, without Dad," I say.

He nods. "It's scary to think he had that much control over you."

"It is." And now that we're on the topic, I can't help thinking about how Miles now has the very same power Dad has if he wanted it. "Are you ever tempted? You know, to use his scent?"

Miles actually looks away from the game, and his eyes meet mine. "No. Never. Sometimes I'm disgusted that I even know the scent—how could I ever want to take away choices from the women I care about?"

I lean on his shoulder, knowing he's absolutely sincere. "I thought so."

"You better." The slight citrus scent he was emitting turns to blueberries. I've always appreciated how he changes scents just for me. "Besides, I enjoy smelling like fruits too much."

After about fifteen minutes of baseball—nearly my max attention span for it—I realize someone's missing. "Where's Graham?"

"Went back to see Allie." He shudders. "Those two can get so mushy together. It's weird seeing him like that after so many years of Violent Angry Graham."

"I can't even picture it." All I can conjure is a scowling Graham with some overly happy girl, and it just doesn't work. "Do they have anything in common?"

"They really like playing board games together. Especially chess."

Words won't come.

Miles laughs. "I know, right? It gets really gross when they start flirting with chess euphemisms."

"Ew. No more."

"You asked for it." Miles looks at his phone, and the smile falls off his face. "It's nice that they do things like that together, though. You should want to spend time with the person you care about."

I can't stand that pout. He has to be thinking about Spud. "Can you at least call her?"

He shakes his head. "She uses a different number every time, hacks them and drops them just as fast. I never know where or when I'll run into her."

"That's gotta be hard."

"I knew what I was getting into. Keeps things interesting." Miles shrugs off the sadness like he can't stand to talk about it anymore, but I can feel how much this bothers him. I watch him—there are circles under his eyes, creases in his brow, stubble on his chin—it seems like Miles has aged years since he first showed up to help me get free of Dad. Where did my happy, carefree brother go?

"How long are you staying?" I ask after I finish another Pop Tart. "The whole weekend?"

"Probably longer," Miles says without looking away from the game.

"Longer?"

"Until my ankle is better at least. Like a week."

I purse my lips, confused. He went out in the desert last night though I told him he shouldn't walk on it—he said it wasn't that bad. Now he's using it as an excuse to stay here? "What about school and work? I thought your Spring Break wasn't until the end of March."

He gives me an epic pout. "What? You don't want me around or something?"

"I do!" But he's so avoiding something. I hope he's not staying here because he's worried about us. I'd hate to be more of a burden than I already am. "I just—"

The doorbell rings. So instead of confronting my brother I get up to answer it. I didn't think The Pack would be here so soon, but maybe they're more eager to know how I got the formula than I thought. When I open the door, I'm met with two men in uniform instead.

"Fiona McClean?" one of them says.

"Yes?" My blood pumps faster. Something is wrong about this.

The man holds up a paper. "You are under arrest for stealing Army property. If you do not comply, we have been ordered to take you by force."

Chapter 15

"What? You can't do that! Where's the proof?" Miles is up from the couch and already by my side, but my eyes are on Mom. Luckily, the open door blocks the soldiers' view of her, and I'm not wearing glasses or hair things to show where I'm looking. Her face sets into surprising innocence while she folds the formula and slips it into her pants.

"There were footprints found," one of the soldiers says. "We have to take her in for—"

"That's it? How do you know they're not old or someone else's?" Miles has moved in front of me, as if he can stop this from happening.

"We're following orders, sir."

"Let me see the warrant," Mom says from behind me. She takes it from the soldier, reading it intently.

All I can do is stand there in shock. My first impulse is to run, except that would make me look even guiltier, wouldn't it? The idea of being dragged to the makeshift military base, thrown in a cell, and questioned about what I did last night isn't exactly how I want to spend the rest of my weekend. And Major Norton…he'll see right through any lie I tell.

"This looks pretty flimsy," Mom says with a sigh. It's definitely not the first time she's seen an arrest warrant—Dad just usually gets his women out of them. She turns to me. "But we have to follow the law and clear up the misunderstanding, Fiona. Let's go."

I gulp, trying to quell my fear. Laws. How could I forget about those? "Okay."

"We'll figure this out," Miles says as the soldiers come forward with handcuffs. "I promise."

I don't answer—all I can see are the cuffs. The soldier looks over me with a confused expression, probably because he isn't sure where my hands are.

"Are those really necessary?" Mom asks.

"I'm afraid so, ma'am." He finally decides to reach for my shoulder first, and my skin crawls as his fingers run down my arm. He latches the cuff and goes for my other shoulder, but I can't take it.

"I'll do it myself." Snapping the other cuff around my wrist, I feel sick. Mostly because this is exactly what I deserve for what I did. I've become so used to getting away with things that I honestly believed this wouldn't happen.

I really hate when Seth is right.

Mom stays by my side as the soldiers guide me to a big truck covered in a cammo pattern. The back is windowless and seems to be fortified just for prisoners with abilities. By now, my neighbors have come out to see what's going on, and all of them stare at us with faces that say, "Not surprised." This doesn't bother me—I'm used to it—but what does bother me is The Phantom standing on the sidewalk, right by my house, smiling.

He clucks his tongue. "Looks like someone was somewhere she wasn't supposed to be."

"You did this?" I say. Of course he did. A simple warning note isn't syndicate style. There's always a scare tactic involved.

"You set her up!" Mom looks so angry I worry she'll actually attack him. "That was way out of line."

"Was it?" The Phantom pops a Radiasure pill in his mouth, and I can feel the soldiers tense behind me. If Graham is right about Radiasure making it so he can take other people through walls, too, I don't want to know what he's planning for my mom. "If I were you, Lauren, I wouldn't step foot on that military base—I told you this was your warning. I'm sure you know all the things I could do with your daughter instead of putting her in an Army cell."

Mom, despite her best efforts, shrinks at the threat. "Asshole."

The Phantom shrugs innocently. "I'm just a concerned, law-abiding citizen."

"Bullshit!" I yell, pissed that he's forcing my mom to stay behind. How am I supposed to do this without her?

"Hey," one of the soldiers snaps at me. "No more talking." They take me to the back of the truck, while Mom's tears begin to fall. The Phantom's laugh fills my ears, and I'd give anything to kick his skinny ass.

The locks on the back of this vehicle are ridiculous—three huge bolts that each need a separate code. The door opens with a puff of air, like it's pressurized inside. When I look into the dimly lit space, I'm surprised to find someone else already in there, hunched over and squinting at the sudden burst of light. One look at his size and blazing red hair, and I know who it is.

Brady.

Now I'm even angrier. It's one thing for The Phantom to mess with me, but with my friends?

"Fiona?" Brady says as the soldiers shove me inside with unnecessary force. They shut the door, and the locks wheeze as they're reset.

"I'm gonna kill that guy." I kick the side of the truck, wishing it was The Phantom's head. Somewhere in my mind I know my rage is disturbingly high, that my need for vengeance could easily get out of control. But I don't care. "What'd they accuse you of?"

Brady doesn't look at me, seeming embarrassed. "Destroying private property."

"Ugh! That land isn't private!" I sit across from him on the narrow bench. "This is ridiculous. They just want an excuse to leech more information, and The Phantom gave it to them."

This doesn't seem to improve Brady's mood. "You should have seen everyone, Fi. They were freaked out. Bea…she was on the verge of tears."

These words extinguish all my fight. "I'm sorry, Brady. It's all my fault."

He shakes his head, a hint of a smile on his lips. "Don't flatter yourself. You didn't force us to do anything."

"Whatever." I lean my head back on the wall, thinking. "We shouldn't talk anymore. Who knows what they'll try to use against us, and we don't know who's listening."

"True."

The ride doesn't take long, and when they open the door I'm surprised to find we're at the school, not their little base at the factory. Truth be told, I'm kind of bummed—I was hoping to at least get a peek at the dig site Seth described. Maybe that's why we're here instead.

Since it's a weekend, the school is abandoned save military personnel. Brady and I step out of the truck, and immediately five more soldiers surround us as if we're thinking of fighting back. They take us to the office, where they've put up bars in the small copy room's doorway.

How they think this would hold any respectable criminal, I don't know. Even I could get through drywall.

After they take off our handcuffs and lock us in the cell, a soldier says, "The Major will be here soon."

"Super." I settle in on the floor. The area has been stripped of the copier and shelves, with only a few blankets and a bucket for I-don't-want-to-think-about-it in the far corner.

"Soon" must be a term for "sometime in the future" in military speak, because Brady and I sit in that room long enough for my butt to start aching. I fold up one of the blankets to sit on, hoping that will help. It's brutal to sit in silence, especially since I would prefer to pass the time joking around with Brady.

I can't stop thinking about The Phantom and his smug grin. What did he tell the Army, exactly? Why is it that only me and Brady got taken in? They had to have seen Seth with us at the very least. Maybe they could only drum up enough fake evidence to arrest us, or maybe...

"Shit," I say out loud. *This is a trap. We're the bait.*

Brady gives me a funny look. "What?"

I shake my head, wishing I had my cell phone so I could text Seth and tell him not to come. Because he's the one they want—they already suspect him of knowing more than he's saying. The Phantom just gave them an easy way to do it. All Major Norton has to do is threaten to harm us if Seth doesn't tell him everything.

And I thought I was pissed before. Now I could punch out that wall without feeling it, I'm so wound up. Stupid Army, they play games just as well as any syndicate.

Hearing a door open, I scramble to see who's coming in. My heart sinks when I see his strawberry hair and blue eyes. Seth looks horrified to see us behind these makeshift bars, but he should be more worried about himself.

"Fiona! Brady!" he says once he gets to us.

I push back tears. "Idiot, you should have stayed home."

Seth gives me a hurt look.

Right then, Major Norton enters the office, as if he was waiting for Seth to show up. "Seth Mitchell. Since you're here, can we have a word before I question our prisoners?"

"Uh…"

"Don't. Tell. Him. Anything," I say through my teeth. Because if this is how Juan and the Army are playing, then there's no way in hell I'm letting them get away with it.

"Do I have a choice?" Seth asks the Major.

"No. Not really." Major Norton's eyes turn cruel, and I know all my guesses were right. Unless one of us caves, we're not going anywhere anytime soon.

Chapter 16

When I hear just how loudly Major Norton yells, I'm not so sure Seth will remember my final plea. The volume makes his threats sound that much worse. He tells Seth that Brady is a danger to people's safety and should be forced into the Army immediately, so that he can be properly trained. He explains that I could be prosecuted for all my past crimes if he felt like it—I'd be locked up for years if found guilty.

But Seth can stop it. All he has to do is tell the Major what we did in the desert last night and why. Easy. Then we can walk away like nothing happened.

Listening to this is too familiar. I feel like I'm back in Vegas, hiding in a closet while Graham threatens person after person. Drop the case, or your clairvoyant daughter will end up in the syndicate. Tell us where the Radiasure is, or you'll never walk again. Keep quiet, or we'll let your wife know about the other woman. If that didn't work, the beat squad would take Radiasure pills to make their pain-causing abilities stronger— sometimes people wouldn't make it out of that alive.

It's always the weakest ones, too. Of course Major Norton didn't go for Brady and me—we have abilities that give us more confidence in protecting ourselves and our loved ones. But he thinks Seth is little more than average, that intimidation will scare him because he's defenseless.

How quickly Major Norton shows his colors.

Silence makes my ears ring after all that yelling. Then there is a mumble I recognize as Seth's voice. Particularly his attitude tone. I don't know what he says, but it has the Major yelling again, "Get out!"

The door opens, and Seth is smiling smugly. "I'll be back with a lawyer next time."

"You step one foot on these premises, Mr. Mitchell, and you'll be the next one behind bars."

He turns back. "So I can't go to school?"

"No."

"Damn. Those last few months of senior year are so critical." Seth rolls his eyes and shuts the office door. He comes to me quickly—we probably have seconds to talk. "I told him his extortion attempts pretty much negate your charges. They obviously don't have anything solid on you."

"I know that." I put my hands on the bars. "It doesn't mean he'll let us go, though."

"Still working on that." He leans in for a kiss, and that's when how bad this is hits. I don't know when I'll see him or my family and friends next, so I savor his lips on mine and try to tell myself there's a way out.

Major Norton bursts out of the office. "Get him out of here now!"

The soldiers scramble to surround Seth, and he's escorted away before I can say goodbye. The imposing Major, face crimson red with anger, turns on me. "Bring her in."

I sit in the same chair I was questioned in just days ago, but this time I'm not so much scared as I am livid. This guy isn't any different from a syndicate leader. At least Juan's men have the decency to be upfront about their crimes. I'll take that over this charade any day. "I wouldn't bother threatening me—pretty much seen it all and it won't work."

Major Norton grits his teeth. "Something was stolen from a secret military operation last night. None of my soldiers reported seeing anyone. How do you think that happened, Miss McClean?"

I'm not stupid enough to answer that question.

"You think being quiet will save you?" He smirks as he slaps a photograph onto the desk. "We have proof."

My heart speeds up. I swear I was careful not to leave a single sign that I was in the area. Maybe it has been a while since I've spied and stolen, but it felt like it came back easily. Not sure I should see that as a good thing. I lean over to get a better look at the picture. My fear dissolves to the point that I have to fight back a fit of giggles. It's an image of a footprint on the muddy bank of the pond. "That's not my foot."

Major Norton's face fills with confusion. "Say that again?"

"Not. My. Foot."

"How do you know it's not your foot?" he goes on, like he can't believe I'm telling the truth even though his own ability proves it. "Maybe you didn't notice you left this print. Because something *was* stolen from us, and there's only one person who could do that."

"Really? Just one?" I fold my arms, confident I have this.

"No offense, but I can think of like ten people who could have done that just as easily as me. Like that ass of a wall walker who turned me in as a scare tactic, for example."

His face twitches, and I know he doesn't have any clue how that formula went missing.

"Besides, my foot isn't that long or wide," I continue. "And if I were on some kind of a mission, I would *never* get anywhere near mud. I've done that kind of stuff enough to know what to avoid."

Major Norton pounds the desk. "But you know why we're here! I can feel it. You and your whole gang of friends."

Mentioning my friends triggers something inside me. A need to protect. To deflect the suspicion solely onto myself. It feels wrong, but giving a piece of information here could at least keep The Pack out of this. "Of course I know why you're here. The Radiasure formula, right?"

His eyes go wide. "You did steal it."

"I knew about the formula way before you showed up," I say, avoiding the accusation. "My father wanted me and my mom to steal it from the guy in China. Why do you think we ran? It was a suicide mission."

"Truth." The Major's eyebrow quirks. "Interesting…"

I don't like the way he says this word. It smacks too much of plotting. "Interesting how?"

"Of all the places you could have gone, you guys came to the town nearest the one Radiasure plant in the entire world. Why is that?"

I stare at him, the question taking me completely off guard. "It's the only one? Really?"

He nods.

"I had no idea this was the only area where Radiasure was produced—I can promise you that. I'm sure my mother and brother didn't know either. Our only goal was to get out of the syndicate."

He has to know I'm telling the truth, and yet he doesn't seem to care. "Maybe you believe that, but I can sense you have what I'm after."

I can't open my mouth. Nothing I say will prove me guilt-free on that account.

"You're not as innocent as you act, and you *will* be telling me what you know one way or another. Guards!"

The door opens, and two soldiers come in. "Yes, sir?"

"Let the Mitchell boy go." He looks at me, his smile turning sinister. "We have everything we need right here."

Chapter 17

This is what I wanted, I tell myself over and over as the days pass in lonely silence. The rest of Saturday, all of Sunday, and now the last bell has rung Monday afternoon while I've been in this makeshift prison cell. They've only given me water, since after I got Brady out I've refused to talk. My stomach groans against my will, revealing my weakness when nothing else can.

"Hungry?" my guard asks. He's the same one I saw at the waterfall, with nasty spikes on his knuckles and forearms. His tag tells me his surname is Tagawa, and that's all I know about him.

"Nope."

"Sure…" He laughs to himself. "Think you're so tough."

Even though I'm tempted to argue with Tagawa, I restrain myself. It'll show Major Norton I'm craving human interaction. No one has come to see me—I assume because they aren't allowed to. I wonder what they're doing, how worried my mom is, if Seth is killing his head watching me.

I have to admit I didn't think it would take them this long to get me out. At night when Tagawa starts to doze, I strain to hear if Mom's out there unlocking doors with her mind.

She could do it easily enough, but after The Phantom's threat to do worse to me than the Army maybe she's scared. If the military is already giving us so much crap, we can't afford to officially break our deal with Juan's syndicate.

Time slugs along. Major Norton brings me dinner as usual. It's a big, greasy pizza that I want to stuff my face with more than anything. "I'd really like to let you eat this, but I need your cooperation first."

"Eat it yourself." I plug my nose so I don't have to smell all that cheese and meat and fresh, hot bread.

"If you insist." He pulls up a chair and opens the box. His bites are big and messy, and I turn the other way in disgust. I swear he enjoys this—I've never seen someone take such pleasure in someone else's pain. Not even Graham or my dad. "You know, I was hoping we didn't have to take this further, but I'm beginning to think you're stubborn enough to starve yourself to death."

"Probably."

He nods, and the fluorescent lights gleam off his bald head. "I know you've 'seen it all' and talk big, but have you ever been tortured?"

I don't answer.

"I didn't think so." He leans back. "It starts slow, something uncomfortable but not unbearable, just enough to fray the senses and weaken resolve. Then it gets worse, both mentally and physically, until you've been violated in every possible way and you'd do anything to make it stop."

Closing my eyes, I tell myself to breathe slowly, to stay calm, to believe in myself. But I still can't suppress a shudder.

"I'm only telling you this because step two begins tomorrow, and maybe you'd like to tell me what you know about the formula and the desert before then." He sets the box on the floor and slides it under the bars. "Don't want you dying. Yet."

There's no way I'm touching that box.

Major Norton clucks his tongue. "You of all people should know integrity died a long time ago."

"No wonder no one trusts the government anymore."

"Fight fire with fire, sweetheart." He eyes Tagawa. "Tell me if she eats."

"Yes, sir."

Even though the night grows dark and quiet, I can't sleep. I hate admitting the Major's threats got to me, but they did. Torture isn't something I plan on sticking around for. My mind runs through plans for escape. It'll be hard, since I'm so weak from not eating.

Tagawa starts snoring, and I roll my eyes. He has fallen asleep every night he's been on duty. The first day I tried to reach the keys latched to his chest pocket, but he was too far away. Pizza smell fills my nostrils, and I wish Miles was here to unleash a nasty smell that would make me too queasy to eat.

I crawl under my blanket and try to sleep, but my body aches from the hard linoleum floor. As I'm finally dozing off, I swear I feel someone nudge my shoulder.

No, I'm losing it.

Another nudge.

I pull the blanket down and recoil when I see a figure standing over me. In the darkness, it's hard to make out who it is. Until I hear the voice. "Someone call for a fairy godmother?"

110

I scramble to my feet. "You."

The Phantom snickers. "Had enough yet, Fiona?"

"You really think it's funny, don't you?" I hiss. "I'll yell for the guard—he'll sound the alarm and then the whole Army will be after you."

"What's new?" he says. "Besides, if you wake that guy up, how will I help you escape?"

My heart skips a beat. "What?"

"They starved you, no?" He looks me up and down, as if he'll be able to tell. "If you haven't eaten, I can make you like me with one touch. No Radiasure necessary, even."

It's tempting—there's no denying that—but I can't help wondering. "How'd you know they starved me?"

He waves his hand dismissively. "Standard procedure."

"Yeah right. You have some kind of spy in the Army is my bet."

"This is not the time to question me, is it? Look, I intended to teach you a lesson about keeping your word, not to permanently imprison you. These idiots were supposed to let you out days ago." His eyes, dark as they are, still pierce me through the dimness. "If they're keeping you, it must mean you know things they want to know. Things *I* want to know."

I keep my mouth shut though he'll take the silence as confirmation.

He nods, then holds out his hand. "Let's go."

I stay where I am. "Why, so I can give you information in return for getting me out of the place you got me into to begin with?"

"You are what they call savvy." He smiles, and the kindness in

111

it creeps me out more than anything. The Phantom is beginning to see me as useful, and that is not a trait I want to have. "I only want to get you out so you don't crack and tell them what you know, but I won't refuse extra information for myself. As a good faith gesture."

"Good faith my ass." I step toward the bars. "Thanks, but I'll get out myself."

He tilts his head. "Oh?"

"Yeah, I'm not owing you anything."

Before I can blink, he swoops in, grabbing my shoulders and pinning me to the bars. The stupid guard doesn't wake up. I struggle to push him away. "I'll scr—"

He punches me in the gut, and it knocks the wind out of me. His fist smashes into my face next, and the pain is blinding. For how frail and ghostlike The Phantom appears, he sure can be solid when he wants to. The guard lets out a loud snore, while I'm left speechless.

"Go ahead. Scream." The Phantom's face is too close to mine, his breath stale. "Have you ever thought owing someone is better than making unnecessary enemies? I would not make a true enemy out of me, Fiona McClean."

"I'm not trying to," I cough.

"If you do anything to help the Army get the element first, then you may as well start picking out your headstone."

Finally getting my breath back, I scream as loud as I can. Tagawa falls out of his chair, but The Phantom is already running for the wall. He goes right through it just as Tagawa stands on the other side of the bars. "W-what's wrong?"

"The Phantom was here," I say.

He snorts. "Good one."

"He was—he attacked me." I touch my fingers to my nose, and there's something wet. "I'm bleeding."

"Yeah right. You're just trying to get me to open the gate." Tagawa calls me a dirty name and goes back to his chair. As I glare at him, a fire ignites inside me. I decide once and for all that Juan or the Army or anyone else who comes will never lay a finger on this merinite stuff. There's no way I can turn a blind eye after what they've done to me. I'll do what I have to in order to stop them.

Chapter 18

I plan on escaping when the soldier comes to clean my waste bucket, but he doesn't show up. This makes me crazy paranoid, as if they somehow can guess my plan, though in reality Major Norton probably just wants to make me more uncomfortable. Hate to admit this tactic is more effective than he knows.

My only chance will be when the Major himself shows up. I'll have to be fast to disable him and Tagawa, but it's not impossible. If I strip down…no, that will only make it obvious I'm preparing to fight.

The outside door opens, and I crane my neck to see if the cleaning guy has finally shown. But it's not him—it's the blond scientist girl I stole the formula from. I raise an eyebrow as she stands in front of my cell, her eyes wild as she searches for my invisible face. I wait for her to speak, but she seems hesitant and uncomfortable with the sight of me.

"What, never seen an invisible girl before?" I say when I can't take it anymore.

She smirks, her eyes never stopping the search for my face. "No, actually. You're fascinating."

This statement makes me step back, because I get the distinct impression she'd like nothing more than to study me. "So did you come to stare, or is there a point?"

"I need you to tell me what you know."

"No way." I head for the corner nearest the bars, where she won't be able to stare at me like a creeper. "Did Major Norton think I'd cave to a girl?"

She sighs. "He didn't want me to come, but I insisted on trying before he…anyway, he thinks it's a risk to the mission for you to see me."

I stay quiet for a moment, taking in that tiny piece of information. Just what kind of stuff does this chick know? Maybe I should be trying to get information from her…"So I guess I can't ask your name."

"Classified. Sorry." Her delicate fingers wrap around the bars. "But if you agreed to help us, that could change."

I grit my teeth just thinking about the idea. "No offense, but there's no way in hell I'm helping an organization who imprisons me based on fake evidence, continues to keep me because of what I might know, starves me, and is now planning to torture me. Call me stubborn like that."

"Major Norton's tactics are extreme, but I promise his intentions are good. Can't you trust me on that?"

My laugh comes out cold. "Why should I trust a person I know nothing about?"

"Because…" I hear fabric shift, and I guess she sat down but I don't look. "I need what you know to do my job. Do you know what happens if I don't do my job, Fiona?"

The tiniest bit of guilt creeps in, imagining the kind of punishments the Major might inflict for failure. I stuff it back down. "You suck at this, you know?"

"I'm normally very good at it, but you seem to be an exception." Scientist girl lets out a frustrated grunt. "If I could just tell you what I'm trying to do, I know you would change your mind."

"Then tell me."

"It's classified. Not even your guard knows."

This top secret information makes me salivate more than I like to admit. I have half a mind to give in just so I can know, but that's exactly what she and the Major want. Whatever information they have, it's incomplete enough that they believe they need me. And that's my only protection, little as it is. "You can't give me even the tiniest hint? There has to be something."

The bars clang from being hit, and Tagawa yells, "Shut your mouth! You're not the interrogator."

"Don't, George, you're not helping," the scientist girl says, and I try not to laugh about Mr. Tough-Guy Tagawa being named George. "I'm afraid there's nothing I can tell you, Fiona. Not even the people closest to me know I'm part of this—it's that secret."

"You should just go, then."

"I guess so." More shuffling, which I assume is her standing up. "Sorry for what will happen to you tonight. I really hoped I could stop it."

I don't answer. Her footsteps fade away, and the door shuts behind her. The only thing I can hear in the silence is Tagawa tapping his spiked knuckles on the wall. Then he says, ever so quietly, "Shoulda talked while you could."

116

When the school bell rings, my jitters start. There are only a few hours left to plan my escape. My face still hurts from The Phantom's attack last night, and I gingerly touch my nose. Sure hope it's not broken. Lying on the floor, I save all my remaining strength for the moment of escape. The idea of smashing my elbow into the Major's face brings way too much joy. Tagawa will be tricky, since I don't know where else he has those nasty spikes.

Dinner time. Major Norton comes in as usual. Today it looks like he brought Taco Bell—he's crazy if he thinks that will be even remotely tempting. I've seen way too many burrito-eating contests since moving to Madison.

He stands in front of me. "Well? Have you decided whether or not you'll talk?"

"I'll talk." I stay absolutely still, determined not to put him on guard.

He seems pleased, as if he thinks he's already broken me. "Excellent. Tagawa, open the cell."

Tagawa does as he's ordered, and I have to force myself to be calm as I walk past him. I can't use my opening move on him, as easy as it would be. The Major opens the office door. "Shall we?"

"Sure." I start for the door, but then quickly turn on the Major with a knee to the groin. He hasn't finished swearing over that when I sink my elbow into his face. There's a lovely popping sound.

Tagawa grabs his gun, but in these close quarters I'm already up in his face and pushing the gun to aim at the Major.

"Get off me, bitch!" Tagawa yells as I feel something pierce my leg.

117

I scream, pulling back to see his sharp knuckles where my thigh was. Not having time to think about the pain, I throw my head into his like I would to a soccer ball. It hurts, but not as bad as my leg. With both of them on the ground, I make for the door as I pull my shirt off. The wound might slow me down, but I can still—

Arms come around my waist, and I hit the floor hard. "You really think it'll be that easy, huh?"

I grunt as I fight against Major Norton's hold on me. He pulls me upright and pushes me towards the office. I try to kick his shin, but he dodges it.

"Did you actually think that would work? I could tell you were lying, but I wanted to see why." He grabs my hair, and I spit in his face.

"You have a fighting spirit, Fiona." He wipes the spit off his cheek and rubs it on my invisible skin. "Looks like we'll be skipping right to step three instead. Tagawa, get the chains to tie her down."

"Yes, sir!" Tagawa heads for the door, and now I'm officially panicking. What will they do to me? I dig my feet into the ground as Major Norton tries to get me into the principal's office. Once I go in there, it's all over. I have no idea if I can keep my secrets under actual torture.

Gunfire.

The Major freezes, and in the silence I can hear yelling outside. My heart skips with hope. Someone has finally come to get me! Is Brady out there destroying the school? Is Bea popping eardrums? Is Mom hurling cars at soldiers? It might be horrible, but I hope they are.

The office door bursts open, and a few soldiers come in, walking backwards with their guns trained on someone. When I see his wild auburn hair and angry face, I'm not sure I've ever been happier to see Graham. He grips the young scientist girl with one arm and holds a knife to her throat with the other.

"How about we make a trade?" Graham says.

Chapter 19

They throw me back in the cell and usher Graham and his hostage into the principal's office. I can't hear anything but mumbles, and yet my hope has never been higher. The Major needs that girl to make Radiasure—he won't let her get hurt. I don't know how Graham found out about her, but for once I'm kind of glad he's an evil genius.

Ten minutes later, Graham emerges on his own and hands a paper to Tagawa. "Major Norton says she's free to go."

Tagawa snags the paper and reads it with a curled lip. Tossing it on the floor, he grabs the key and unlocks my cell. "Shoulda guessed your syndicate family would come for you eventually. Bunch of crooks."

"Speak for yourself," I spit back.

"C'mon, Fi." Graham grabs my shirt from the ground and hands it to me. For the first time, I'm not scared when he picks me up and flies out the door. He shoots into the air before the soldiers outside can react. I shut my eyes and hold onto him tight. "You okay?"

"Yeah," I whisper, but him asking brings on tears. "Thank you. For coming to get me."

He puts his hand on my cheek, all brother-like and concerned. "They hurt you?"

"The Phantom hit me when I refused his help to escape. They just starved me."

He snorts. "Just? Because going without food for four days is nothing."

"You know what I mean." I venture a peek at his face, and it seems full of regret. Though I can't quite place my feelings, I think I might see the brother Graham used to be when we were kids. And more than that, I'm surprised by how much I want him back. "How did you know to hold that girl hostage? Maybe I'm horrible, but it was pretty brilliant."

He looks away, shrugging. "Did some digging. I've been taught to hit people in their weak spots for a long time. Kinda second nature, unfortunately."

"I get that, about the second nature thing." Thinking about everything that's happened since Juan's men and the Army showed up, it feels like going back to the crime life is as easy as slipping on a pair of sandals. "Right and wrong…I still don't know which is which."

"Not sure anyone does these days."

"Guess so."

"What matters most to me now is making sure the people I care about are safe and happy." Graham squeezes me tighter. "Whatever happens, Fi, I hope you know I've only been trying to do what's best for you. I've screwed it up a lot, but that's the truth."

"I know. It's okay." And I mean it—Graham and I will be fine eventually. With my eyes closed and that trouble so far

121

below us, for a second I feel safer than I have all week. I breathe out the tension and let myself lean on Graham. "I'm so tired."

"We're almost home. You have to at least eat before you sleep."

"Okay."

The descent is as horrible as usual, but at least there's nothing in my stomach to lose. Before Graham can grab the knob, the door flies open. Mom screams my name and then more people join in. It looks like the entire Pack is here, and I frown. "Wait, so you all let Graham go in there on his own?"

"He insisted!" Hector says.

Miles scratches his head. "He was the only one who could have done it with no consequences, since he's already a wanted criminal. Plus, it saved Mom from breaking The Phantom's deal, and it makes it look like you're still working with Dad to boot."

"Sometimes my shitty past pays off." Graham sets me down, and I wobble. Mom and Seth are immediately by my side. "They starved her, Ma."

Mom puts her hand to my face, and it stings. "Oh, sweetheart. Let's get you something to eat."

"Are you hurt anywhere?" Seth nudges me to the kitchen, where Mom already has plain crackers and a glass of water out. She must not trust my empty stomach to handle more. It sounds like everyone follows us, and I have to admit I appreciate the concern. "Did they torture you?"

"Um, no, but I got cut on my thigh trying to escape," I say, just remembering he can see my wounds when no one else can. By the sound of his voice I wonder if it's worse than I think.

Mom grabs the first-aid kit from the laundry room. "Where's

your cut?"

"I'll do it," Seth says, but then immediately blushes. "Um, if that's okay with you."

"Of course." Mom smiles.

He opens the kit and grabs the cleaning cloths. "Where's the wound, Fiona?"

"Here." I take his hand and put it on my thigh where it stings, though I know perfectly well he can see it. He cleans it gently, feeling the cut more than necessary. As I watch, my heart feels like it's about to burst I missed him so much. Maybe our secret isn't always ideal, but right now I treasure it—no one else can understand what we share.

"It seems pretty long." Seth rummages in the kit, pulling out some butterfly bandages. "It could scar."

"Oh no, not a scar." I take another cracker. It feels so good to eat that the pain in my leg hardly registers. I want to eat forever even though my stomach couldn't take it.

"Sounds like you're fine. Attitude is still intact." He pokes my ribs, and I lean my head on his shoulder, happy to have him back just the way he is. But as much as I'd like to revel in this moment of return, there are more important things to discuss.

"So The Phantom paid me a visit while I was locked up." Everyone's faces fill with horror. When no one answers, I figure I may as well go on. "He wanted to help me escape, but I told him no. Then he roughed me up a little."

"Oh, Fiona." Mom crumples onto the counter.

"What else was I supposed to do? I would have been in his debt."

"I know." Mom pulls herself back up, rubbing her temples like I've given her an instant headache. "What did he say to you?"

"He figured the Army was keeping me because I really do know stuff, and he told me if I tell them I'm dead." I try to grab the cracker box, but Mom snatches it away telekinetically. "It's not a big deal because I'm never telling the Army anything after what they did to me. That Major Norton is a massive asshole."

Carlos snorts, and everyone looks at him. "Sorry, I got this picture in my head and—"

"We know," Bea says. "No need to explain."

I sip at my water. "What have you guys been doing?"

"Besides trying to get you out?" Miles looks like he hasn't slept much in the past few days, and I feel like it's my fault. "We've taken turns trying to figure out that formula you didn't steal."

"Anything?"

Mom pulls the formula from her pants pocket, and I wonder if that's been its permanent home since I got arrested. She points to a bunch of symbols I don't really understand. "The key is this element: merinite. It's a very stable liquid I've never seen on the periodic table, I assume because it's top secret. It looks like when you combine merinite with this large compound it inhibits radiation."

"Is there any way to test if something's merinite?" I ask, thinking of that scientist girl and her tests at the waterfall.

"Yeah, Hector's been working on performing it," Seth says as Mom flips to the right page to show me. "We should be able to pull it off if we get a sample."

"And what, exactly, will you do if you discover this secret place of yours does have what they're looking for?" Graham asks. "Destroy it?"

"I don't see why not," Hector says.

Graham purses his lips. "Why not just take it out now, then?"

"Because," I say, hesitating as I think of those beautiful pools that hold so many good memories, "it's an amazing place. It shouldn't be destroyed if it's not a threat to anyone. I want to know for sure before that has to happen."

"Me too," Seth says.

"Sounds sentimental to me." Graham floats higher up, reclining in the air.

"It's not all sentimental," Brady defends. "We know nothing about this element. What if we do something wrong with it and the whole place explodes? We need more information before we try to destroy it. If we even *have* it."

Graham nods. "I guess that's true. But you don't have much time to figure it out."

"Nope," I say as this pit forms in my stomach. My whole being craves revenge for what The Phantom and the Army put me through, but there are other people I have to think about, too. "If you guys don't want to be involved...I understand. You've seen what can happen now, and I'm afraid it's gonna get worse from here on out because I'm not stopping. If you help me, it might be you locked up next time."

Bea's dark eyes seem hesitant. "What are you trying to say, Fi?"

Part of me doesn't want to admit it, because there's no going back and they might abandon me. But my mind is made up: I have to do the right thing. "I'm saying I'm going vigilante here. Look at how much violence just the search for this merinite element has caused—can you imagine how much worse it'll get if they find it? There's no way in hell I'm letting anyone make Radiasure again. And I'd love to have you all on my team, but I'm not forcing anyone."

Shocked silence.

I look down, embarrassed. "I know I've made fun of those vigilante groups, but I think I'm starting to get it. Someone has to fight back against all this shit. Why not me? Why not us? We're strong. You can't tell me we aren't."

Still no one answers, and I'm waiting for them to walk out on me. Covering our tracks was one thing, but going on the offensive is another. Finally, Carlos clears his throat. "I just have one question."

"Yes?" I say tentatively.

"Do I have to wear a dorky costume?"

I roll my eyes. "Um, no."

"I'm in then!" He strikes a pose, puffing out his chest. "What're we gonna call ourselves? The Justice Coalition?"

"Hell no." Hector smacks the back of Carlos' head. "We'd need a better name than that."

I raise an eyebrow. "We don't need a name at all—but does that mean you're in, too, Hector?"

Bea punches my shoulder. "Of course we're all in. Being in your gang is better than someone else's. At least we'll get priority."

"It's not a gang!"

Seth gives me this look that is one part worry and two parts pride. "It kind of is, but that's okay."

I sigh. "Whatever. I'm just making sure you know I'm not expecting you to follow me on this, because I know I'm being crazy."

Brady holds his hands up. "As long as you know."

Mom gives me a knowing smile. "Your family will always have your back."

"Okay then. Let's plan," I say, though my heart races with fear. As much as this feels right, it's the craziest thing I could possibly do. I ran from my crime life, and now I'm officially jumping right back into it.

Chapter 20

Since Seth is banned from attending school, he spent all of yesterday at my house taking care of me. It's nice spending so much time with him after being locked up, and Mom is able to go to work without worrying so much about me and my gimp leg. But this morning he's late, and I get a text: *Dad being stupid. Be there once I get him to work.*

I'm okay. Miles is here, I send back, knowing he'll stress if he thinks I'm alone. "You're not going anywhere soon, right, Miles?"

He looks away from the baseball game just briefly. "Wasn't planning on it, why?"

"Seth is gonna be late."

"Ah." He sits up straighter and flexes his muscles. "So I'm on guard duty."

"Whatever."

"Someone has to keep an eye on our leader—you're a prime target."

For some reason, I'm not in the mood for his jokes today. They used to be fun, but now it feels like they're hiding something. I can't help but ask, "It's been over a week and your ankle is fine. Won't you get in trouble if you miss more work?"

"I quit. It was getting in the way of school." He makes it sound like no big deal, but I don't buy it.

"But you're missing classes, too, aren't you?"

He turns off the TV. Finally I have his full attention, but his expression is clearly annoyed. I'm not sure if it's because of the questions or interrupting him while a game is on. "What are you trying to get at?"

"It's just…I feel bad that I'm putting you in harm's way when you've already sacrificed so much for me and Mom. I know you're worried, but if you want to go back to Tucson—"

"Fiona, I'm not just here because I *have* to be, okay? I *want* to. I *need* to…" Miles' phone makes the sound of a baseball hitting a bat, and his eyes about pop out of his head. He grabs it, and by the way he looks at the screen I can only assume it's one person.

"Is it Spud?"

He nods, reading the message intently.

"Can I see?"

He looks hesitant, but then shows me the screen. *Sorry, babe. Things are bad here. I have to take out this chick first.*

I frown, not fully understanding the context. "What does that mean?"

"It means she can't help you like I asked. Gotta admit I kinda hoped she'd say yes, because then maybe I'd get to see her. Last time was the hack on Dad." He sighs, and it sounds so sad I can't help but hug him. He squeezes my arm. "Do I look as pathetic as I feel?"

"No," I say, imagining how I might feel if I couldn't see Seth for three months. "So does that mean there's no way she can

129

help? Because if we're going on the offensive Spud would be a huge asset."

He shrugs. "I don't really know. She's had to take on a lot of extra work lately, which is probably my fault."

This surprises me. "Why would it be your fault?"

"Think about it, Fi." His tone is sharp. "Dad knows she's tied to me."

"Oh." A pit forms in my stomach. If Spud was on my Dad's hit list before, now she must be at number one. She ruined his plans, helped us get out, and is probably paying the price. Which means that whatever reason she can't come now is likely my fault.

"Not tonight," Seth says when I insist we have to get to the cave as soon as possible. He sits at my bedside, where I've slept most of the past three days when I'm not eating. "You're still weak, and Brady really tore the place up. It'll be more like a hike than a run."

"What if they find it?" I eat the ham sandwich he brought me. "Bea said it sounded like the Army was expanding its search, since they aren't finding what they want at the factory."

While I recover, my friends use their skills to cull information. Hector overhears that Juan's men are planning to break into the factory grounds. Carlos sneaks around at night, using his vision to get the locations of Juan's patrol guys. The Pack also has the school covered, watching everything the Army does and relaying anything they hear. Graham surveys the town from above, Mom flirts thugs into telling secrets at the bowling alley, and Miles trawls the internet with his newfound hacking skills thanks to his girlfriend.

They're pretty much as awesome as I knew they'd be.

"At least one more day." Seth puts his hand on my leg where Tagawa ripped into it. "That cut was pretty bad."

"Brady can carry me," I offer. "Or Graham can fly me."

He shoots me a look. "Graham is *not* coming."

I frown. "He put his ass on the line for me, Seth. Kidnapped a girl, stormed the school by himself, and he got me out. What more does he need to do to gain your trust?"

"I don't know." He turns away, but I can still see anger on his face. "Maybe it's easier for you because he's your brother, and because you never saw exactly how much he hurt you when he got violent. I can't forget that, no matter how much I try. Someone who treated you like that will always be a threat to me."

"Fair enough, I guess." I take his hand and pull, the memory of lying in his bed begging to be recreated. "C'mere."

He smiles widely. "If you say so."

Our arms wrap around each other, and I breathe out some of the stress I've been holding since officially forming a vigilante group. "I suppose I like to think people can change—it gives me hope for myself."

Seth sighs. "Maybe people can change, but it doesn't hurt to be careful."

"You can be careful for me." I kiss his cheek. "How about I don't bring up Graham helping as long as we get the sample tonight?"

He glares at me. "You drive me crazy, you know that? In pretty much every sense of the phrase."

"Is it a deal?" I bite my lip, knowing how much he likes when I do that. "Please?"

"Only if…" He leans in. I'm more than ready for an extended make-out session, but right before our lips meet he pulls back, wincing. Then he covers his eyes and starts swearing like a sailor. My mind immediately goes to him not being able to control his vision.

"Is it happening again?" My voice betrays my panic.

"Yeah." He pulls himself up, blinking rapidly. "It's been acting up ever since, but not as bad as that first time."

"Why didn't you tell me sooner?" I try to remain calm. But if this has happened more than once since he pushed his ability too far, that's not good.

"You weren't here, remember? And then…what the hell?" He squints as if staring at something he can't make sense of.

"What?" I ask, looking at my desk because he is.

Seth shakes his head, the episode seeming to have gone as quickly as it came. He stands and reaches behind my desk for reasons I cannot guess. When he holds his hand up, there's a black dot on his pointer finger. He looks at it closely, and then to me. "Tell me this isn't what I think it is."

I get up and stare at the little device. It's a bug. My room's been bugged for who knows how long. I pick it off his finger and rush down the stairs to the stove. Turning on the gas, I throw it into the flame and it sparks as it dies. Seth's look of terror must mimic my own, and I grab a pen and notepad from the counter.

Look for more, I write.

He nods, and I follow him through the house as he peels

132

back layers with his eyes. One in the kitchen and living room. Another in Mom's room. One in the guest room. I burn them all before we talk again.

"We have to find out who planted those," I say quietly, still fearing listening ears. I feel sick, thinking that someone could know not only my secrets, but Seth's and the Navarros' and my mother's. "If this was Juan's doing…"

"The Phantom would have already taken you out if he heard the stuff we've said," Seth says. "Same with the Army. They'd know about the cave and wouldn't have bothered keeping you."

My eyes narrow. "What are you saying?"

"Maybe we have a mole." He looks down, and I get the feeling I know exactly who he suspects.

"You think it's Graham, don't you?"

"Think about it, Fi." He puts his hand over his mouth, like he doesn't want to continue. "Why haven't we seen your dad's people here yet? It doesn't make sense, unless he's already getting all the information he needs by listening in on everything you say."

"No…" I can see Seth's logic. Graham could be a plant. My dad could be playing along with us "being out of the syndicate" because it's useful to him to have us here. But it can't be. "My dad shot Graham—that wasn't just for show! If we'd gone back to Vegas, I have no doubt Graham would be dead right now. You saw how clearly my dad viewed him as a traitor. There has to be some other explanation."

"Like what? You don't think someone in The Pack would do this, do you?"

"Of course not!" I put my hands over my face, trying to calm

133

down. Then I remember something. Snapping my fingers, I say, "The Phantom said Juan's been keeping tabs on us for a couple months! It has to be a spy, not a mole."

Seth seems skeptical. "But then they'd have to know where the cave was, or at least that there was a cave. Juan's guys aren't looking out in the desert—they're letting the Army do the heavy lifting and spying on them."

"And us."

"Look, I know he's your brother and you guys are finally starting to see eye to eye—"

"I don't want to hear it!" I put my hands in the air, my temper about to go off. "If Graham wanted to spy on us he could have stayed *here*, but he went to Tucson with Miles. I suppose you think that was to throw us off the trail?"

He gives me a "duh" look.

I let out a frustrated grunt. "Can we think about the last time I decided not to trust Graham? You got shot!"

"That doesn't mean he has good intentions now!"

The doorbell rings before I can get out my next defensive point, and I trudge for it despite the pain in my leg. When I pull it open, Brady and Bea stand there with a brown box. They give me a surprised look.

"Whoa, I can feel your angry face," Brady says.

Bea laughs. "Definitely."

I take a deep breath, wishing I could prove them wrong. "What's in the box?"

"A major score, that's what." Brady steps inside and heads for the kitchen table, Bea following behind.

I shut the door and come over. Seth's already pulling out

test tubes, beakers, and chemicals that look like materials we'll need to test the cave water. "Sweet. How'd you get this stuff?"

"We had to take turns sneaking into one of the school science labs," Bea explains. "One is on serious lock down, but the other two still have classes going on. Carlos took one thing during biology, I took another during chemistry, and so on and so forth. Now all we need is a sample of the water."

"Perfect." I shoot a glare at Seth, who gives it right back. "We'll get it tonight. Brady, you're taking me even if Seth refuses to 'let me' go. He can look for more bugs at your house and the Navarros' place."

"What?" Bea and Brady say at the same time.

Seth puts his hand on the table, eyes all fire. "Oh, I'm coming. Who else will make sure you don't get hurt?"

I grit my teeth. Bea and Brady step away from the table slowly. Seth doesn't back down one millimeter. I hate that it kind of makes me want to jump him. "Fine."

Chapter 21

"So Graham broke into the Navarros' and planted all those, too, huh?" I say to Seth as we begin our trek into the desert. Brady really did do a number on the landscape. What was once fairly flat now looks more like rolling hills.

"It's not impossible," Seth grumbles. "He was in Madison last Friday."

"He never went in the back rooms."

"That you know of."

I scowl at him. "And how did he get into your house again?"

Seth doesn't answer because we found five bugs in his place. He knows chances are low that Graham could have bugged all three of our houses. Juan spying on us makes a lot more sense, even if they aren't using the information they should have got.

It's so dark tonight that we probably should have flashlights, but it's too risky. So we slowly make our way through the new landscape, trying to be as quiet as possible. There are more signs of others out here than I'd like to see—tire tracks here, dig sites there, and even lights far to the right. My cut leg trembles as I attempt to climb a four-foot cliff made by Brady's fists. It gives out on me, and I land in Seth's arms.

"Told you to take another day off," he says. "You're pushing yourself too hard."

"You're one to talk." I wiggle away from him, even though I know I'm being mean. But after all we've been through, how much we've changed to be together, I thought he'd have more faith in my family than he does. "Brady, I'm sorry, but I think you're gonna have to help me."

"Here." Brady holds out his hand from where he stands on top of the small cliff. I take it, and he lifts me like he's lifting a stuffed animal. He carries me the rest of the way. The trip goes much faster.

When we get to the giant boulder hiding the cave, my heart begins to flutter with all the memories I have of this place. Brady pushes the rock aside, and I can't help but remember the first time I watched him do that. It was a night I thought my dad was coming for me, one filled with fear and yet hope, too. My first steps into the tunnel are shaky, and a hand I know is Seth's finds mine. Part of me wants to pull away, but how can I when memories of us together in the water swirl in the cool air? I can't count how many times he's kissed me here. There isn't a spot in the world that means more to me than this one.

The blue light grows brighter as we near the pools, and I hate how glaringly obvious it is that this is what everyone's looking for. This is merinite. I want to pretend I don't know just a little longer. As Seth pulls test tubes from his backpack, I say, "Maybe we should just destroy it now, even if it's risky."

Both boys look at me, horrified. Brady especially. "It might not be merinite. We don't know for sure. We've never been hurt by swimming in it."

I fold my arms, knowing a glare won't mean anything to him. "Do you really believe that?"

"Yes…" He looks away, an awful pout on his face. "It's just that this place has been my hideout since I was a kid, since my father told me what I did to my mother. I ran out after that and planned on never coming back—that's when I found this place. It made me feel better, and I was going to live here forever."

"Except I followed your divot trail," Seth says, a small laugh escaping. "There was no way I was about to let you go all Peter Pan out in the desert."

Brady tries not to, but one side of his mouth curls, making his dimple show. "I offered to let you stay with me."

"Then I reminded you of the merits of air-conditioning." Seth dips one of the test tubes into a pool. "And you called me a bed-wetting pansy."

"That's right!" Brady sits next to Seth and puts his hand on his brother's shoulder. Now that I'm around them so much, I sometimes forget all they had for a long time was each other. "I stand by that statement."

"Psh." Seth tries to shove Brady, but it doesn't work very well. "You came running back the second you needed a toilet to—"

Brady covers Seth's mouth. "Okay! Fi's heard enough!"

I laugh, my heart warming at the sight. No, I can't take this place away from them permanently if I don't have to. There has to be a way we can protect it, because I want to keep them and these secret pools forever. Walking over, I sit by Seth and lean on his shoulder.

"Being nice again, huh?" he says as he fills another tube.

"For now." I want so badly to dip my feet in the water, but

now that I know it's probably not just water it seems smarter to stay away from it. "No fighting at the pools. Especially if it'll be a while until we can come back."

They both grow still.

"I guess this could be our last time, huh?" Brady says. "If I have to bury it."

"I hope not." Seth finishes off the samples and takes my hand. "We'll find another way, bro."

"Well, just in case…" Brady shoves his hand into his pocket and pulls out a worn picture. My heart skips as I catch the figure of a woman with bright red hair. "I think I should leave her here to watch over this place."

Seth's hand tightens around mine. "You sure?"

Brady nods slowly.

"Is that…?" I'm hesitant to ask, but I want to see the picture up close.

"Our mom? Yeah." He extends his hand out to me, and I gently take the wrinkled image. "She was pretty, huh."

"Beautiful," I say as I study the picture. Their mother has the same big smile as Brady, dimple included, but she is tall and thin like Seth. Her red hair is wavy and vibrant. She holds a guitar while she stands at a microphone. "She liked to sing?"

"In her journals it says people called her a siren," Seth says. "I guess she had perfect pitch, to the point that sometimes people would become obsessed with hearing her. She could have been famous, but the stalking freaked her out."

"Stalking isn't fun." My mind goes straight to The Phantom appearing in my jail cell, and I cringe. "Is that how she ended up in Madison? To hide?"

Seth nods. "My dad grew up here, and when she came into town he fell head over heels. Guess her voice was pretty powerful, because he's still…well, you've seen it."

"No talking about him here either." Brady snatches the picture from me and stands up. "As I was saying, I feel like carrying this picture made it so Mom could watch over me. Maybe leaving it here will let her watch out for this place."

"Then who will watch out for you?" Seth asks in his sarcastic tone. "You'll be all alone."

Brady rolls his eyes. "Don't be a smart ass."

"He's incapable of being anything else," I say.

Seth pulls me close, his lips on my ear. "Don't make me throw you in the water."

"Do you want me to be mad at you forever?" I poke his sides, and before I know it we're on the verge of a tickle fight. He makes it way too easy to forgive him.

"You guys are weird." Brady walks towards another pool, holding up his mother's picture. "I'm gonna find a good place to put this."

For some reason things feel weird between Seth and I when Brady is out of hearing range, as if we're both waiting for the other one to apologize. It sure as hell won't be me. Doesn't seem like Seth is budging on it either. Finally, he lets out a long sigh. "You know Brady sees you as a sister, right? You're like part of our family."

I raise an eyebrow. "Um, random?"

"It's just…I'm trying to say I…" He shakes his head and zips up the backpack. "Never mind. We should get these samples back to test."

140

"Okay…" A familiar awkwardness comes between us—it seems to be doing that more often—and I'm not sure why. What's his problem?

Seth calls for Brady, and then we make the trek back to town. When we get to Madison's borders, we're more careful to look out for Juan's men. No way he'll rat us out this time. I constantly feel like I have eyes on me lately, and tonight is no different even if the coast seems clear. By the time we reach their street, I'm ready for bed. But the test awaits—then the decision on what to do next.

Seth's steps slow drastically, to the point that I have to look back to see what the hold-up is. His arms are spread wide, and he walks as if he just went blind. My stomach drops. "Again?"

"Just…um…" His voice is shaky, and I can tell he's doing his best to look normal. "Shouldn't talk out here."

I walk back to him and put his arm around me, so I can guide him. "This is really not funny."

"Tell me about it," he says through gritted teeth.

"Do you need to go home?" Brady asks. "I can have Hector start without you guys."

"Maybe that would be…" Seth trails off, his eyes on his house. By his expression, it's clear he sees something he doesn't want to be seeing. I'm starting to understand just how much his ability must have sucked when he was a kid and couldn't control it well. "There's someone in there with Dad."

"What?" Brady is clearly confused. "Who?"

Seth closes his eyes tightly, but still I see tears at the rims. "It's one of Juan's guys."

Brady shrugs. "So he's buying more drugs, what's the big deal?"

"No." Seth looks at his brother. "Juan's guy gave Dad money—not the other way around. Which means he's doing something for the syndicate."

Chapter 22

"No way…" Brady stares at his house as if he can see what Seth does. "He's too drunk or high to do anything useful for *anyone*. You must've seen it wrong. Maybe he was giving him change."

"A thick stack of bills is change?" Seth says through his teeth.

Brady shrugs. "All ones?"

I don't know what to say. On the one hand, I'd like to point out that their dad could be the spy who planted the bugs, so Seth shouldn't be so harsh on Graham. But when I look at Seth, it's obvious he already knows. And more than that, it's tearing him apart inside. I want to take away the betrayal he must be feeling—I know all too well how deep a wound like that can go.

"Let's go before that guy comes out," I finally manage to say.

"They're still talking." Seth doesn't take his eyes off his place. "Damn, I need to learn lip-reading."

I grab his arm, worried he'll overuse his already-unpredictable ability. "If Juan's guy comes out and sees us we'll be hosed. C'mon."

Seth doesn't move. "If he's…I didn't think I could hate him more. How could he do that to his own sons?"

"Stop," Brady says, still seeming firmly in the denial camp. "You're reading too much into it."

Seth shakes his head, but tromps towards the Navarros' house. Brady and I follow him in nervous silence. Sure hope he doesn't take out his anger on Hector, Bea, and Carlos. Though I guess it wouldn't be the first time they've dealt with a rampaging Seth. He opens the door without knocking, and we find them in the living room watching late-night TV.

Hector raises an eyebrow when he sees Seth. "What's wrong?"

"Nothing. Just stressed about this test." Seth sets his backpack on the coffee table and pulls out the tubes. "You have everything ready to go?"

Hector sighs, as if he knows Seth isn't telling him something. "Yeah, in my room."

"Let's get this over with." I head for the hall. May as well find out once and for all if we have what everyone is looking for. After that we can figure out who bugged us and what Mr. Mitchell is up to, if anything. I'm still on the fence like Brady—I've never seen the man sober and can't imagine anyone trusting him for reliable information.

Though, well, the information *hasn't* been reliable, has it?

Hector has a hot plate set up on his desk. There's already a beaker on it filled with a clear liquid. A thermometer sticks up out of it. He turns on the heat. "I've already mixed the right chemicals together for the test. Just have to heat it to exactly one hundred and thirteen degrees."

"Why one hundred and thirteen?" I ask.

He shrugs. "That's what it said in the formula. Merinite doesn't like to bond with other substances, and apparently they found the temp helps."

"Huh." I'm glad I have smart friends.

"So are we actually cooking Radiasure?" Carlos asks as he plops on his brother's bed. "Because if Mom and Dad catch us we'll never see the outside of the confession booth again."

Bea rolls her eyes. "Nothing new for you."

"It's not Radiasure, anyway," Hector says as he checks the liquid's temperature. "This is only part of the process for making it—the part that primes the merinite so they can use it."

"How are we supposed to know if it's right?" Brady asks.

"If it's merinite, it'll bond and the reaction will make the substance thicker and brighter."

I nod. "That's what their scientist girl said at the waterfall, too."

"Good to know." Hector doesn't stop watching the temperature rise. "Do you know anything else about her? Maybe we can find some of her research, see what kind of stuff she studies."

I clench my jaw just thinking of my one conversation with her. "She wouldn't tell me anything—said even her name was classified and no one she knew in real life had a clue she was doing this."

Seth gives me the look. "You never said she talked to you."

"When I was locked up. But like I said, it was useless. She wanted me to talk. I wouldn't. She left me to my impending torture. The end."

Seth folds his arms, thinking. "If security on her is locked down so tightly, I wonder how Graham found out she was the best person to hold ransom. Unless he already knew."

My eyes narrow. After what he just saw at his house, he still has the gall to imply that Graham is up to no good? "There are plenty of ways to get supposedly secure information, and that was pretty much my *brother's* job since he was ten. So."

"It was also your *brother's* job to drag you back to Vegas every time you left."

My jaw drops, but before I answer Bea stands between us with her hands out. "Whoa, whoa, whoa. What's going on here?"

"Oh, nothing," I growl. "Seth just thinks Graham's behind the bugs."

"No way!" Bea says at the same time Carlos exclaims, "That makes perfect sense!" Hector is the ever-level-headed one with, "We can't rule it out, though it doesn't completely add up."

"Ugh." I don't need more opinions on this topic, because I want to trust my brother. He shouldn't be the first one I suspect every time something bad happens. "How long will this take? I'm tired."

"Almost there." Hector measures the right amount of cave water and pours it in. "The reaction takes about three minutes."

Also like the scientist girl said. This comforts me because any way we can match her test means we're doing it right. I may not know much about her, but I'm sure she's brilliant. Otherwise she wouldn't be so important to Major Norton. The seconds feel like they've stretched out as we all stare at the beaker. The liquid is slightly blue now, but not as much as the cave water on its own. Just how bright is it supposed to get?

"This must be how it feels to wait for a pregnancy test," Carlos says about two minutes in.

Bea smacks the back of his head, though she bites back a

smile. "Dumbass."

"What?" Carlos seems genuinely surprised at her reaction. "If that thing glows blue in three minutes our lives will be changed forever! *It's the same.*"

It takes surprising effort for me to suppress a laugh. "And how do you know so much about pregnancy tests?"

He tips his chin up. "I take health class very seriously."

"It'd be nice if you'd take *this*—" Seth starts, but then he stops because something is happening to the stuff inside the beaker. The color has gone from barely blue to intense ultramarine, and a distinct aura of light emanates from it. It feels as if my insides have been flipped upside down.

We have merinite.

Hector takes a spoon and dips it in the substance. Sure enough, it coats the utensil like a thick syrup. "Well, I *think* it worked."

"Really? What tipped you off?" Seth looks sick.

"I wasn't sure until the glowing," Carlos says sarcastically.

"What do we do with it now?" Brady says. "It's not like we can pour it down the drain, and that stuff is bright as a lamp!"

Hector turns off the hot plate. "Good question. Didn't think that one through. Guess now we have to figure out if it can be destroyed safely."

"Great idea," Seth says. "Small test before dealing with the cave."

"That's all nice, but what do we do about the Army and Juan now? We really do have what they want, and they already suspect us so much," I say, putting my hands on my hips. Seth and I both told Brady that there'd be a way to protect the pools without burying them, but as the merinite swirls like a lava lamp I can't help but think destroying them completely is the only way.

We gather in a circle on Hector's floor to strategize. Maybe we could barricade the place—no, that wouldn't stop them from using sensors to analyze the subsurface and finding the cave. Maybe we could empty the pools and take the merinite somewhere else—we'd just need a couple semi-trucks, a giant pool vacuum, and a new location. Not likely. Or we could guard it by making the area look haunted. Or booby trap the entrance. The longer we talk about it, the stupider the ideas get.

Brady leans his head back on Hector's bed, sighing. "Let's face it. There's only one way to guarantee people won't find it. I have to bury it."

Seth purses his lips. "You're probably right."

"I hate to say it." Hector stirs the merinite. "But if it's safe to do so, caving in the place would contaminate the merinite with dirt and rock, which would make it a lot harder to find and extract. It may even destroy whatever process is happening there to create it in the first place. That's probably the best we can do."

"Are you sure?" Bea puts her hand on Brady's arm. "That place…"

"It's okay." Brady gives us a big smile, and I'm surprised it's not his fake one. He takes Bea's hand. "I have you."

A big grin spreads across her face. When she leans her head on his shoulder, Hector and Carlos make gagging sounds.

I roll my eyes. "We'll have to meet up at my place tomorrow, see if my mom can help figure out how dangerous destroying the merinite might be."

Hector nods. "She was a huge help with this test."

After saying our goodbyes, I head to my car parked in front of Seth's house. Miles took Mom to work so I could have it, and for once I'm glad to drive home by myself because I don't know where Seth and I are at. He watches me unlock the car door, and when I glance at him our eyes meet.

"I don't like fighting with you," he says.

"Then stop." I open the door, but he grabs me before I can get in. I don't hug him back. "So you're mad at me but hugging me?"

"Be safe. Keep your phone on." He squeezes me tighter, then whispers, "I don't want to sleep in the same house with him, but I have to, don't I?"

I bite my lip, the frustration fizzling. My boyfriend is scared. Of his own father. Our lives are starting to be similar in ways I'd rather not have them be. I wrap my arms around him. "Yeah. You be safe, too. We'll look into it tomorrow."

"Okay." He kisses me once, and there's something sad about it, as if he's unsure of whether I want his lips on mine or not. Then he heads for his house, and I watch him until he disappears behind the door.

As I drive home, I wish I could turn off my brain. I'm tired of thinking, of worrying, of making sure no one is following me. By the time I've pulled into my driveway, I feel like I could sleep for weeks. I drag my feet towards the front door, telling myself I need to be on my guard but knowing my reflexes are shot from fatigue.

So when a person wearing black emerges from the bushes pointing a gun at me, I almost expect it. It would be the perfect time for an attack. I pull out my phone and call Mom. "I'm dialing the person inside who can rip that gun right out of your hands, so if you're gonna shoot you better do—"

"Fiona!" a feminine voice says from behind the mask. She puts the gun down. "Thought you were at Bea's, sorry."

I quirk an eyebrow. "Do I know you?"

She shrugs. "Miles might have mentioned me once or twice."

Well, now I'm wide awake. "Spud?"

"Yup. Ah, there she is." Spud aims the gun again. This time she pulls the trigger, and the silencer hides most of the sound. I turn just in time to see a person hit the ground. I stare at the fallen body, horrified that my brother's girlfriend is a killer. Does he know this?

"What the hell?" I step back from her, scared.

"Oh, come on. You think I've survived this long without fighting?" Spud heads for the street, and I feel obligated to follow. Besides, maybe she'll explain what she did, because right now I'm not sure my brother should be with a girl like this.

"Sorry I had to do this in front of you." Spud kneels down next to the corpse, typing something into a fancy-looking phone. "This bitch was too smart for her own good, going completely off the grid. It was the only way to intercept her."

I don't want to look at the body—the thought alone makes me ill—but when I finally get the courage to face whoever Spud shot, my eyes go wide with horror. This can't be happening. Short brown hair, hazel eyes, perfect skin that can change to any shade she pleases—I know this woman. "Noelle."

She used to teach me how to steal and hide. She's from my dad's syndicate.

Chapter 23

As I take in the reality, I don't know what to feel. Noelle was like a mentor to me—as a chameleon, she could almost understand how I felt being invisible. She would tell me I'd find myself eventually. She taught me how to use my ability in ways no one else could teach me. But at the same time, if she was here tonight then it means she was on a mission for my dad. Finally, there is a hint that he's not ignoring what's happening in Madison—and Spud just protected us from him.

Maybe I should feel grateful. But it seems horrible to be grateful someone is dead.

Spud searches Noelle's body, for what, I don't know. All I can see is the blood pooling in the street. All I can feel is the urge to cry and throw up. Spud reaches into Noelle's bra and pulls out a small box. "Always in the bra," she says. "Is that protocol or something?"

It takes me a moment to find my voice. Still, it comes out weak. "Um, not that I know of."

"You probably didn't wear a bra on your missions, so how could you?" Spud opens the box, and even in the dark I recognize the contents: knock-out needles tipped in purple and killing needles tipped in red. And here I thought Dad only made those for me—another reminder of his lies. There is also a piece of paper, which seems to be what Spud is after. She smirks. "Written in code. Cute. I dream in code, idiots."

"What does it say?" I ask.

"Directions to the mark: your address, best ways to break in, the location of Miles' room." She throws it in the blood. "Nothing about her superiors, though, damn it. I need to take out the puppeteers, not the puppets."

I lost her at "Miles' room." My mind reels—his injured foot, the extended visit, the overall sullenness…Why didn't I see it earlier? Now everything makes perfect sense.

My dad is trying to kill Miles.

Covering my mouth to hide a sudden sob, I take a few steps back from the body. Poor Noelle, yet another victim of Dad's twisted plots. There's only one thing that could be more important to my father than Radiasure, and that's making sure no one can challenge his power. Of course he wouldn't let Miles live now that he can replicate the mind controlling scent. Just how many times has he tried to kill my brother? My gut says this isn't the first.

"Fiona?" Spud's voice floats into my mind. "You can go inside if this is making you sick. My people will be here to clean up in a couple minutes."

"Your people?"

She nods. "They don't know who I am, but they pretty much worship me and would do anything to be associated with me. May as well take advantage."

Our front door slams, and soon Mom and Miles appear in

the driveway. Mom must have heard my call before I hung up. Spud stands and takes off her head mask. Her black hair tumbles out and brushes at her shoulders, and her big smile is beyond stunning. She waves excitedly at my brother. "Hey, baby!"

Miles does not seem to share her enthusiasm. His eyes are filled with horror as he takes her in. "Lee Seol…what're you doing here?"

She pouts, pointing to the body. "She went off grid. Excuse me for making sure you didn't die tonight."

"What?" Mom says in a high-pitched tone.

Miles pinches the bridge of his nose, and then Spud—who apparently has an actual name—puts her hands on her hips. "Oh for serious? You didn't tell them yet? You said you would!"

"I couldn't find the right time!" Miles cringes at the body still in the road. "Maybe we should go inside before you keep yelling at me?"

"Fine." Spud tromps to the door like she owns the place, and I get the sense that this kind of confidence is normal for her. Just as I'm about to go inside, a black van breaks in front of our house. A group of masked men get out, put the body in the back, and clean the street. I wish I could do more for Noelle—give her a proper funeral—but I can't, so I shut the door.

"…Could you not tell us? We're supposed to stick together. We can't do that if you're keeping *assassination attempts* a secret!" Mom already tears into Miles, while Spud taps her foot furiously.

"I wanted you and Fiona to have a normal life for once,"

Miles says quietly, like he knows he can't escape the lecture. "Is that so horrible?"

Mom grabs him by the shoulders. "Yes. You dying is horrible. I don't want normal if you're dead."

"Me neither," I say.

Spud gives him a steely look. "Told you."

He sighs. "Graham and I were doing fine for a long time—it's only gotten bad recently."

This doesn't quell Mom's anger. "Graham knew?"

"Ugh," I say. "That's why you took him back to Tucson with you so easily. He was your backup. You guys expected this to happen!" Stupid brothers. I should smack them both.

"So they've been after you since you left?" Mom asks.

"Pretty much." Spud sits on the couch, typing again. "And after that hack I did for the Radiasure info, the O'Connell syndicate has gone crazy old school. No cell phones. Hardly a blip of computer use. I've had to hack security cameras, radios, and other peripheral devices just to get anything on these chicks. It's pissing me off. Why does it have to be so hard to keep my boyfriend alive?"

So that's what she's been busy with. Not running from my dad herself, but watching out for Miles.

"I'm sorry, okay? I honestly did think I could handle it." Miles sits next to Spud, scoops her up and kisses her even though now is so not the time. I figure I should cut him some slack, since they rarely see each other.

"When did it get bad?" Mom asks, not seeming to mind the sight of them together.

"About three weeks ago." Miles doesn't take his eyes off

Spud, as if he can't believe she's in the same room as him. "Lee Seol has a *real* database of syndicate-affiliated people: their pictures, names, abilities, what type of illegal work they do most. But that's not the best part—she's made a program that can identify their faces on any camera she can hack into."

She smiles mischievously. "I made that when I was like ten. Comes in handy when everyone's out to get you. Literally."

He rolls his eyes. "You're way too proud of that. Anyway, the program sends her warnings when questionable people are spotted in places within a certain radius of her...or anyone else she decides to watch out for."

"Like my annoyingly self-sacrificing boyfriend." She snuggles into him, and I have to resist the urge to ask how in the world they got together. Because it's way too late already and I have a big day tomorrow. After what I just saw, sleeping is the closest I can get to blacking out and forgetting.

"So your program flagged people in Tucson?" Mom asks.

"Further than that—I have visuals in every airport in the U.S. I'd catch them flying into Phoenix at first. It was easy to scare them off with enough time to prepare..." Spud scowls, and it's kind of scary how such a tiny girl can look so mean. "But then they changed tactics, going by road, and I'd catch them at gas stations. They started getting into Tucson, and I'd have to warn Miles each time."

"Graham and I were usually able to shake them off," Miles continues. "But then Lee Seol was sending warnings every day, then every hour—they were closing in on us, so we had to leave. We hoped they wouldn't follow us here, but looks like Dad's broken the deal entirely now."

"Well *that* didn't take long." I collapse onto the floor, unable to maintain an upright position with all this information pounding me. "What're we supposed to do about this?"

The front door unlocking makes us all jump after what just happened. Spud looks at her device, which must be some kind of custom smartphone. "It's Graham. Good."

Sure enough, Graham floats through the door. He looks confused as he takes us in, but then he seems to put the pieces together. "This must be the infamous Spud, which means something bad happened tonight and everyone finally knows what's up."

"Yup." Miles eyes Graham. "And where the hell were you for so long?"

"With Allie. She came to visit me, got a hotel room in Saguro for the weekend since there's not much room here."

Miles raises an eyebrow. "And you didn't stay the night with her?"

"I came back to get a few things." He glances at Spud, then back to Miles. "Or do you want me to stay in the guest room with you? Do you need an extra guard?"

Miles shakes his head rapidly. "Nope! We're good."

I groan, not wanting to think of my brothers and their girlfriends and—gross. "Please stop now."

"Yes." Mom seems as squirmy as I am. "If we're safe for now, I think we should all get some rest before the sun comes up."

"Safe as far as I can see," Spud says as she looks at her screen. "Of course, I can't account for Juan's dudes in the area, but the O'Connell syndicate isn't here."

"Good enough for me." I pull myself off the floor, ready for bed. But when I get there, my mind won't shut off like my body has. Because if Graham knew about Dad going after Miles and helped protect him, how can I possibly believe he's spying on us for the syndicate? Which means there's only one person I suspect, and if I'm right I don't know how Seth will handle it.

Chapter 24

I wake up sore and grouchy and wishing I could get the images of Noelle's dead body out of my head. That's why, when I drag myself out of bed, I determine to do something I haven't done in years. Because I need to feel real and capable and maybe this will help. Mom's downstairs messing around in the kitchen, so I sneak to her bathroom and scoop up an armful of her makeup. Then I run to my room and lock the door.

Staring at the foundation, blush, mascara, and more doesn't have the effect I want. All I can remember is the last time I put this stuff on, and how awful Graham made me feel about it.

I was twelve, and when everyone went out on Friday nights they'd keep me locked in the penthouse where I was "safe." So I did what any girl would have done—I turned on musicals, ate whatever I wanted, dressed up in my mother's fancy clothes, and slathered my face in makeup.

It never lasted long, fading as my skin absorbed the color. And it looked weird because I still didn't have hair or eyes. But for a girl who doesn't know what she looks like, it was just enough to keep me going.

One night, Graham and Miles came home early from some

party and found me dressed up. Graham burst out laughing. "You think you look like a person in that stuff? Don't kid yourself—you look like an invisible girl trying to be something she isn't."

Tears ran down my face as I rushed to my room, filled with shame. When I looked in my mirror, I saw Graham was right. My tears had streaked the fading makeup, turning me into a pretty disturbing ghost-like creature. It was then that I realized makeup wouldn't show me my face, not really. So I never put it on again.

My hand shakes as I reach for the foundation. Screw Graham—I want to see myself today, and this is the best I have. Opening the cap, I pour the creamy color into my palm, where it seems to float in the air. I dip my fingers into it and begin spreading it over my face. It makes my heart race, seeing my features come into view bit by bit. A soft jawline, cheekbones, my button nose. I even put it on my lips so I can see how full they are.

I stand there, staring at this person I don't know in the mirror. This face doesn't look like the one I had at twelve. It has more angles and less round cheek. I try to see what Seth sees when he looks at me—imagining my golden hair and hazel eyes to go with this muddy mask in front of me.

Don't see it.

Grabbing the lipstick, I use it generously in hopes that maybe it'll make this flat image more realistic. It does a decent job, so I add blush and eye shadow and pretend this is enough.

But it's not.

I head to my closet in hopes of covering all the still-invisible parts of me. I put on a long sleeve shirt, gloves, tight pants, and sunglasses to hide my hollow eyes. As I stuff the beanie on my head, I look in my long mirror.

The makeup is already fading, but I try to take myself in. Maybe I do look like Mom. Maybe Seth isn't over exaggerating when he says I'm beautiful. Or maybe this is all stupid. It *does* feel fake, even without Graham here laughing at me. I pull the hat off and throw it on the ground. Then the gloves and shirt and—

Someone knocks on my door.

"Fiona?" Seth's voice is muffled through the wood.

My face burns. He better not be looking through. "One sec! I'm not dressed!"

"Sorry for just showing up—you didn't answer your phone. I was worried something happened," he says as I run for my bathroom to scrub my skin. I don't even want to know what he'd say to seeing me with makeup on.

"It's okay!" I call, though I do find it slightly annoying. After I throw on a dress, I open the door with a smile. "Good morning."

He gives me a suspicious look. "What's wrong?"

"Nothing." He comes in, and I shut the door behind him.

"That smile was the fakest thing I've ever seen your face do."

He might be right, but I still find this statement offensive. "Do I have to tell you everything?"

This was clearly not the right thing to say, because Seth now looks like a wounded puppy. "Don't you *want* to tell me everything? I *like* that I can tell you anything."

I look away, unsure about whether I should feel bad or not.

160

"Every time I tell you about wanting to see myself, you don't understand. So why bother?"

Seth purses his lips, but says nothing.

Wrapping my arms around my stomach, I try to keep it together. This fighting thing is getting out of control, but I can't seem to reel it back in. "That's not important right now anyway…"

"It isn't?" His voice cracks, and I know I've done something really wrong.

I can't deal with this on top of everything else. "My dad is trying to have Miles murdered, and it would've happened last night if Spud didn't show up."

He tries not to be interested, but he is. "So that girl downstairs…Miles said her name was Lee Seol, but that's Spud?"

I nod.

"Whoa."

"Don't tell anyone. Not even Brady. Miles will probably be pissed I even told you."

"Of course I won't." He scratches his head, the information seeming to quell whatever issues we have. "So does this mean she's, like, going to help us now?"

"I have no idea." I grab my checkerboard bag from its peg and sling it over my shoulder. "I wanted to ask her at first, but she's already working so hard to keep Miles safe. How can I demand more than that?"

He nods. "Good point."

"So are we looking into your dad today?" I ask, since we're finally on to business. Business is so much easier. "If so, I figure we should check his office."

Seth gives me the smallest smirk. "You read my mind."

The Mitchell Construction office is in an old strip mall that also houses a laundromat, tax place, and the one dentist in Madison. Pretty much the worst combo of businesses ever. But though I know where it is, I've never actually been inside. For some reason I was picturing something a lot nicer than the one room filled to the brim with files and blueprints.

"Wow," I say as I take in the mess.

"I know." Seth goes to a desk buried in paper. "And this is actually pretty clean. My dad is supposed to keep up with the finances, but Alejandro usually gets slammed with it all. He should probably own the place."

"Are they out on a job?" I can't help but notice that Alejandro's desk is the one organized spot in the whole room.

"Yeah. They only come here for scheduled consultations, paperwork, or designing." Seth is already digging through the files, organizing like this isn't his first time.

"So what are we looking for?" I ask.

He shrugs. "I've come here plenty of times, and I know the numbers better than my dad. So I guess I don't really know. Something that seems off?"

"Okay…" I help him go through the papers, which all seem to be money related: supply orders, estimates for customers, final payments needed, etc. A few hours go by in this mind-numbing boredom. I get us some vending machine candy from the laundromat. We start scouring the computer files.

A little past two, Seth finally leans back, clearly frustrated.

"There's nothing! I've seen these accounts a million times and they're the same as ever."

"Hmm." I start reading the spines of binders on the shelves, all of which are labeled with years going back to before I was born. All the way back to the 1940s, in fact. This sparks my curiosity. I pull out the oldest one, labeled 1945. "Your family has been building houses around here since before Radiasure?"

He nods. "My great grandfather started the company when he got back from the war. Why?"

"So did they help build Radison before it was blown to bits?" My heart pounds at the thought. Maybe Seth's father *does* know more than he lets on.

Seth pauses, the gears turning in his head. "I…don't know. My grandpa died before we were born, and you know how my dad is about the past. It's not something I ever thought to ask, but it makes sense that they would have, right? At least if he lived in this area at the time."

"Miles said Madison didn't even exist until after the drug wars, so yeah." I open the binder, suddenly curious to see what the Mitchells were building in 1945. "There's nothing here."

"What?" Seth comes to get a closer look, as if I can't tell the few yellowed papers are blank. "I never thought to look at these. I was always looking for money that didn't belong. And of course hiding places for drugs, which I always find. Why do you always show me answers I've missed for years?"

"No clue." I go for the next year and the next. Those are empty, too. Something about seeing nothing in these binders makes me uneasy. "Seth, if there was nothing to put in these binders, then why have them?"

He nods slowly. "I know where you're going with this. The information has been removed, which is suspicious. But the most logical answer is that it was confiscated after Radison was destroyed…"

"What?" I don't like the angry expression he's giving off.

"Think, Fi—who would have taken these? Would they have destroyed them or would they have kept them?"

It clicks. "Ohhh, shit, you think the Army…?"

He drops the empty binder on the desk and puts his head in his hands. "I don't know what I'm thinking, but it sure seems like Major Norton has had me targeted from day one. Maybe there's no coincidence at all—maybe he's worried we know stuff about the old city."

I can't seem to get enough air. It's not impossible. The Army clearly has some kind of intel about the factory. For years no one ever thought to dig it up, and that's the first thing they started to do. They must have known. Maybe they even have the blueprints. "You think your family helped with the factory?"

"No idea." He leans on the desk, wincing at what I'm sure is another headache from his glitching vision. I want to reach out to him, comfort him, but I still have no idea where we stand. "But this doesn't make my dad look *innocent* by any means. For all I know, he could be selling info to whoever wants to pay."

"Maybe…but then where's the money?"

"In his veins." Seth's voice is cold.

"He couldn't have spent that much on drugs. That kind of info would come with a huge payoff. He'd have to have a whole room full of painkillers." I purse my lips, the wheels turning but getting nowhere. "Something is beyond fishy."

Wearing an expression I can't read, Seth goes to the desk and digs through the papers again. "I'll keep looking through this stuff. I know you're probably bored—you can check up on Hector's progress with destroying the element if you want."

For some reason his words make me uneasy, or maybe it's his pain-filled expression. It's obvious he's hurting in more ways than one, and I don't like the idea of him being alone with all that stuff on his mind. "Is your vision still being weird?"

"It's fine," he says, though he blinks rapidly.

"You don't *look* fine. Can't you tell me what's wrong?"

He shoots me a biting look. "We don't have to tell each other everything, right?"

Anger flares, hearing my own words used against me. "Seriously, are you gonna be like that right now? I'm worried about you!"

"And I'm worried about you!" He pinches the bridge of his nose. "You're getting...I don't know, like, distant from me lately, and now you won't even tell me what I've done wrong."

My eyebrows rise. "You haven't done anything wrong."

"Really?" Seth leans on the desk, staring me down. "Then why do you always pull away from me when you should want to be close? And you can't seem to stand the thought of me seeing you undressed. Not that I'm incapable of waiting, but how do you think it makes me feel to see you recoil like that?"

I fold my arms, not expecting this sudden change in topic. "I don't know what you're talking about."

"You're doing it right now!" he points out.

Crap. My hands drop to my sides. "This really isn't the time—"

"When is the time then?" Seth rounds the desk and grabs my hands. "I can't do this. I have to tell you everything, and you should tell me what's wrong because if this keeps going... what then?"

I know he's right. There's no way I'll get past this invisibility barrier without telling him how strange it is for me, but I'm so scared of how he'll react.

"Fiona, please, tell me." His eyes beg me so badly that I have to look away.

"Sometimes...when we're...it's just..." I can't seem to get words past this lump in my throat. But he wants me to tell him. He's asking for it. "Sometimes it's weird, okay?"

Seth's brow furrows. "Weird? Like, me touching you is weird?"

I wince, but force myself to nod. "I mean, I can't see what you're touching or kissing. It's just you and the air and..."

"Oh." He drops my hands as he steps back. I have never seen him look this embarrassed, and I regret even the few words I said. "Well, I'm sorry it's so weird to be with me. Not sure I can fix that."

"No, Seth, that's not what I meant." I try to grab him, but he jumps behind the desk.

"Maybe you should go." He sits in front of the computer, not looking at me. "I need to think. By myself."

"Um, okay." I head for the door slowly, hoping that maybe he'll call me back. But every time I turn to glance at him, he's still staring at the computer screen. So I leave, and I manage to keep my tears in for five whole blocks. But when they come I can't seem to get them to stop.

Chapter 25

When I compose myself enough to talk without breaking down, I call Bea. Though it's only the late afternoon, the short winter days make it so evening is almost upon me.

"Hey, Fi! What's up?" Her voice is warm and happy when she answers, and it makes me want to be with her even more. Maybe some of that will rub off on me.

"Oh, just wondering if you could pick me up at SuperMart." That's as far as I made it before I realized walking from Mitchell Construction to my house would take longer than I wanted it to. With the ever-watchful eyes of Juan's men to follow me the whole way to boot.

There's the smallest pause, and I picture her confused face. "I thought you were with Seth."

"Well…um…he needed some space." I hope this is enough information for her to understand that things aren't exactly going well, because I'd rather not explain more.

"Aw, Fi, of course I'll come get you. Except now I'm worried. Just hold tight—I'll be there in like ten minutes, okay?"

"Sounds good." I lean back on the bench, wishing I could close my eyes and put my guard down. But I can't, not with the two Jaguar-tattooed men standing just on the other side of the SuperMart entrance. They don't even pretend not to see me; their glares are strong and unwavering. Finally one puts a cell to his ear. Great.

I haven't seen or heard from The Phantom since he offered to break me out of jail Monday night. It's only Saturday, but it feels like a long time with everything that's happened this week. And if Juan was the one behind the bugs, you'd think they would have come after us by now.

Or maybe they're waiting for us to make a move.

Bea arrives very loudly, honking Sexy Blue's horn way too many times. As I get in, she says, "Juan's guys are really pissing me off. I'd pop all their eardrums if it didn't also hurt you guys."

I can't help but smile. "That would be awesome."

"So is everything okay? You sounded upset." Bea peels out of the parking lot at her usual breakneck speed.

"It's not okay. At all." I lean towards the window to get more air, since the afternoons in Arizona are still warm even in winter.

"Say no more. I know what you need." She heads to the main street diner, and we sit at the bar. Bea orders the biggest ice cream sundaes they have—it might be a small gesture, but it really is just what I need. She's the best friend a girl could ask for. "Alright, we have sugar. Now spill it, chica."

I sigh, wondering where I should start and how much I can tell. Sure would be nice if she just *knew* Seth could see me, then I wouldn't have to give half truths. "Lately I don't know how Seth feels about me anymore. Like, there's all these little things that aren't a big deal on their own, but together it's just…"

Bea frowns. "He's crazy about you. It's probably all the stress from what's going on. You should have seen him when you were locked up. He was a mess."

I know she's trying to comfort me, but I don't feel like being comforted. "Maybe, but that doesn't mean it was easy before this happened."

"I get that." She digs into her sundae, and I do the same. The cool ice cream is perfect after sitting out in the hot afternoon sun. It makes everything just a little bit better. "Did something happen?"

I pop a maraschino cherry in my mouth to stall. Seth took my admission about our physical relationship so hard—the last thing I need is for Bea to tell me I'm being stupid. "Yeah. I think I really hurt his feelings, even though he asked me to be honest with him when I *knew* he'd get upset."

"Hmm, what did you tell him?"

"Well…" I cringe just thinking about how Seth pulled away from me. "I told him sometimes it's weird to see him making out with me when it looks like he's kissing air."

Bea coughs on her ice cream. "You really told him that?"

"Yeah." I put my head on counter. This is bad. I can tell by her reaction. "What if he wants to break up with me because we haven't…you know?"

It feels like an eternity before Bea answers. "I don't think Seth's like that, but he's probably not feeling so great about what you said."

"I messed everything up." I stuff more ice cream in my face. "I shouldn't have said anything."

"No, you have to be honest about it." Bea looks away from me, seeming embarrassed. "I mean, it's hard to take sometimes.

Brady is always pushing me away physically because of his worries about hurting me. And I know that's a real fear for him—that I *should* be respectful of it—but it doesn't mean I like having to deal with that distance."

I stare at her in surprise. I never would have guessed they had issues at all. "I didn't know you felt like that."

She shrugs. "I didn't know you felt weird about the invisible thing. Now that I think about it, that'd be really hard."

"You and Brady don't have it so easy, either, though." My ice cream is beginning to melt, so I take a last bite because I can't stand when it gets goopy. "Gotta admit I've been kinda jealous of you guys, getting to take pictures together and stuff."

"Aw, chica." She leans in to whisper. "And I'm jealous you and Seth can make out without risk of death!"

To my own surprise, I laugh at that. Bea does, too. I'm so glad I called her, because while it doesn't take away my problems it's nice to know that she has some as well. Maybe that's just how it is, trying to be with someone who has a crazy ability. "Wouldn't it be nice if we didn't have to deal with these stupid abilities?"

Bea nods. "If only. People with minimal mutations don't know how lucky they are."

"Seriously." My life would be so much easier if I weren't invisible. Sometimes I wonder why it had to happen to me. It sure isn't fair. "It would be way easier to be with Seth if I could just see myself."

"You guys will be okay," Bea says with confidence I can't even begin to muster. "You're just going through a rough patch, and all this syndicate crap isn't helping. Once this is over, you'll both chill out and be back to your happy selves."

"I hope so." Because the alternative is something I'm not prepared to deal with. As mad as I can get at Seth, the thought of not having him in my life is the worst possible thing.

"Don't wor—" Before Bea can finish her sentence, someone in the diner lets out a horrible screech. By the time I turn towards the noise more people are screaming, and that's when I notice two hands coming through the glass windows just behind me.

I grab Bea's arm and run for the door just as The Phantom's face appears through the wall.

Chapter 26

I keep waiting for The Phantom to grab us, but we make it outside with no problem. Which is when I see those two guys from SuperMart. They not only followed us, but they brought a whole bunch of other friends with them, too. Several of them swallow Radiasure, which only proves they're here for a fight. As if we weren't outnumbered, now we have to deal with power-boosted abilities.

The Phantom's dark eyes almost meet mine, and I wonder if he can sense my fear as he grins. "Someone has been a very busy bee since she got out of that jail cell."

I gulp. "If by busy you mean sitting around my house recovering from starvation, then yes, super busy."

The smile drops off The Phantom's face. "The queen bee doesn't have to move to get work done, does she? That's what her…" He glances at Bea. "…workers are for."

"You've been watching us—all we do is go to school," Bea says with a heavy helping of attitude. "Stop making up crap just so you have an excuse to bother us. Don't you have anything better to do?"

"School, yes." The Phantom tips his chin up. "Where there

is a lab full of supplies."

Shit. Maybe he can't see my expression, but Bea's is enough to give her away.

He takes a few steps closer. "You think I don't have eyes in that school? Don't think for one second that this town is yours, because there's only one syndicate boss around here and that's Juan."

The men around him cheer, and I get the sense that they're not here for show. They're here for blood.

My heart raccs, but I try to steady myself. "Can you at least tell us what you're getting at before you attack us?"

Bea glances at me. I hope this hint has her ready to scream, because we don't have a chance otherwise. The Phantom looks from side to side, as if he's unsure about talking in the street. In broad daylight, no less.

"We know your friends stole lab equipment and chemicals from the school," he says. "What could they need such things for?"

This is not good. Either there is a student or teacher who's a spy at the school for Juan, or they have someone there posing as an Army official. That would be even better for them, so I'm betting on that. "I don't know. Maybe you should tell me."

His upper lip curls. He has reached the end of his patience with me. "Seems they needed to test something. A certain element, perhaps."

"What element?"

"Playing dumb won't work. The Army already suspected you knew where it was—this proves they were right. I suggest you cooperate with me while I'm still feeling merciful."

Part of me wants to give in, because I know all too well what outright defiance of a syndicate will do to us. If Bea and I run now, none of us will be even remotely safe. I can't make this decision for everyone, but I have to.

"Let's make one thing clear, Phantom," I say, though it doesn't come out quite as strong as I'd like it to. "*No one* is getting that element."

His eyes go wide. "Excuse me?"

I grab Bea's arm. "Bea, remember what you said in the car?"

She nods.

"I'm plugging my ears." I slam my hands on the sides of my face and brace for the sound. It's just as horrible as I remember, indescribable in its pitch and ability to cause pain. But it levels Juan's men. Several already have blood coming out of their ears when Bea stops.

"Let's go!" Bea runs for Sexy Blue, and I'm right behind her.

The Phantom barely picks himself off the ground as Bea revs the engine. His lips move, but I can't make out what he says over Sexy Blue's roar and my ringing ears. It doesn't matter—I already know things are about to get violent. As Bea makes a sharp U-turn, I already have my phone out.

Upset as I am at Seth, still he's the first one I think to text. *Phantom ambushed us. Knows about test. Had to fight out. Coming to get u.*

Seth's text comes quickly. *Are u ok?*

Stupid, confusing boy. Still worried about me even when he practically shoved me away. *Yeah, but we're in big trouble.*

Calling Brady. Hector texted me and said element probably wouldn't explode. We need to destroy it now.

I couldn't agree more. *Okay.*

By the time Bea and I pick up Seth, I've gotten a hold of Hector, Carlos, Mom, and Miles. Graham has his phone off, and I keep trying back every couple minutes. It's the first time I wish I had Allie's number, because they must be together. I don't know her, but she's in danger for being with Graham anyway.

Seth sits directly behind me in Sexy Blue, and it's annoying because I can't see his face or tell if he's still hurt by what I said. I want us to be okay. I shouldn't be thinking about this right now, but it's all my brain wants to focus on.

"We'll need Bea, Hector, and Carlos to come up with some kind of diversionary tactic," Seth says. "They'll be tailing us for sure if they can."

Bea nods. "We'll watch your backs until you get to the edge of town, then figure something out."

"Sounds good," I say.

The Pack is already outside when we get to Seth's house. They cram into the car, and the extra weight makes it difficult to go as fast as Bea usually does. Everyone is quiet as we head in the direction of the cave, mostly because they're playing lookout. Hector has his eyes closed, focusing on sounds none of us can hear. Carlos scans the quickly-dimming horizon, his diamond pupils expanded and round like a cat's.

"Looks clear," Carlos says.

Hector nods. "But it won't stay that way."

"Yeah," I say quietly as a new wave of panic washes over me. "Don't get cocky, okay? They way outnumber us. If you can avoid a fight, do."

Bea pats my knee, then says in my voice, "We know the difference between diversion and attack."

"Do we?" Carlos asks. "Because I've been wanting to beat up Juan's dudes for years."

"Don't be stupid," Hector says. "Seriously."

Carlos makes a face. "It was a joke, man. You know, trying to lighten up the situation. Being tense won't get us anywhere."

"We have to be on our guard." Hector runs his hands through his hair, and I wonder if he's more scared than he lets on. He tries to act tough, but the more I get to know him the more I don't buy it.

Bea slows to a stop at the city limit. Hector and Carlos take a few minutes to listen and look before they clear Brady to start running. Once they do, Brady carries Seth and me to save time, and we're off at a ground-breaking pace. The sun has just set over the distant mesas, making it harder to see because the moon isn't quite up. Everything is gray and hazy and passing by so quickly I barely have time to prepare.

The pools. They're about to be gone. I want one more chance to swim in them. One more chance to be there with Seth when we're not in this weird place, but happy like before. This is happening too fast. I'm not ready to say goodbye.

But what else can we do? If we don't get rid of them tonight, chances are The Phantom will figure it out. He's already too close.

The mountain that hides the pools grows bigger and bigger as Brady closes in, but about a mile off he skids to a stop, spraying pebbles everywhere. He doesn't put us down. Just stares out at the shadowy landscape with a blank look on his face. Seth digs his knuckle into Brady's head. "Uh, earth to

Brady? What's the hold-up?"

"I…" He squints. "Is it just me, or can you guys see the blue, too?"

"What?" I say, my eyes immediately on my best guess for the cave's location. "There's no light anywhere."

"Are you sure?" Brady says. "I know that mountain like my own house, and I swear I can see the cave opening. Opened. Am I nuts?"

"Maybe you're just so used to where it is that—"

Seth swears under his breath. "More to the left, Fi. That's definitely brighter than it should be."

I turn my head, looking for what they see. It's very faint, but I finally catch the soft, deep blue spot against the mountain's shadow. My stomach threatens to lose it as the implications set in. "Oh no."

Someone moved the boulder.

Someone else found the pools.

Brady puts us down, and we all stand there for a second in a shocked daze. After that wears off, all I feel is regret. We should have caved it in yesterday. But no, I was selfish and wanted to keep something I knew was dangerous. Now we're paying the price.

"What do we do?" Brady says quietly.

Seth clenches his jaw. "There's only one thing to do—finish our job."

I look at him, surprised. "Are you sure?"

"I'm sick of drugs. I'm sick of these people doing whatever the hell they want. And I'm sure as hell sick of this getting in the way of our lives."

I bite my lip, positive he's referring more to our last exchange than anything. But he's right; this Radiasure race has made our lives even more difficult than before. "What if there are a bunch of people there? I don't think Brady wants to bash heads in."

Brady cringes. "Please, no."

"We won't know until we get there." Seth starts running, and I'm not sure where this new zeal is coming from. Did he find more at his dad's office? Or is this a reckless way to blow off steam from all our issues? There's no time to ask—even the sound of our footsteps feels too loud now that I know there is someone in our cave. Someone potentially dangerous.

The closer we get, the slower and quieter we move. My hopes are high when I make out only one unmarked truck, which looks like it was used to move the boulder because the chain is still wrapped around the rock. There can't be more than a handful of people. Of course, their abilities could make it much worse.

"They didn't leave a guard," Seth whispers. "Seems stupid."

"Or they're strong enough not to worry about it," Brady says.

"Maybe." Seth squints in a way I now know is him looking through something. My guess is the truck and nearby brush. "Ugh, I wish I had Carlos' night vision right now. It looks clear, but the shadows cover a lot."

"I'll have to go down there," I say, dying to know who found the cave and how.

"No!" they both say at the same time. Seth adds, "I'll just look through the rock like before and—"

"Hell. No. If you pass out like last time, we're screwed." I look down, nervous to display any concern after what happened.

"Besides, I can't stand to see you go through that again."

His eyes soften the tiniest bit. "But I can't handle you in danger again."

"I didn't get hurt—and I didn't get caught, either," I point out.

This doesn't satisfy him. "You got put in jail and nearly starved, not to mention getting beaten."

"That was The Phantom's doing. They didn't actually have evidence on me, just his tip."

"She's right, bro," Brady finally chimes in. "We have no idea what will happen to you if you use your ability, and it's already been acting up a ton since you did it last. I don't want you ending up brain dead or something."

Seth grits his teeth, but says, "Looks like I'm outnumbered."

Brady pats him on the shoulder, probably having no clue about our fight. "Sorry. I'll go unhitch the truck from the boulder while Fiona scopes things out."

He sneaks off, leaving Seth and I alone for the first time since we were in the office together. Seth turns around immediately. "I'm not looking. Should I go somewhere else just in case you don't believe me?"

"Here is fine," I say, though his words sting. I take off my clothes. Try to convince myself maybe it's okay for him to see me like this, but I still can't get myself to say it out loud. "I'll be back once I see who's there. If it's more than twenty minutes, come looking."

"Be careful, okay?" Maybe I'm imagining it, but I think his voice shakes.

"Of course." I head towards the cave opening, feeling a surge of confidence now that I'm on my own.

The steep, rocky tunnel is difficult to climb down without moving a single pebble. Every time something shifts beneath my feet, I fear it will make a noise loud enough to alert the people at our pools. Even though I'm invisible, this part of the cave is narrow enough that they wouldn't miss running into me.

As I get closer, I begin to hear muffled voices. This makes my blood boil. Maybe the pools aren't technically ours, but it feels like they are. Brady found this place. It's supposed to be secret. As far as I'm concerned, whoever's here is trespassing—and we have a right to stop them. Maybe I sound like a syndicate leader, but I don't care.

It's hard to make out any of their words, and I guess that they're whispering. Not sure why. Are they worried someone might hear them?

When I make it to the bottom, I peek around the corner and see just two people at the nearest pool. Even at this distance, it's impossible to mistake who I'm looking at. That long, bright blond hair and lab coat can only belong to one person—the scientist girl from the Army. She is bending over one of the pools and filling vials with samples of merinite.

But that's not the worst part. Beside her is a muscled guy with auburn hair who floats just above the ground: Graham.

Chapter 27

I thought I knew what betrayal felt like. Heaven knows I've seen plenty of it in my life. But to earn our trust like this, to pretend to protect us…From the way Graham and that girl talk, it's clear they know each other. He didn't bust in and save me when I was in jail—it was all a setup. I can see the plot they had in my head: let her go and we'll follow her around until she leads us right to it.

I've forgotten how important it is to look up. Graham must have followed us last night, and all that crap about being with Allie was a cover. He was out snitching to the Army and ruining all my plans.

Anger wells up inside me, boiling over as I stagger forward. It might not be the smartest move, but I don't care. "How could you?"

Both of them freeze, and Graham slowly turns around. Of course he can't see me, but the fear on his face is clear. He better be afraid. He's not my brother anymore, just another enemy I plan on taking out.

"F-Fiona?" he says quietly.

"How could you!" I scream it this time, and my echo bounces

all over the cavern. I take the opportunity to move so he can't begin to guess my position. "You betray your own family over and over! You're the worst kind of person. We took you back after everything. Miles, Mom, me...we trusted you. But you really are a traitor!"

He flies up higher, frantic to find me. "Fi, it's not li—"

"Shut up!" I'm about to explode from the rage building inside me. "I don't want to hear any more of your lies. You were the one who bugged us, not for Dad but for the Army. How could you sell out so fast?"

He gives me a convincingly confused look. "Bugged? What was bugged?"

"Don't try." I watch the scientist girl, who is still taking her samples. It's sad she thinks I'll let her leave with that. "You being here says more than any words can."

"It's not what you think!" Graham yells back at me.

I don't answer, but instead stalk towards the scientist girl. I hate her so much it's disturbing. She'd do anything to get this stuff, including ruining my family. I shove her away from the pools, and she cries out. My sympathy is gone. I pick up the vials and smash them to the ground. "You shouldn't have come here, because now I have to keep you quiet."

Before I land my fist into her pretty face, Graham swoops down and grabs her. They're too high up for me to get.

"Come down here so I can beat your traitor ass!" I scream.

Graham is more consumed with the scientist girl than he seems to be worried about me. He puts his hand on her face gently. "Are you okay, Allie?"

I stop at the name. No. No way. His girlfriend is...

Rocks begin to tumble out of the tunnel, and soon Brady and Seth appear. When they see who's down here, their faces fill with horror. Surely they have put the same pieces together I have, because then they get angry.

Brady balls his fists. "Oh, it's gonna be really hard to hold back now."

"Seriously?" Seth says. "I knew you were a dick, but *seriously*? You're with them?"

Graham has the gall to roll his eyes. "Can you give me three seconds to explain?"

"No!" I say. "Brady, grab them out of the air if they won't come down on their own. I want them tied up."

Brady steps forward. "Sounds good to me. I'll try not to break anything."

Graham looks to the exit, but Seth backs up so he's blocking it. "You can't take on more than one person, right?"

Graham snarls. "You guys are still morons."

"And you're still an asshole," I say.

"He didn't know, I swear!" Allie says, looking over the cave as if she could find me. "Fiona, I'm sorry I couldn't tell you who I was, but Graham didn't know what I was doing either, not until that day he got you out. Major Norton wouldn't let you out even though Graham was threatening me, so he promised to follow you as long as the Army didn't actively search for the element."

She thinks she can sway me? Sad. "I'd have rather starved to death than be betrayed."

"I'm not betraying you!" Graham flies higher up and away from Brady, as if that'll keep him safe. But Brady can jump *really* high. "I'm trying to *help* you!"

"I don't think you understand the meaning of 'help,'" Seth says.

"Will you just listen? I didn't know what was going on either—I just went to see my girlfriend last weekend and she was gone. I didn't know when I was tracking her down that I'd find her here. I thought Dad had kidnapped her to get back at me." He holds Allie to him like there's nothing in the world he cares about more. "I was scared to death."

Allie frowns. "I'm so sorry, hon."

He shakes his head. "It was a relief just to find out she was safe, okay? At that point I didn't care what she was doing or who she was doing it for as long as it wasn't Dad. And we hoped she could get you out."

"I tried to convince the Major to let you go, Fiona," Allie says. "I promise. But you've seen how he is. This mission is his *life*."

"And mine, too," I say back, more determined than ever to keep the Army from getting merinite. "You aren't taking the element, but if you want to be buried with it feel free to stay."

Graham lets out a frustrated grunt. "What are you, some syndicate boss now? Are you seriously threatening to kill us?"

"Why not? You've threatened me plenty of times. Good intentions or not, I refuse to let Radiasure be produced again." I'm tired of listening to lies. Every time I let him in just the littlest bit, I get burned. "Brady, go for it."

"Yes, ma'am." Brady leaps into the air, and Graham barely dodges him.

"Wait!" Graham yells. "She's not trying to make Radiasure!"

"Graham! Don't!" Allie covers his mouth, her eyes wider

184

now than at any time I've seen her. This piques my interest. So there is someone she's told her top secret information to.

"Then what is she trying to do, huh?" I ask.

"She's—" he tries to say through her hands, but she snuffs out the rest of the words.

"No, you can't! I'll get in huge trouble!" Allie says.

Graham wrestles his way out of her hold. "We're already in trouble, and Fiona will never let us go if she doesn't know the truth, trust me. But if we tell her, maybe she'll actually *help* you."

Allie doesn't seem to like this assessment. She looks me over skeptically. I can't begin to imagine what she's hiding, but it must be big.

Brady looks in my general direction. "Fiona? What're you thinking?"

"I don't know, I'm kinda curious," I say. "Seth? You wanna let them talk more?"

Seth shrugs as he shakily puts his hand to the wall. Crap, his vision must be messing up again—if he loses it Graham and Allie will get away. "They don't seem to stop."

I let out a long sigh, knowing we have to stall while Seth recovers. "Okay, Graham. You have one chance to convince me not to lock you and your girlfriend up forever. Use it wisely."

Graham looks to Allie, and she gives him the smallest nod. He floats down slowly, as if he's that confident in what he has to say. "She's not trying to *make* Radiasure, Fi. Allie is trying to *cure* the mutations."

The words bounce around in my mind as I stand there speechless. It feels like the world I know is crumbling under my feet, replaced with something I can't even begin to imagine. "That's not possible. They've tried for years."

Allie looks hesitant. "They've also never had merinite—it's the missing key. I've studied Radiasure my entire life, trying to figure out the process of mutation and how to reverse it. I have formulas to test. I just need the element to do it."

"Are you saying…you can make people normal again?" I breathe out, the idea too tantalizing for my own good.

Allie nods. "That's the goal."

I put my hand over my heart, which is fluttering faster than it should. Normal. That would mean I could see myself. It would mean I wouldn't have to deal with syndicates ever again. Seth and I wouldn't have to fight over my invisibility. Everything I've ever wanted could be possible. And a lot more than that.

"If you want out of here," I say, "then you have to swear to me you'll never tell the Army where this place is located."

"I swear." Allie puts her hand on her heart. "On my own life. If you let me use the merinite—I'll die before I tell them where it is."

Her sincerity is shockingly clear, and I get the sense that she wouldn't work for the military if she didn't have to. All she wants is to make a cure, and she'll side with anyone who can make that happen. I am now the one who can do that—so she's on my side. Little does she know, I'm on hers, too. "Okay, then. You can take a small sample, but if you want more you have to come through us."

"Of course." Allie goes back to the water. "Though Major Norton may not be so easy to convince."

"You better make it happen, because we can ruin this place."

She looks at me, horrified. "Don't do that."

"Then don't betray my trust." I watch her take samples, suddenly excited by the prospect of what that merinite could become. Maybe too excited.

A cure.

Who could pass that up?

Chapter 28

As I head downstairs the next morning, I can't quite believe what happened last night. Was it some kind of horrible, wonderful dream all wrapped into one? I don't think so. Allie really did say she was trying to cure mutations, and from everything I know about her that makes much more sense than her being on some kind of power trip. She's too soft for that.

Seth didn't seem too happy that I let them go once I knew what they were doing, but he'll understand eventually. This could change the world in a much better way, and it would definitely change *my* world.

The kitchen is still abandoned and dark. No coffee going yet. I decide to start it for Mom so she doesn't have to wait. Then I pour myself a glass of milk and pull out the only thing I've eaten for breakfast for years. I'm still not tired of blueberry Pop Tarts. I wonder if I'll ever get to the point where I can't stand them because I've eaten so many.

A muffled giggle comes from the ceiling above me, which I can only assume is Spud. Trying not to gag over what might be going on up there, I rush to the living room and turn on the TV, volume on the verge of excessively loud.

The longer I sit in there by myself, the more uncomfortable I become. It feels unsafe, being alone like this. Even with other people in the house, I can't help thinking I'm vulnerable. And after what happened with The Phantom yesterday…if he gets word about my cooperation with the Army I'll be number one on his hit list.

In fact, I better just assume he's already planning a horrific death for me.

My phone buzzes, and I open the text. It's from Graham. *The Major would like to see you tomorrow. Is that okay?*

The thought of seeing Major Norton again makes me sick, but the possibility of a cure outweighs that. I have to know if it can be done. *Sure. So I can go to school without being jailed?*

A minute later I get *Yes. Seth is also cleared now.*

I'm sure he'll be so happy. Or beyond pissed.

Is he ever happy?

Do you ever tell the truth? I type back, still mad that it had to come out like this. Why couldn't he have told me upfront once he knew what was going on? That flight after he "rescued" me comes to mind, how he said even if it didn't look like it he had my best interests in mind. He knew then how mad this would make me, but he picked Allie's secret over me.

"Who're you texting?" Miles says from the stairs. Spud is right behind him, and she's dressed in one of his baseball shirts. She's looking at her device as usual, her eyes flitting back and forth rapidly as she takes in the information.

"Just my other stupid brother." I shut the phone, since it seems Graham doesn't have a reply for my last message. "He says the Major wants to talk with me tomorrow."

I told Mom and Miles everything last night when I got home. I expected them to be more worried about the situation, but they were both too excited about the idea of seeing me that everything else seemed to fall on deaf ears. Can't say I was upset about that—I want them to see me, too.

"Sounds like a fun reunion." He kisses Spud on the cheek. "Continue with your hacking, dear—I'll make breakfast."

She grins as she plops down on the couch next to me. "Some good prospects today. Assholes have been low-balling me lately. This twenty-mil job even looks interesting."

Glad she can't see my jaw drop at the idea of twenty million for one job.

"Good. You're mean when you're bored." Miles heads into the kitchen, and I sit there staring at her. I feel like I should be able to talk to this girl who has so much of my brother's heart, but I don't know where to begin. I'm still not quite over how easily she shot Noelle.

Finally my curiosity gets the better of me, and I have to ask, "So, Spud, how old are you exactly?"

Her eyebrows pop up, but she doesn't look away from her screen. "Don't call me by my hacker alias. It's Lee Seol. If I let you see me like this—you're automatically my friend, okay?"

"Lee Seol…" It feels weird on my tongue, calling her by her real name.

She smiles. "There we go. And I'm twenty-one."

Huh, older than Miles by two years. Not that I could tell, since she's so petite. Even without seeing myself, I feel huge next to her.

"To answer your next questions: I'm Korean. My parents left

190

the country when they figured out what I could do, since the peninsula is pretty much Chinese-syndicate controlled. They were murdered as we kept running. I never live in one place for long, even now. Miles is my first boyfriend. Probably my last."

I blink a few times, surprised at all the information she freely gave. "Uh, I wasn't going to ask anything like that, but okay."

Now she looks at me, curious. "What were you gonna ask then?"

"About that thing you always carry." This close to her, I can tell it's more than a cell phone. It has the same sleekness, but there are all these layers or something. "Is it…a computer?"

Lee Seol gets this proud look on her face, like she's about to talk about her child. "It's *many* computers. Well, more like a central hub for all my hidden servers. It's easier to travel and stay inconspicuous this way."

"Wow." I watch as she pulls out several more thin glass screens.

"It was a bitch to make, let me tell you." She presses a button, and a projector light shines onto the wall. "Code is easier to read than English or Korean for me, but the hardware side of technology I've had to learn the hard way."

"Never seen anything like it." I want to ask if I can hold it, but I'm pretty sure she'd say no.

"Of course you haven't—I make syndicates look like angry caveman mobs. I have everything in the world at my fingertips, if I wanted." The way she says it sounds…exhausted.

"So you understand all that stuff?" The screens are filled with letters and numbers and symbols in what looks like a jumbled mess to me.

"Oh yeah." She holds it closer to me. "This is computer code, but it's also encrypted so only I know what it's really saying. Just in case this ever falls into the wrong hands, you know?"

I have to admit she's just as impressive in real life as her legend. Smart, beautiful, powerful. "How do you understand all that?"

She shrugs. "It's like my language. My father was a programmer, and I'd always mess with his books as a toddler. It wasn't until I was three that they realized I was *reading* them. That's when they put me on a computer to see if I could use what I was reading, and let's just say it was like I could finally communicate how I wanted to."

"That's really cool."

"I guess." She slides the extra screens back into place, and then she gives me a look that says she knows everything about me. "So, when are you gonna ask me to help you out?"

My eyebrows pop up in surprise. "I wasn't."

She purses her lips. "Oh? But Miles said you needed me."

"I do." I fiddle with the remote, feeling inadequate in her presence. "But you're already watching out for my brother. That's why you couldn't help earlier, right?"

She nods. "Not gonna lie, making sure Miles is safe has taken up tons of time lately."

"That means a lot to me—that you would protect him so fiercely. Now that I know you're already working so hard for my family, it feels wrong to ask for more."

This answer doesn't seem to go over well, at least that's what I'm getting from her stink face. "Just so we're clear, I'm watching out for Miles because *I* don't want the only living person I love dead. Not because you asked me."

"Oh." I'm not sure what else I'm supposed to say, but knowing she cares that much about Miles helps me trust her.

"I only do things I'm asked when there's a big price tag attached to it. Free things? Well, those are things I *want* to do." She starts to type into her super phone, as I've decided to call it. "Miles is worried about you, so that means I am, too. I know you haven't met me until now, but I've considered you family for a long time. You're up against some serious powers—I think you know that with me your odds would be evened out some."

I almost can't believe what I'm hearing, but I'm not stupid enough to hesitate. "That would be amazing. I'd love to have your advice, since you deal with these people a lot."

"Well, first off, I've used what I had on me to protect your house, but the surveillance options are shitty in this town. You need more security badly." She pulls up some images on her screens that are familiar: the school library, the bowling alley, the diner, and a bunch of SuperMart. "I've found all the cameras I could access easily. First I thought there were more old-school ones not connected to any network, but I'm starting to wonder if there are hardly any cameras *at all*. We need to fix that."

"How?" I completely agree with her—I just don't have the equipment.

"I have the stuff. Trouble is getting it here without being tracked. I may be the best hacker, but I sure as hell ain't the only one."

"If you can get them, I can hide them."

She smiles wide. "I don't doubt that. After better surveillance, we'll have to focus on mapping out Juan's base in town and what the Army has."

"The Army will be easy, with what happened last night." I already have a bunch of info I could tell her, but some of it involves Seth's ability so I decide to wait.

"Yeah, get me what you can tomorrow. If you see any cameras I didn't show—"

Miles comes into the room holding two plates full of pancakes. "You better be hungry, Lee Seol."

"Yum!" She sets down her super phone and digs in. "Oh, this is so good, baby."

Miles beams. "I hate that I love having you here."

She rolls her eyes. "This is where all the fun is. I'm not going anywhere."

Miles lets out a long sigh, seeming torn about the news. I know he's worried about her safety, but I wish he'd enjoy being with her while he can. He used to be so good at letting go. Now he carries the world on his shoulders, and I feel like it's my fault. If he never would have copied Dad's scent...

My phone buzzes, and the message surprises me. It's from an LS: *Don't tell him what we talked about. He doesn't want me that directly involved, and I prefer to let him think he can boss me around ;P*

I can't help but grin. I think I'll like having Lee Seol around. *We'll both keep him safe*, I reply.

Hell yes.

Chapter 29

"This is the last of what I have on me right now," Lee Seol says as she attaches a tiny microphone to my glasses. It looks just like one of the glittery decals on my chunky white frames—no one could guess it was a bug. "You better not lose it, okay? Those really tiny ones suck to make."

"I won't." I slip my messenger bag over my head carefully, trying not to stress about the impending negotiations.

Mom seems more jittery than usual. "I wish I could go with you, sweetie, but The Phantom is already on to us. If he figures out we're not with a syndicate, he won't hold back."

"I know." She keeps saying stuff like that, even though we're in so deep already that I don't think it would make a difference. Deep down, I wonder if Mom is a bit of a coward. This isn't something she's willing to put her neck on the line for. But it's just as well—I'd rather have her stay out of it because that means she's safer.

"Make sure it's clear they're not getting the merinite unless we know everything they're doing with it," Miles says, his eyes intense. He wants to go, but his girlfriend won't let him. He's too big a target, and Madison isn't wired enough to watch him.

Lee Seol puts her hands on her hips, seeming unhappy. "I wish I had video, but I used my last ones on the roads and your house so we'd be able to see people coming. My Spudlings should be coming through on more soon."

"Spudlings?" I say.

Miles makes a face that might be jealousy. "Her hacker minions."

Lee Seol seems to like Jealous Miles. "I prefer to work alone, but I don't mind the help when I need it. Crisis always comes through when I'm in a jam—he's a mechanical savant—said he'd make me a few things, though I didn't tell him why I needed them."

I want to ask about a billion questions about this guy named Crisis, but a familiar honk sounds from outside. Seth and Brady are here. "Better go."

"We'll be listening," Mom says.

"Okay." Better make sure Seth and Brady know that, otherwise they could accidentally reveal Seth's ability to my family.

Seth doesn't even say hi when I get in the truck. I don't have to ask to know he's still mad at me. But not talking is fine. If he doesn't talk about it he can't break up with me, and that's the last thing I want.

"It'll be okay," Brady says in the silence. "Besides, school hasn't been the same without you guys."

Neither Seth nor I answer. I don't exactly want to go back, but we have to come to some kind of agreement with the Major, because if they won't let us have some control over the "cure" then we won't provide the element. Graham and Allie swore they wouldn't tell the Army the cave's location—that means we control the merinite for now.

Brady sighs. "Fine. Be tense."

Last Monday I was still locked up in a makeshift cell, so when we pull into the school's parking lot I feel like I had one Pop Tart too many. Seeing The Phantom on the other side of the fence doesn't help. He looks like he's about to pounce as we get out, and the Army guards seem reluctant to close in on him.

"Going back to school, huh?" he calls.

"What tipped him off? The backpacks?" I mumble to Brady as we walk towards the buildings of Madison High.

"You think I don't know what this means?" he yells as we get further away. "If you go in there, not only is our deal off but I know you're not working with the O'Connells. Your father would *never* go to bed with the Army!"

I stop, knowing The Phantom has me. If I go in there, I'm telling him exactly where I stand—and worse, I'm showing I don't have a syndicate's protection. Am I ready to make him my clear enemy? Because there's no going back after this. Syndicate people are really good at holding grudges.

"Fiona! You're back!" someone calls from up ahead. It's Bea, with Carlos and Hector coming up behind her. Seeing them clinches it. I'm here to protect them and everyone else in town. The Army may not be my favorite organization in the world, but if I have to pick sides I'll take them over Juan.

So I keep walking.

"You better be prepared for war, little girl!" The Phantom screams.

I guess this is it—war.

I refuse to go back into the front office. Major Norton clearly finds this annoying, but he pastes on a fake smile because it seems Graham and Allie have made good on their oaths of silence. Maybe she's not so bad, after all. "Then where do you suggest we talk, Miss McClean? I'm afraid out in the open courtyard won't happen."

"What about the lab?" I suggest.

His eyes narrow. "I don't think—"

"I don't mind," Allie offers with a smile. "There's nothing in there that they don't already know about."

"It's the least you could do, after what you put my sister through," Graham points out.

This seems to put the Major in an even worse mood. "Obviously my actions were justified, but I suppose we can authorize it…this once."

Once? He wishes. With Allie on my side I'm sure this will go my way. Seth, Brady, and I follow them to the science lab that has been cordoned off and surrounded by more guards than even the office. The soldiers part at Major Norton's command, and we enter a darkened lab with way more fancy equipment than our school owns. This must be all the stuff they were rolling off the truck that first day.

"How 'bout we sit down and have a little chat?" the Major says as he pulls out a lab stool.

"If that's what you want to call it," Seth grumbles. "I was thinking more like a negotiation. Maybe we should write up a treaty while we're at it."

The Major grits his teeth. "You act as if the source of merinite belongs to you, when I'm certain it doesn't. What makes you think you can stop me from finding it with my forces?"

I scoff. "Why did you even ask us here if that's what you think?"

"As a courtesy," he shoots back.

Allie steps forward, head held high. "If you do that, sir, I'm sorry but I won't be working with you anymore. Maybe they don't have official ownership, but who does? They found the pools, and not only that but they're willing to *cooperate*. Why are you making it more difficult?"

Major Norton blinks a few times, seeming surprised at Allie's assertiveness. Then he clears his throat and looks away. "Fine then. If that's how you would like to proceed—we need you more than anyone else."

Allie seems pleased by this, and I'm flat out impressed. "Thank you, Major."

He nods. "I only want this mission to be successful."

"So you'll stop treating us like ants to step on?" Seth pulls out a seat for himself. I sit next to him because I don't want Major Norton suspecting that we have issues.

"I'll try." The Major wastes no time getting down to business. Which I'm glad for, because I'd rather not spend my whole day in his presence. "What we need is access to the element and complete silence on what we're attempting to create. If syndicates were to catch on, it would be devastating. So what do you think is a fair trade?"

"Hmm." I let the silence work its magic. The longer I hold back an answer, the more worried he'll be that I won't go for his simple terms. "The way I see it, this is a straight up informational trade. We have knowledge of the element—you have knowledge about this cure and what went down in Radison, right?"

The Major's eyebrows rise, wrinkling his forehead. "What makes you interested in the old city?"

"Seems you've been interested in the Mitchell family since you got here," Seth says. Brady looks beyond confused, and I assume Seth didn't tell him what we found at their dad's office. "I think there might be a bigger reason than you let on."

The Major shakes his head. "If you expect me to tell you about every classified file I have, you better be enlisting."

And there it is—he knows something. Seth curls his fingers around his knees, anger wafting off him. "Hell. No."

"You okay, son?" The Major looks like he's enjoying Seth's frustration. "You don't look too good."

I turn my full attention on Seth. Sweat beads at his forehead, and it's subtle but he's shaking. My stomach drops at the thought of him having another painful vision episode. And now of all times. "I'm fine," Seth says through his teeth.

Despite our fights, I can't help putting my hand over his. I won't let his secret be revealed before he's ready. "Fine, whatever. That information isn't that important—we were just curious," I say.

"What?" Seth glares at me, and I don't think it's because of his vision. But we have to drop it and get him out of here.

I move on to the other topic of concern. "You want the merinite and our silence about the cure. We're willing to provide that, but we also need to form some kind of mutual protection agreement."

"You want security?" The Major purses his lips. "I can understand that, seeing as The Phantom probably has a big target on your back. We could provide guards."

I shake my head. "That would make us a bigger target right now—I was thinking more like intel on his forces and base, so we know what we're up against."

The Major sighs. "I'm afraid I can't give you anything there. We haven't been able to get a good idea ourselves. We can't even find the networks they're using or where their central base is."

"Damn," I mutter. After what The Phantom said when we got to school, I can't help feeling I need to be even more cautious. "It sounds like we know more than you do."

This seems to pique the Major's interest. "Really? Because we can't get into town for the most part. They've got us surrounded here at the school, and they follow my soldiers who go into town, harass them. I could use help rooting them out, and it seems like that wouldn't be bad for you, either."

I mull it over. "I think we may have found our common ground. So we give Allie access to the pools and keep her work secret, and you allow us to know about the cure. Also, we both agree to collaborate on eliminating The Phantom's presence in the area."

There's a lot of nodding. Even Seth seems to agree—or maybe he just wants to get out of here because of his vision. I hold out my hand to the Major, my charm bracelets showing my action. "So you agree?"

Major Norton squeezes my palm hard. "It's a deal."

Chapter 30

I get one good night of rest, but the next night I'm woken by a rough shake. When I open my eyes, all I see is a black figure. I almost scream, but then I hear Lee Seol's quiet voice, "You better not freak out, because there's no way anyone will get into this house undetected on my watch. You should know it's me."

I gulp back my yelp. She seems more serious and deadly in the dark, and it reminds me of the first night I met her. "What's going on?"

"We need to scout the town for surveillance locations. I'm tiny and dressed in black. You're invisible. I figure we'd make the best team."

Glancing at the clock, I pull myself up to sitting. "It's one in the morning."

"Best time to lurk." She throws my covers off. "Get naked, Fi."

I take off my tank top, though the idea of going out this late isn't appealing. It'll be freezing without clothes. "I'm telling Miles you made me undress in front of you."

She snorts. "You don't think he'd go for a threesome with his sister? Damn."

"Oh, gross, you went there."

"Don't play dirty sarcasm with me—I'll win every time."

"Lesson learned." I tug my shorts off, the sensation of being exposed lasting for only a moment. No Seth means I'm safe and invisible as can be. "Thanks for doing this, by the way. We'd be toast without you."

She shrugs. "You didn't think I'd pass up on all this fun, did you? Much to Miles' distress, I like having my hands in the dangerous stuff, and nothing is more dangerous than this."

"Fair enough." I look around my room, feeling the urge to take something in case things go bad. Not that I can bring much while invisible. Then I remember Noelle's one possession. "Hey, did you keep that little box you found on the woman you shot?"

"Yeah, why?"

"It had knock-out and killing needles in it—thought it might be handy to have that box in my mouth. Just in case."

She nods slowly. "Is that what they were? Glad I didn't touch them. They're in my bag. I'll be right back."

Once Lee Seol gets the tin for me, I slip it into my mouth and we head into the chilly night. I'm not entirely sure where we're going, but now that we're on the move I don't dare talk. This feels like it could be any other mission for my dad's syndicate. But this time no one is controlling me. I'm back in this world because I chose to be.

It better be worth it.

After we cross the street into the older section of Madison, I assume we're headed to where my boyfriend and closest friends live. We definitely need eyes in this area. They are major targets, both for their abilities and their relationships with me.

Lee Seol is incredibly good at sliding from shadow to shadow, crouching in small places, and not making a single sound. I feel like I'm trying to follow a ninja, and I'd be doing a horrible job at it if I weren't invisible. She picks a wall of bushes and waves me over.

"I need you to mark a few things for me," she whispers.

"How?" The word sounds funny with the needle box lodged in my cheek.

It's hard to see in the middle-of-the-night darkness, but she pulls something from her pocket. "These are clear stickers. We should be able to find them though they aren't conspicuous, and it'll give me an idea of how many cameras I need to get. Give me your hand."

"Here." I put my palm on her knee, and she puts stickers on me.

"You need to get that stop sign under the street light, the mailbox on the corner, and that car on cinder blocks in the driveway across the street."

I squeeze her knee instead of talking, and then I'm off. I don't like how the stickers are slightly reflective in comparison to me, but even if anyone is out at this hour chances are low that they'll see them. The stop sign is my first mark, since I want to get the one in lamplight over with. The other two spots are easy in comparison.

We do this one more time before we're right in front of Seth's house, where lights are still on. Please be his dad and not him. Not that he looks through walls all the time, but who knows when his eyes will glitch out lately?

Lee Seol settles behind a trash can and begins to talk, but I cover her mouth. Her eyes pop open in surprise, so I whisper right into her ear, "Hector's been going without his ear plugs a lot. He might be able to hear us."

She nods, and I step away from her. We'll have to be mind-readers from here on out.

When she points at the basketball hoop above the garage behind us, I jump up as quietly as I can. Then she creeps to another location and we begin a strange charade—I can't figure out what she wants, and I'm about to tell her that when headlights round the corner and shine on me.

I instinctively duck down, as if the tiny clear sticker on my hand will give me away. The car slows to a stop in front of Seth's house, and I hold my breath as two men get out. In the dark I can't tell who they are, but based on the last time Seth saw someone in his house so late it has to be a couple of Juan's guys.

They walk up the path and open the door like this is totally normal. I, on the other hand, am freaking out. Rushing back to Lee Seol, I whisper, "Do you have any kind of phone on you?"

Her eyes narrow. "Why?"

"Because two thugs just walked into my boyfriend's house and I'm worried they're gonna hurt him. You heard what The Phantom said when I went back to school."

She sighs as she pulls out her super phone. "I can make it look like it's coming from your cell."

"Perfect."

With a few codes entered, Lee Seol hands over her phone. Seth picks up after three rings. "Fiona? Is everything okay?"

"I'm fine, but a couple of Juan's guys are in your house right now."

"What?" He sounds much more awake now. There's a pause, in which I imagine him looking through a few walls. "How the hell did you know that? Where are you?"

"Shh," I say. "They might hear you."

"Fiona." His voice is quieter, but that doesn't mean it lacks intensity. "Are you outside my house?"

I really don't want to answer that question, and then Lee Seol's grabbing her super phone from me anyway. She puts it to her ear. "Seth, try to listen to their conversation for us, okay? We need to move before the chance is lost."

She hangs up and waves frantically at me. "C'mon, we gotta get in that car!"

"*What?*"

"They'll go back to base eventually." Lee Seol springs up like a baby tiger and bolts for the beat-up Buick. I follow behind, my heart pounding at the thought of throwing ourselves right into The Phantom's den. But what else am I supposed to do? We need to find his hide-out—I won't get a better opportunity.

She tugs on the car door handle, and to my surprise it opens. Maybe they don't expect anyone in this town to dare steal their car? Lee Seol climbs into the back and lies on the floor. I assume she means for me to take the large back seat, since they won't see me there. So I crawl in and shut the door as quietly as possible. This is insane, but I can't help thinking at least it's a little warmer in here. I can hardly feel my feet.

I'm not sure how much time passes. We don't speak or move. Who knows what Lee Seol is thinking, but I sure hope Seth hasn't tried to look for me. He'll kill me if he sees me in this car.

Finally I hear muffled voices and footsteps. The two men

hop into the front seats, and the driver starts the car. Sure enough, they have the trademark tattoos. Other than that I don't recognize them. As they speak to each other in Spanish, I try to catch what I can. Too bad my five months of Spanish 1 aren't enough to get more than bits and pieces of their rushed speech. Something about a building...? And maybe girls. Or one girl. The guy in the passenger seat said he has to pee. I understood that no problem.

Why doesn't Senorita teach us useful vocabulary about spying and murder and theft? I have a feeling I'd understand a lot more that way.

The car slows to a stop, and lights shine brightly through the windows. I risk a peek—ugh, just the gas station. I highly doubt The Phantom is running his operation from here. He's got too big a crew.

The guy who has to pee gets out. While he's gone the driver sings to the song on the radio and pulls out a cigarette. He paws at the console between the seats, I assume looking for a lighter. Then, to my horror, he puts his hand right on Lee Seol's hip. He whips around without hesitation and grabs her by the arm.

She doesn't scream, only tries to free herself.

"What do we have here?" the man says. "A spy?"

Leo Seol tries to head butt him, but he dodges.

"Diego!" he cries from the open window, but his buddy is already inside. There's only one thing to do, so I spit out the needle box and grab the first one I see. Sure hope it isn't a killing one.

The man catches sight of it just before I shove it into his forearm. His eyes go wide as understanding registers. Maybe

207

he can't see me, but he knows there's only one person who could have gone unseen. I pull it out—the tip is purple under the faint layer of blood—and he slumps in his seat.

Lee Seol scrambles for the door, and I'm right behind her. The moment we're out, someone yells from behind us, "Hey! What're you doing?"

It's the other guy, Diego.

We bolt, but he's right on our tails.

Chapter 31

Lee Seol is faster than I expect her to be, but not quick enough in comparison to the guy running after us. Even I can't run fast enough—he has to have some kind of mutation that makes him quicker. He closes in on us after just a block, grabbing Lee Seol around the waist and dragging her behind the nearest building.

"Get off me!" she screams, and I wonder if she thinks I've left her. I just wanted to get off the main road in case there are more of Juan's guys patrolling.

"Who are you?" Diego yells back as he tries to pull off her mask.

She steps on his foot, but he's so much bigger than her that it doesn't do much good. I slip the box back out of my mouth and grab a knock-out needle. For a moment I think a killing needle would be smarter—fewer people to identify us—but I push back the thought. That's exactly what my dad wanted me to be, and I refuse to go that far.

Creeping up to him, I stick the needle in his neck and he drops to the ground. Lee Seol whirls around, looking for me. "Took you long enough."

"Better to leave a body in an alley than on the street." I kneel down next to the guy, deciding I should search him for anything useful. We already lost our chance to find The Phantom's base, but maybe he'll have something that'll make this night not a total loss. I find a cell phone in his pocket. "Can you do anything with this?"

Lee Seol grabs it. "It's password locked, but I can get around that easily. We probably shouldn't do it here, though."

"You think?"

She tries to point the phone at me, but misses by several degrees. "Don't get smart with me."

"We better go before they wake up and rat us out." That's the biggest problem. We got away, sure, but these guys aren't drunk—they'll remember that I had something to do with it, and I'm not stupid enough to think The Phantom won't retaliate. Just wish I knew *how*.

We head for the house as quickly as we can, which isn't very quick with all the creeping and fatigue. I need two weeks of sleep after all this crap. But when I see the lights on at home, I kiss any hope of sleep goodbye.

Miles is lying on the couch watching some infomercial when we get inside. He doesn't look at Lee Seol, and he seems pissed. "Welcome home, honey."

"Did you make me cookies?" She sits on the couch next to him and pulls out the cell phone we got. "You know how much I love cookies after causing trouble."

Miles clenches his jaw. "Because you weren't already in enough?"

"How'd you know we were gone?" I ask. Miles can sleep

through just about anything, so I have a hard time believing he just randomly woke up.

He shoots a glare in my direction. "Seth called me."

"Snitch," I mutter.

"He mentioned something about you guys following some of Juan's people?"

Lee Seol rolls her eyes. "It wasn't a big deal. We just hopped in their car so we could find The Phantom's base, but they found us first, Fiona knocked them out, and we got this cell phone as a prize. Cool, huh?"

"So they saw you?" Miles' voice goes up an octave, and I worry he might actually explode. "If they figure out you're here…"

"Relax, baby. They probably thought I was Bea—we're about the same size." She plugs her super phone into the regular one, I assume to better hack it. "I had my mask on, anyway. Stop treating me like I'm stupid. If you haven't noticed, I'm pretty good at what I do."

"That doesn't make you a god!" Miles stands and points at me. "And now you're encouraging my sister to do even more dangerous stuff than she's already doing?"

"Miles, don't blame her," I say, grabbing a blanket from the couch to wrap around my shivering self. "I would have—"

"Don't," he cuts me off, fuming. "I gave up my freedom for you. I put my girlfriend's neck on the line to get you out. Now I'll never have a normal life, and you're throwing away everything I did like it means nothing!"

The tiniest bit of guilt creeps in, thinking about how trapped Miles is now. Being number one on any syndicate's list is not much of a life at all. He did so much for us, but… "So because

211

you got us out of the syndicate, you get to decide what I do with the rest of my life?"

That question makes him hesitate. "No...though I think I'm allowed to be worried about your safety."

I shake my head in disbelief. "You know who you sound like? Graham."

Miles stares at me, speechless.

"Don't be too hard on him, Fi," Lee Seol says nonchalantly as she continues her work on the phone. "He's just annoyed because he has to hide out instead of doing useful things. Guys don't like to be protected, especially by girls."

"That's not..." Miles slumps back onto the couch. "Okay, maybe that's a little bit true."

Lee Seol smirks. "You know I don't love you because you can protect me, right?"

"Why do you again?"

"Because you're you, and you make me happy." She puts her hand over his. "Also, you're hot. And usually, you don't ask me to be anyone but myself."

Miles leans his head on her shoulder. "Oh yeah. Just promise me you won't take on more than you can handle, okay? I do hate that I can't help."

Lee Seol smiles. "I promise. It's just simple surveillance, plus trying to find their den of evil. That's only like two things."

"Yes. Two teeny tiny things." Miles laughs.

So they're disgustingly cute together. I decide not to say this, but instead to sit next to Lee Seol. "You find anything on this cell yet?"

She nods. "Broke through the password, downloaded all

texts and messages on the memory, but it's connected to a majorly protected network. This thing will probably take me a few days to crack."

My heart speeds up at the thought. "Does that mean it's probably a syndicate network?"

"That's my bet. The Phantom probably has more tech than we think, with what he seems to know and how quick. He'd need a super secure network to stay in touch with Juan and other leaders in the syndicate."

"So once you get into that network, you'll know where they're hiding?"

"I should be able to track it down." She finally looks up at me, and when she does I'm surprised to see her eyes full of excitement. There's no doubt in my mind that she's having the time of her life. "Make some coffee? Once I get on a code I have a hard time quitting until it's broken."

"Sure." I get up and start the coffee maker, then I go up to my room to get dressed. Grabbing my phone, I flick it on and see twenty messages. All from Seth. I guess he does still care about me, even if he's not showing it much lately. After seeing how upset Miles was, I feel bad for making him worry.

I want to ask if he overheard anything when his dad was talking to Juan's guys, but tonight I have a feeling that won't go over well. It takes me several text drafts to figure out the right words, but I finally settle on: *I'm safe. Sorry I couldn't explain. I know I must've scared you.*

Seth's reply comes quicker than I expected, it being four in the morning and all. Has he stayed up worrying since I called? *Glad you're okay. You know I'd go crazy if I lost you, right?*

The words mean everything right now. Maybe we'll be okay. *I know. Same here.*

Good. See you in a few hours.

Right. I settle into bed, wishing it was a lot more than a few hours. Not because I don't want to see Seth, but because I'm way too tired to go to school and deal with the Army after a night chasing The Phantom.

Can't a vigilante catch a break?

Chapter 32

I should probably be trying to catch up in class, but I can't stop looking at the texts from Diego's phone. Lee Seol printed them out, and Bea sits next to me translating the longer ones from Spanish. She hands me another paper, sending her words right into my ear, "Some of these look more useful."

I grab it, hoping our history teacher doesn't notice. So far the texts have been stupid or too vague to help—but I keep hoping one will tell us where to look for The Phantom's base, what Seth's dad is doing, or what kind of attack we need to prepare for.

Delivered the money to JM. Says he'll cooperate. Will report info after doing my rounds.

JM—that could be John Mitchell. It probably is, since the date on this is the same as when Seth saw one of Juan's guys in his house. There's no denying he's telling them *something*, but it's hard to know what. If Seth's dad is behind the bugs—and I'm sure he is—he should know a lot more than what Juan's people do.

Keep telling him to send for Ted. Bitch would never get past his infrared, but he won't listen. Never does.

My stomach turns; this one is about me. I hate infrared devices because they're a pain to get around, but at least they can be dismantled or destroyed. People who see that way? I'd be in big trouble if The Phantom got past his pride and asked for help.

There's not much else, and the bell rings anyway. We meet up at our usual lunch table, where Seth and Hector are already eating. I sit next to my boyfriend, wanting to be closer but unsure because he looks beyond stressed. I haven't even asked him if he heard something last night. He'll tell me when he's ready, right?

"Find anything interesting?" he asks through a mouthful of pizza.

"Just this." Rather than saying outright that his dad's probably guilty, I show him the texts Bea translated.

Seth sighs. "We should probably find out who exactly this Ted guy is."

"Yeah." I take a small bite from my salad, my appetite minimal.

"And it only confirms my…" Seth's hands go to his head, the words turning into cussing. These vision glitches are getting ridiculous, and I have a feeling they are more frequent than he's telling. He puts his head on the table as I watch The Pack stare at him in confusion.

"What's wrong?" Hector asks. "Did you realize something bad?"

"No…" Seth's voice is weak.

"Must be a sudden headache," Brady says in a feeble attempt to cover. "You know how he gets those."

Carlos purses his lips, not seeming to buy it. "Looks like one hell of a headache."

"Maybe you should go to a doctor," Bea offers.

"No!" I blurt out. That was so not the right thing to say, because now they look even more suspicious. "Uh, I mean…"

"What's going on?" Hector's face is serious, and I worry he's heard more than he lets on with how often he goes without his ear plugs lately. "I get the sense you guys aren't telling us something."

Carlos nods. "Something majorly important. That's not cool—we're supposed to be in this together."

Brady and I cringe at the same time, but what are we supposed to say?

Bea frowns at Brady's expression. "Wait, *is* there something you're keeping secret?"

"Guys, don't worry." Seth picks himself up from the table, trying to look like he's fine. Too bad his eyes flit back and forth rapidly. At this rate there's no way he'll be able to keep his secret, no matter how much he wants to. "It's just—"

"Fiona!" someone calls from behind. I turn to find Allie waving at me, a big smile on her face. She comes up to the table, panting and excited. "There you are! I was hoping I could steal you away for the rest of school, get started on things. What do you think?"

"Oh, sure," I say evenly, though I'm afraid she'll notice Seth's pain. She is a scientist; she has to be observant. "Seth can come, too, right?"

"Of course!" She nods toward the office building. "Should I check you out now?"

I wasn't aware she was allowed to do that, but I tell her she can, anyway. "We'll meet you over there, okay?"

"Perfect." Allie practically skips off.

As I help Seth up and head for the lab, I'm happy for the excuse to leave because I'm not sure The Pack would have stopped pressing for answers. "That was close."

"Yeah." He's shaky still, and I'm not sure his vision has fixed itself yet. It's been a while since he held onto me this tightly. "Do you have the microphone today?"

"No. Mom took it to work with her. Lee Seol is hoping to get more intel on The Phantom's base, since we have the Army covered."

He nods. "It's getting weird, Fi. I'm seeing through things I never did before."

This is not good news to me. "Like what?"

"Just…there's more subtlety, I guess. Like instead of pulling back all skin layers I know I'm pulling back only a few. Or with trees—I can pull out particular rings in the trunk. And with Allie's hair just now, I think I saw through her hair dye, because it was brown instead of blond."

I take in this information as we walk the halls. "And you couldn't do that before?"

"No. I'd just see straight through something, not midway." He puts a hand to his eyes. "It hurts like hell."

I wish I could take care of him, even though I'm not sure he'd let me. Maybe we came to some kind of truce last night, but we're still dancing around our physical issues. "It sounds like you're going through some kind of ability growth spurt."

"Maybe." He appears a little stronger now. "Better than

thinking I'm messed up."

"It's not unheard of." The lab is in sight, and Allie waves to us from where she stands by the guards. "Lots of people with mental abilities don't fully master them until they're older. My mom spent years honing her telekinesis."

We get to the lab before he can answer, and Allie clears us with the guards. The lab is mostly the same, except now the vials of merinite give the room a blue aura. These must be the samples she got when we discovered her and Graham in the cave. Speaking of which, "Where's my brother? I haven't seen him in a few days."

Her smile gets dreamy. "He's been doing a lot of security flights around the school, your house, and factory, watching for any of Juan's people."

"I see." Sounds like something Graham would do. I'm pretty sure it's impossible for him to shake the guard dog tendencies. Not that it's a bad thing—I feel safer knowing he's up there looking out for us.

"So…" Allie holds out a hand to the vials. "I've started analyzing the merinite, and it's looking like my theories all these years have been correct."

"What theories?" Seth asks in his grumpiest tone. He must still be in pain, either that or he hates the idea of a cure way more than I thought.

Allie's smile drops slightly. "I've been studying Radiasure since I was a kid. Well, at least the formulas I was able to get a hold of. They never added up to me, and I postulated in one of my high school papers that there was a missing element. Everyone thought I was crazy, because the element I described didn't fit anything in existence. I tried to get enough Radiasure to study, but people would rather use it than donate it to science, you know?"

I nod, imagining how horrified my dad would be at the thought of breaking down perfectly good pills to study. "So you kept researching as if there really was a missing element?"

"Well, it's a long story, but a few people noticed what I was doing and believed me. Major Norton was one of them." She runs her fingers over the smooth table top. "If it weren't for him, I'd have never made any progress. He convinced the military to let me use confiscated Radiasure—I was able to confirm a missing element, but unable to extract that element from the drug. Everything broke down each time I tried."

"So that's why you owe the Major," Seth says. "Even though he's an ass."

Allie nods. "Now that I have merinite, I should be able to build the antidote from the ground up. I probably know more about how Radiasure works than anyone, and I finally get to put that to good use. Thanks to you guys."

Seth doesn't seem to buy this, but I can't help liking Allie. She seems so driven and smart and good—I see why Graham is crazy about her. I head for the vials, curious to see more of what could make me visible in the near future.

"What made you devote your life to this so early on?" I ask. "Seems like a pretty dangerous choice in occupation."

She smirks. "I guess you're right, but it's personal for me."

"It's personal for everyone," Seth says. "What makes you so special?"

"Nothing, really." She seems uncomfortable with Seth, and I

want to tell him to stop being so rude. "So many people focus on the extraordinary abilities from Radiasure mutation, but people forget that our infant mortality rate is higher than it's been in centuries. Many babies die from deformities or deadly abilities that kill both them and their mother. And if they do live, their lives are often painful and difficult."

Allie gets this distant look in her eyes, and I recognize it as the same look Brady often gets. I hesitate for a second, but then say, "You lost someone close to you because of a mutation, didn't you?"

She nods, unable to pull her eyes from the floor. "My little sister had a rapid growth mutation. My mother went through an entire pregnancy in a few weeks, which nearly killed her, and then my little sister spent a year growing so quickly you could literally watch her age. But only her body grew—she was still a baby in her mind. It tore my mom and dad apart, going through life in fast forward like that. I decided I had to find a cure, impossible as it seemed. Too many people have suffered because of this drug."

I couldn't agree with her more. "How long do you think it'll take to make a cure?"

"It depends." Allie goes to a drawer and pulls out a bunch of papers. "I've created a lot of theoretical drugs based on what I know about Radiasure and the missing element—if one of these proves to be a good start then it could take just days to create."

"Seriously? That seems really fast," Seth says, seeming a little more interested. "What do you know that all these other scientists over the years don't?"

Allie sighs, like explaining this is tedious. "It's not just me—many scientists agree that Radiasure isn't what its creators thought it was. Epigenomics was barely a science when Radiasure was developed, and they got in over their heads."

"Epige-what?" I say.

"There is the genome..." Allie grabs one of the three-dimensional DNA models from the shelf. "...and then the epigenome. Your genes are kind of like a musical score with all the different notes and instrument parts—the epigenome is like the annotation of how those notes should be played. They are chemical instructions that tell your cells what part of your DNA should be used and how much and when.

"Radiasure is the first and worst of its kind: a drug that acts like an epigenetic tag to control your genes. Originally it was supposed to turn off a human's sensitivity to radiation, but the FDA approved it without enough testing or knowledge of epigenetics." Allie stretches out the DNA model, frowning at it. "Scientists knew there was a risk that Radiasure's epigenetic tag would transfer generation to generation, but since most of the tags don't they took the chance. Everyone hoped that even if it wasn't ultimately safe, the drug would only affect those who chose to take it. But it actually added an extra, permanent chemical to the epigenome. That's why mutations are genetic, but we can't predict what that tag will tell a person's DNA to do."

I can barely follow what she's saying, but it seems like Seth grasps most of it. He puts his hand over his mouth, thinking. "So if you can get rid of the tag, you get rid of the rogue mutation?"

Allie nods. "That's the idea. It may not work for every debilitating mutation, but even in those situations it should

222

prevent it from being passed on. There are scientists that have known this for a decade, but they haven't been able to do it because they don't have merinite. I really believe that will make the difference."

My heart pounds at her words, and I crave for this drug to be real right now. If it could take away whatever in me is stopping me from being visible, then every problem that's haunted me my whole life would be gone.

Allie could save me.

"But how will you test it?" Seth doesn't seem to be impacted by the amazingness of her work one bit. Probably because he has no interest in giving up his ability. "Give rats Radiasure until they mutate and then see if the drug works?"

Allie bites her lip. "We don't have that kind of time, or enough Radiasure to do that. But we have a small group of volunteers within the Army forces here."

Seth's eyes go wide. "You're testing on humans right away?"

"We don't have much choice."

Seth is saying something, but I can't hear over my own thoughts. I might not have to wait years or even months... what if I could see myself next week? The idea makes my eyes water, and I say, "Can I volunteer?"

Seth and Allie stop arguing, staring at me in surprise. Allie takes a deep breath as she puts her hand on my shoulder. "Did you say you want to be part of the study?"

"No, she didn't," Seth growls.

"Yes," I say at the same time. "Please. I need to be."

Allie's eyes glitter with excitement. "All the volunteers have more minor abilities. It would be amazing to observe the impact

223

on what's probably a very complex mutation. If you're willing, I'm afraid I can't say no."

"I'm more than willing." *I'm desperate.*

"First you throw away my one chance at getting the factory information, and now this?" Seth stomps away, slamming the door as he leaves. I know I should care, but I don't.

Chapter 33

By the time the weekend rolls around, Lee Seol has gathered the necessary surveillance equipment from all over the country. We just have to pick it up under the interstate bridge, where the river has carved a gorge in the rocks. Despite her insistence that only she and I should go, Seth is determined to stay at my side. I wish I could say it was out of affection, but I'm pretty sure he thinks I'll do something stupid.

"Why are you wearing clothes?" Lee Seol stuffs a dagger into her pants' side pocket.

I glance at Seth, who has acquired a pair of brass knuckles from Carlos of all people. He knows the black dress is because of him. I need the barrier after how he reacted to my volunteering for Allie's tests. "Last time I nearly froze to death. I can have this off in seconds if I need to."

Lee Seol nods. "Fair enough. It's colder at night here than I expected."

"Are you sure we're enough?" Seth asks as he zips up his black hoodie. "What if we get attacked?"

"A drop-off is supposed to be about stealth. No one will attack us if they don't *see* us," Lee Seol grumbles as she pulls her hair back.

"Given how things have been going with The Phantom, I don't think it would hurt to have backup," he insists.

Lee Seol gives him her stink face, which I'm starting to learn is what she does when she agrees but doesn't want to admit it. I thought Juan's guys would have gotten us back by now for knocking out their men, but two days have passed with nothing. The longer it takes, the more afraid I get for what they might be planning.

I shake the box of needles. "I'll have these just in case. They might be tiny but they are lethal."

"They kinda freak me out, honestly." Lee Seol slips her arms through a backpack, which I assume is to carry the new equipment. "We just need to be careful is all. There shouldn't be any problems."

Miles, who sits on the couch, clears his throat. "Too bad you haven't cracked that network yet. What if they know more than we think?"

Her glare doesn't seem to scare Miles like it does me. "Oh, I'm gonna crack it. And I'm gonna find their hide-out and shut their power down for good measure."

He smirks. "I can't believe you haven't gotten in yet."

"It's not my fault they got a better programmer!" she yells.

"Actually, it probably *is* your fault."

"Shut up!" She throws a pillow at him. Then they're making out. Lovely.

"Guess we're not the only ones who do that," I mumble to Seth. He pretends not to hear me. I shove him. "Did you hear that? Or are you deaf now?"

"Just because I hear you doesn't mean I have to reply. Not like you ever listen to me." He slips his fingers into the brass knuckles, not a single wisp of teasing in his voice. I'm starting to feel like we've gone back to that first day I met him, when he made me angry and confused and scared all at the same time.

I wait for his eyes to meet mine. When they do, my heart twists.

"What?" he asks.

"Can you give me my boyfriend back? I miss him."

Seth looks away from me. "Only if I can have my girlfriend back, because I'm not sure I recognize her anymore."

"What do you want me to do? Give up the things I want in favor of what you want for me?" I lower my voice to a whisper, though Miles and Lee Seol are surely too occupied to overhear. "I know you don't like the risks I'm taking, but can you at least respect that it's my choice and maybe you can't understand why I need to do what I'm doing?"

Seth folds his arms. "Then explain it to me. Because I'd really like to know the logic behind taking a drug that could do who-knows-what to you—death included."

It's been a long time since he's spoken to me like this, and instead of making me mad it just makes me want to cry. "I have explained it to you. Over certain drawings you hate to do. At your dad's office when you kicked me out. It's not my fault you don't want to hear it."

Before he answers, Lee Seol is standing in front of us again. No embarrassment in sight. "Okay, *now* I'm ready to go. Maybe you two should kiss, too. You're tense. Tense is bad for secret missions."

"We'll be late if we don't hurry." Seth heads for the door. I follow, since I couldn't have said it better myself.

Though we're supposed to meet these Spudlings at the interstate bridge, we don't take the roads to get there. Seth and I know exactly how to navigate the desert so that we end up at the drop-off, and Lee Seol seems happy to let us take the lead.

The night sky is darker than usual, thanks to the considerable amount of cloud cover. It's been a while since we had a storm roll in, and I'm not sure whether the darkness is a good or bad thing. Either way, I speed up.

"What's the rush?" Lee Seol says through labored breaths. "They know to wait until I get there."

"If it rains I'm screwed."

She curses. "I'll suck it up then. You people and your long legs."

After another mile or so, I can feel the humidity saturating the air. It's easy to pick up on, since usually Madison is beyond dry. Thunder growls in the distance, and my heart begins to race. Just a little further. We'll pick up the stuff and leave. Simple as that.

"Almost there," Seth says quietly, and my heart flutters because I know he senses my nerves and is trying to comfort me. Stupid boy. I'm sure he still cares even though he's acting like a jerk.

Even though the gorge under the bridge is nowhere near Grand Canyon height, I still get jittery as we approach. A fall off this cliff would mean death. We've slowed to a walk, the dark outline of the bridge's pillars in clear view.

Lee Seol sounds exhausted when she says, "They should be right under there, in the space between the interstate and cliff."

"Fabulous," I grumble. "A chance of rain plus heights? Best night ever."

I can't see her eye roll, but I swear I can feel it. "I'll go by myself then."

She takes off, and I immediately feel guilty for complaining. All she's done since she got here is help me out—she doesn't need my crap. I run after her, Seth next to me. We're closing in on her when a dark figure appears from the bridge's shadow. Looks like the Spudlings showed as promised.

The figure sets something on the ground, and Lee Seol slows to a stop. She goes for the box, and that's when the guy points something at her. The sound of the silenced gun isn't much, but it still pierces me. I skid to a halt, shocked, as I watch her hit the ground. This can't be happening. She'll get up and fight back. She has to.

She's not.

Miles is going to kill me.

"Fi." Seth puts his hand on my shoulder, and my eyes go to him. "Take your dress off."

"Right." I get to it, though my body floods with terror because Seth is running towards the guy instead of away. What does he think he'll be able to do? The guy has a gun, and we don't even know what ability we might be up against. But we can't leave Lee Seol there, and whoever that is can't get our equipment.

Seth throws a surprisingly decent punch, but the guy dodges just in time. Though I'm closer, I still can't make out much of our enemy besides his clearly male lines. Seth tries to grab him, but the man turns out of it and slaps the back of Seth's head. Not a hit, but a slap.

"That the best you can do?" the man says, his voice muffled from his black mask.

"Shut the hell up!" Seth punches. The man bats his hand away. He kicks. The man grabs his leg and makes him trip. Seth charges. The man flips back, landing perfectly, like a cat.

Why he hasn't used the gun yet is beyond me.

I can't help feeling like this guy is playing with Seth, which doesn't make sense after he shot Lee Seol right off. I creep closer, trying to decide the best way to get a jump on him. His reflexes have to be enhanced, because he seems to anticipate Seth's moves. Not that Seth is some amazing fighter, but still.

The man doesn't seem to notice as I approach him from behind. He's bulkier than Seth by quite a bit, and he carries a confidence that screams super ability. I slip the needle box out of my mouth. I don't want to use a killing needle, but it might be time to do it.

"Tsk." The man stands in front of Seth, who is panting from the effort. "I can't believe The Phantom's having trouble with such a pathetic group."

"It's not all about physical strength, is it?" Seth says.

"But you're not—"

That's when it starts to rain. Hard. The water shows my outline, and the man immediately notices. He wastes no time charging me. My heart races, but I prepare to stab him with my needle. Before he gets to me, Seth closes in and tackles him. He shoves his foot into Seth's stomach, and Seth falls to the ground with a loud thud. Then the man gets up and comes for me.

I try to stab him, but he avoids me thanks to the rain.

"Shoulda known…you'd…bring…" He grabs my wrist and squeezes so hard I lose the needle, but I won't go down without a fight. I grab his mask with my other hand. May as well get an I.D. if we can't beat him.

But when I see his surprised face, mine fills with horror. I know him.

It's always one thing to suspect someone of doing wrong, but another thing entirely to see the living proof.

"Dad?" Seth coughs.

"Are you really surprised?" Mr. Mitchell looks at his son. I take several steps back, not a single clue what to do now.

Chapter 34

"Why?" is all Seth can say as he stares at his father. Better than I can do, because I still can't find a single word. My brain is stuck in "holy crap his dad really does work for Juan" mode. Also, he just shot Lee Seol.

"*Why?* Because you idiots destroyed my bugs and I needed more. Easiest way to get it is to steal it." His dad picks up the box and looks behind him, spotting me easily in the rain. "Don't you dare think about attacking me again. I *will* hurt you next time."

Seth is on his feet now. "Don't talk to her like that."

His dad glares at him. "The same goes for you, too, son. My perfect balance makes me a better fighter than you could ever hope to be."

"You just keep finding ways to suck at being a father, don't you?"

He lets out a long sigh. "Do me a favor? Stay the hell out of this from now on. You're getting in my way."

Seth balls his fists. "Good. I want to be in your way."

"No, you don't." He hefts the box onto his shoulder. "I'm gonna pretend I didn't see you this time. Use it wisely."

Seth just flips him off and heads for Lee Seol, who is sprawled out on the ground. His dad walks away, and I wait until he's a long way off before I move. Taking my place next to Seth, I carefully pull back Lee Seol's shirt to see how bad the wound is. There's blood everywhere, but he got her in the stomach. "This is really bad, but she's not dead."

Seth nods, angry tears streaming down his face. "How did he know we'd be out here?"

"No cl…" Then something comes to mind. "Lee Seol mentioned another hacker named Crisis—maybe your dad knows him and paid for a tip?"

"Maybe." He wipes at his eyes, already stuffing whatever he's feeling back inside. "I'll get your dress."

"Okay." I watch as he walks off, but my attention is quickly back to Lee Seol. I put my ear to her heart. There's a beat, but it's slow. I pull off her mask and wad it up to try and stop the blood. She needs help, but I don't know what to do because she'd kill me if I brought her to a hospital. The other option isn't much better…if I bring her home like this Miles will explode.

Seth tosses me my dress when he gets back, and then he sits on the other side of Lee Seol. "We should take her to Rosa. Lee Seol will have to reveal her identity, but there's nothing else we can do."

I slip my dress back on as I say, "You're right. She'll be pissed—that's better than dead, though."

He looks at me, his eyes sad. "We've been keeping so much from The Pack, Fi. I can't deal with that anymore—they're the only family I have. I already keep too much from them as it is."

Those words hit me hard. After tonight, can I blame him

for thinking any differently? "You could tell them about your ability, you know."

"Not yet." His eyes are on the horizon, and I'm not sure he even considered what I said. "I need you to do something for me right now, though I know you won't like it."

"What?"

"Go see if he killed the Spudlings?" He gulps and then buries his head in his knees. "I don't think I can see it for myself, but we need to know what we're up against."

I suck in a breath. He's the only person I'd do this for. "Okay. You call Brady—we don't have time to carry her out of here. Tell them to bring Sexy Blue."

"Okay."

As I force myself to walk towards the bridge, I can't help feeling like this was The Phantom's revenge. It sends a pretty clear message—he knows what we're doing. He might even know Spud is here. Or at least helping us out. Who knows? One thing's for sure: this is just the beginning.

I don't have to go too far under the bridge to see what happened here. There's blood everywhere—bullet holes in precise, fatal places. These aren't the shots of a novice. The wounds scream hit man.

No wonder Seth's dad is always high or drunk or both.

I look away, my heart racing at the thought of Mr. Mitchell doing this. I've been in that house, so close to him, more times than I can count since I've been here. He could have done this to me months ago…which means there's probably a good reason he didn't. He also could have killed Lee Seol—his aim seems perfect—and yet he didn't. I wish I knew what to think of that.

When I get back to Seth and Lee Seol, I think he already knows, but still he asks, "So?"

"Five guys. All shot dead."

He purses his lips. "I guess our dads have more in common than I thought."

"Seth." I take his hands. "How can I make it better? Please. I hate thinking about you in pain."

He squeezes my fingers, and his head finds my shoulder. "I seriously don't know."

I put my arms around him, because I can't think of words that would help. We lost the equipment. Lee Seol is badly hurt. Seth's dad is a freaking hit man. Hours ago I thought we were making progress—now it seems like we're screwed. So we hold each other, and for a second I remember that Seth is the one person in my life who can make me feel like it will be okay even when it's not.

Headlights appear in the distance. "They're here," I say.

He pulls me closer. "Don't let go. Not yet."

I want to say I'll never let go of him, but I don't.

Bea and I cradle Lee Seol in the back seat, while Brady drives over the rough terrain. No one has said anything yet, but I can tell by Bea's face that it won't last long. I get the sense that she's known all along that I've not been telling her stuff—she's just been the bigger person and not gotten pissed about it.

"Fiona…" Bea looks down at Lee Seol, whose head is in her lap. "Who is this? I feel like I have a right to know, if she might find out what my mom can do."

"You're right. She didn't want me to tell you, and she's not exactly someone you argue with, you know? But now I don't have a choice and I hope she doesn't get mad at me because—"

"Fi," Bea cuts me off. "You're rambling. Just tell me."

I gulp. "She's Miles' girlfriend. You remember who his girlfriend is, right?"

Bea's eyes go wide, but it's Brady who says, "Holy shit. Are you serious?"

"Yeah. Dead serious." I lean my head back on Sexy Blue's grimy old seat, exhausted from the things we haven't told them yet. "I can't say more here. I don't know who could be listening to us after what just happened."

"I wish we were all telepathic," Seth grumbles.

"No kidding." I'm so tired of my life. But once I'm not invisible anymore, I won't have to deal with this at all. I have to keep my eye on that invaluable prize.

Lee Seol moans when we hit another bump. She's been going in and out of consciousness, but this time she opens her eyes. "Miles? Where's Miles?"

I put my hand on her face. "He's okay—you're the one who got shot."

"Oh yeah…" She clutches her stomach. "Feeling it now."

When we get to the Navarros' house, everyone is awake and waiting for us. We lower Lee Seol onto the couch. She winces at every move, and I can tell she feels uncomfortable with so many eyes on her. Bea's dad doesn't look particularly happy about this, and I'm proved right when he says, "I'm still not convinced we should do this. We know nothing about her."

"Do what?" Lee Seol says weakly.

All the Navarros hesitate to answer.

236

"I know it's a lot to ask," I say. "It's just...this girl means everything in the world to Miles. I can't bring her home like this." At my words, Hector and Carlos exchange glances. Clearly that's all they need to get who Lee Seol is.

"Miles will worry when I'm not home. I can't stay here forever," Lee Seol says, since she clearly has no idea just what Bea's mom could do for her.

"Just tell us who you are," Bea's dad insists. "Miles' girl or not, why can't you go to hospital for this?"

Lee Seol looks to me with wide, panicked eyes. I gulp and say, "Can't you just tell them? I promise it'd be worth it, and they are the most trustworthy people I've ever met."

"They better be." Lee Seol sighs in defeat. "You might know me by the name of Spud."

"What?" Bea's dad turns to his wife. "She could tell the whole world about you!"

"Alejandro, calm down. If she's with Miles I don't think she's like that." Rosa kneels down by the couch. "I have always wished I could share my gift with the world. God blessed me with this miracle—I'm happy to use it when I can."

Bea's dad sighs. "I wish the world wouldn't punish you for having such a gift."

"I know. Perhaps someday." Rosa looks over the wound before she asks, "Is the bullet still in there?"

"Think so," Seth answers. "We need to get it out, right?"

Rosa nods. "It will be difficult and painful, but I'll get the tools."

"Tools?" Lee Seol says in a high-pitched voice. "What's going on?"

I want to explain to her, but it's not my place. All I can do is hold her hand and say, "It'll be okay, I promise."

Rosa comes back with a long pair of tweezers, but she doesn't look excited for what she's about to do. "This is the hard part."

"I'll do it." Seth grabs the tweezers, and before anyone else can object he's already at Lee Seol's side. She looks terrified as he pulls the black mask from her wound. Too bad I can't tell her that he's the best possible person to find that bullet inside her. It's clear from the way he approaches the wound that he's confident in his ability to retrieve the metal.

Lee Seol screams as Seth pushes the tweezers into the torn hole in her skin. I try to hold both her hands, but it's more like she's crushing mine. Seth cringes, and I can't imagine what he's seeing. "I know it's hard, but can you try to relax? The muscles contracting are making it worse."

"Oh sure, easy!" she yells at him.

"Almost…" Seth pinches the tweezers. "I think I got it."

Sure enough, he pulls out a round object covered in blood. Lee Seol whimpers at the sight of it. Hector lets out a low whistle, eyeing his best friend. "You sure did that easily. Like a freaking surgeon."

"I got lucky." Seth gulps, and I wonder if his best friend is starting to put things together.

"Alright, dear, it's almost over." Rosa cuts her finger, and a few drops of blood splatter onto Lee Seol's stomach. As I watch her heal before my eyes, I can't help but think of Rosa saying her ability is a gift from God. To me it seems so strange to attribute my ability to a higher being, but I suppose I can see why Rosa is so religious.

"Holy. Shitballs." Lee Seol stares at her now perfect stomach, and I think I see understanding cross her face. "Did that really just happen?"

I nod. "You'll keep it secret, right?"

"Of course," she says breathlessly. "Hell, is everyone in Madison keeping secrets like this?"

I look right at Seth—he won't look back. Sighing, I say, "Who knows? But we better get going."

"I'll take you guys home," Seth says. "And, um, Rosa? Can me and Brady stay here for a while? My dad…he's…"

I can feel him struggling for words. Of course he wouldn't want to stay in his house when a paid killer lives with him. He must want to tell them what we saw tonight, but how can he?

"He's been wasted for days," Brady picks up. He seems to get that there's more to it, but for right now this is all the excuse he can give. "We're both getting tired of dealing with it."

Alejandro curses in Spanish. "John has been useless at work lately, too. Most of the time he can at least pretend to look normal, but these last few days…"

"Of course you can stay. But let me make one thing clear." Rosa stands, pointing at Brady. "You are not to go near Bea's room. Don't think we haven't figured out you two have a thing."

"Mom!" Bea's face fills with horror.

Brady goes stop-sign red. "I would never."

"I'll hold you to that," Bea's dad says sternly. "You better get home, Fiona. I'm sure your mother is worrying."

"Yeah." I help Lee Seol off the couch. He has no idea just how worried she probably is, knowing this mission was going down tonight. And we're definitely late on return. "Thanks for your help."

"Of course," Rosa says as we leave.

The night is quiet and dark, but the light is on at Seth's house. He glares at it, and I'm sure he's looking through walls to see where his father is. Lee Seol pulls away from me, seeming to have gotten her strength back. "So when are you gonna tell me what really happened post-shooting?"

"At home," I say. "It's...complicated."

After Seth and I tell them what happened, Mom, Miles, and Lee Seol sit there in a daze. Clearly no one saw this coming. Then Lee Seol says, "He can't be with Juan—he sounds like a free agent to me. A contract worker."

"Why's that?" Seth asks. "We've seen him around Juan's guys twice now."

Mom sighs. "He's probably working with them currently, but he'd have tattoos if he were initiated into the syndicate."

"It's not that uncommon," Miles points out. "You want something done quietly—you hire it out. Would explain him knowing Crisis, too. There's no other way he could have found the drop-off info."

Lee Seol taps on her super phone. "John Mitchell wasn't flagged in my database as a person of interest, but he is now. He must be damn good at his job. Even I didn't see any red flags."

Seth lets out a wry laugh. "Great. My dad's a top notch hit man. That makes it a little better."

I frown. "I don't think that's what she meant."

He shakes his head. "Whatever. I better go."

"Are you sure that's a good idea?" Mom asks. "He knows

240

you know. Even staying at the Navarros', I don't like the idea of you being so close to him. Maybe you should stay here."

He raises an eyebrow. "You're okay with that?"

"Do I have a reason not to be?" She eyes him suspiciously.

"Nope!" I stand quickly and grab him by the hand, pulling him up the stairs. This is exactly what we need right now. Me and Seth. Alone. "We'll be good, I promise!"

"He better sleep on the floor!" Mom calls after me. "I will be checking!"

"Okay!"

The second I shut my door, I'm kissing him. He doesn't resist, but he does say, "I thought you said it was weird to do this with me."

"Only sometimes," I say between kisses. "Do you want me to stop?"

"No." He relaxes a little, but not much. "But aren't you mad at me?"

"Nope." I wrap my arms around him. This will make it better. At least for a tiny moment. "You're mad at me, and I'm okay with that because I won't change my mind. I just hope you get over it soon."

"I hope so, too." He kisses my neck, and soon his tenseness is gone. I push him towards my bed. Maybe we won't go all the way, but after the shit that happened earlier this feels good. For one second it feels like we're back to how things were before The Phantom showed up that day at soccer practice.

I hear my mom's footsteps on the stairs, and I push him back. "She's coming."

"Damn." Seth grabs the extra pillow and the blanket at the

foot of the bed. He hits the floor just as she opens the door, and I hold my breath.

Mom lets out a small laugh. "Better stay there."

When the door closes, I wonder if Seth will listen or not. I even consider asking him to come back. But then the insecurity creeps in. Maybe after I'm visible. I smile just thinking about it.

Definitely after I'm visible.

Chapter 35

"Still shacking up with the Army, huh?" The Phantom yells on Monday as we walk into the school. "Saturday night wasn't enough for you?"

I don't look back.

On Tuesday, Mom has to fight her way out of work because Juan's men try to kidnap her. Graham sets up guards at our house and personally watches the area from the air.

Wednesday, it seems like everyone in town is leaving before things get worse. My neighbors pack up their stuff. Half the students at school are absent—same with the teachers. Gunshots are heard outside far too often. There's no doubt The Phantom is prepping for something huge.

On Thursday, I consider not going to school at all. Seth watches me while I decide on glasses, the tension between us a little less thanks to that make-out session. Too bad Mom wouldn't let him stay more than one night. Maybe our whole relationship would be fixed by now. I can tell he's watching me in the mirror, and I can't help but ask, "What?"

He shrugs. "I just hate that you have to wear glasses all the time. You look better without them."

I smile a little. "Well, if this cure works, I won't have to wear them ever again."

"You're really obsessed with that, aren't you?"

"Yes." And I'm not apologizing for it, either. The more I think about all the ways it will improve my life, the more I'm willing to do just about anything for it.

He lets out a long sigh, and the expression on his face screams impending apology. I hold my breath, hoping that he'll finally say he's okay with this. Because I need his support more than I can tell him. "I guess I just—"

My door flies open, and Lee Seol enters in a fit of excitement. "I'm IN, Fiona! I AM IN!"

It takes me a second, but then I gasp. "Wait, like, you cracked the network?"

"Duh!" She points her finger at her super phone. "Take that, idiot programmer. I told you I'd beat your ass and now your secrets are MINE. Damn, I can't wait to mess the shit out of his system."

She laughs maniacally. Seth and I exchange a worried glance.

Miles appears in the hallway, looking one part proud and one part exhausted. "Are you done gloating yet?"

"Nope." She types furiously into her phone. "Why hello, list of assholes on this job, don't mind if I download you. Oh, and what's this? SuperMart! These bastards are trying to hide their network by making it look like the company's. They must have found someone decently good to think of that."

"Is that for sure?" Seth says excitedly. "Could I tell the Major that?"

"Hell yes. Tell this shit to whoever you need to."

"You swear a lot more when you win," I say.

She smiles wide. "You shoulda heard me when I stole that Radiasure info from your dad."

Miles groans. "That was ridiculous. So what if it took you twice as long as expected? You still prance around victorious."

"Because *I won*." Lee Seol has her super phone right up against her nose, her eyes moving rapidly as she takes in the information. Then her eyebrows pop up, and she freezes in place. "No. Way."

"What?" we all say at the same time.

"Crisis is working for Juan! I'd know his handle anywhere." She goes off in what I can only assume is Korean. It doesn't sound like she's saying nice things. "No wonder I couldn't get in as fast. And that explains why they so easily jacked up my drop-off. Juan must be paying him a shit ton of money."

This is the second time she's mentioned this Crisis dude. I put my hands on my hips, thinking. "Is he really that good? I've never heard of him."

"Not as good as me, but he's getting a name for himself. You know, now that he's given up on principles and started taking money from whoever is offering. That's when things got interesting for me, too."

"So he's being paid by Juan to keep you out?" Seth asks.

She smirks. "Maybe. Don't know the particulars. I just know he's the one with the network's puppet strings. Well, he *was*—now they're mine."

"This is perfect." I slip on a pair of black frames, taking care to put the little microphone in place. "Maybe the Army will be able to fight off Juan's men now that they know where they're coming from."

"Right now all I have is the location, but that doesn't mean it'll be easy to storm SuperMart and take them out, you know?" Lee Seol heads for the hall, not looking up from her machine. "My bet is there's major security in place, complete with secret bunkers. You're gonna be late if you don't go now."

"Oh! Right." Once I grab my things, Seth and I hurry to the truck, where Brady has been waiting for us.

"Took long enough." He puts the car in drive and hits the gas.

"We got a break on info from you-know-who," Seth says. "Should be enough for the Army to fight back Juan's forces."

Brady raises an eyebrow. "Yeah?"

He nods. "Who knows? Maybe the Major will even let us see the factory. I really think we need to push for all of us to see it, Pack included."

"That'll be hard to convince them of," I point out.

Seth doesn't seem pleased with my statement. "So? You got what you wanted out of all this—my requests are nothing in comparison. I just want to know if my family has anything to do with the factory."

I sigh. "You're really still upset I didn't fight for that? You know why I was trying to finish up quickly."

He purses his lips, knowing I have the microphone so we can't talk about his vision. "Whatever. You still made time to get everything *you* wanted out of the deal."

"Excuse me?"

"Guys, stop." Brady grips the steering wheel, seeming uncomfortable with us fighting. I feel bad, thinking about how Seth said Brady sees me as a sister. Is he worried we'll break up? It sure would make friendship with The Pack pretty difficult if we did.

As we approach the school, it's clear this day won't go well. Instead of a small group accompanying The Phantom, there's a whole fleet of Juan's guys lined up at the fence. The Army has an equally large group of soldiers defending the opposite side.

When we pull into the parking lot, my heart races as Juan's men stare. Maybe they're really here to mess with the Army, but I can't help feeling this is personal.

The moment we get out, a soldier I recognize as my jailer, Tagawa, is by our sides. "Miss McClean, the Major requests your presence in the office. Immediately."

I look at Seth and Brady, beyond worried now. "They're coming with me."

Tagawa nods. "Of course. Your friends the Navarros are already there waiting for you."

"Okay…" I head for the school, wondering what exactly Major Norton wants from us. Seeing as The Phantom has a horde of people out there today, maybe the Major is concerned about our safety. I definitely am.

Going back into the office makes my skin crawl, especially as I pass the makeshift cell they held me in. But I push back the feelings and head for the principal's office. Major Norton sits at the desk. Bea, Hector, and Carlos sit in the chairs facing him. Allie and Graham are there as well, and when I see my brother a wave of relief washes over me.

"I take it something bad is about to happen," I say as I sit.

Major Norton nods. "Nice to see you again, too, Miss McClean. It seems Juan's men have gotten wind of what's

247

going on in regards to Allie's research. You wouldn't know anything about that, would you?"

My jaw drops. Is he implying what I think he's implying?

"Are you seriously blaming us for that?" Seth says while I try to find words.

"Of course we don't know," I say as he finishes. "They've been threatening us every day just because we walk into the school, and you think I'd help them?"

The Major watches my every move, I assume to see if he can sense any lie in my words. "It's not impossible—maybe someone is leaking information to keep them from going after you."

Bea glares at him. "We'd rather die than help Juan do anything."

"Damn straight," Carlos spits. "That's downright insulting."

Hector tips his chin up. "Ever thought that you might be the one with the leak, Major? You have a lot more men than we do."

Major Norton stands, his face turning red. "I've interviewed every one of my men personally. There's no way a spy could get past me."

I glance at Seth, wondering just how true that is. He got around Major Norton's questions—who's to say someone skilled enough could avoid suspicion entirely? But I'm not interested in pointing fingers right now, especially when it seems futile to root out traitors when everyone has ulterior motives. "You know we're not lying, so can we just get to the part where I tell you I know where The Phantom is operating from?"

The room goes still, all eyes on me.

"How'd you find out?" the Major says.

"I have connections." Folding my arms, I try to savor his

surprise. Must thank Lee Seol for this moment. "He has some sort of base at the SuperMart. I don't know the extent of the facility, but I've confirmed it's there."

Allie smiles wide, standing up, as if she can't contain her excitement. "That's great!"

Major Norton, though much more reserved, seems to share Allie's sentiment. "I called you here to inform you that we have to move Allie's research to the factory, due to the clear threat from Juan at the school. But this information will be vital in helping form an offense against Juan's syndicate."

"And good news!" Allie hops over to me. "The first round of testing is ready—today could be the day, Fiona!"

My heart stops. "Really?"

She nods.

"What's going on?" Bea asks. "Testing for what?"

Allie looks to the Major, who rolls his eyes. "Go ahead. They'll all need to be under our protection from now on, anyway."

"Testing for a cure to mutations. Today you could see Fiona with your own eyes, if things work out," Allie says, beaming. Bea, Hector, and Carlos look dumbfounded. "Are you ready, Fiona?"

Am I? When I see how scared Seth is, part of me wants to say I'm terrified by the possibility. But then I think about how great it would be to see my own reflection in a mirror, and I smile. There's only one answer: "Yes."

Allie smiles back. "Then let's go."

Chapter 36

The beating of helicopter propellers fills the air as we head for the back field, and my hair whips around in every direction. The helicopter isn't the small kind, but one of those big ones that have propellers in every possible place. My ears hurt as we get closer, and I glance at Hector. He crams his hands against his ears, clearly in pain.

When I climb into the nearest open door, Graham's right there strapping me in. Usually I'd protest, but I've never been in one of these and he makes me feel safe. He hands me a set of headphones and moves on to the others.

My fingers dig into my knees as the helicopter lifts into the sky. I close my eyes, figuring I already know where the factory is so why freak myself out more? What really matters is seeing what they've done to the place in the weeks since they've been here. My bet is we won't even recognize it.

The descent is awful but quick. By the time I open my eyes the helicopter hits the ground with a jolt.

An extremely tall—abnormally tall—woman in uniform heads straight for The Major and Allie, who listen intently while the woman speaks in hushed tones. Allie comes towards us. "Let's get you comfortable while the Major deals with the escalation of violence in town."

The word "violence" hits me, and I begin to panic. Sure wish the mic on my glasses worked both ways. "Will you get my family out? What about the Navarros? They'll probably both be main targets for The Phantom if we're gone."

Major Norton stops his conversation with the crazy tall woman. "Don't worry, Fiona, that's what I'm about to do. Graham, if you could come with me—we'll probably need your help."

"Yes, sir." Graham puts his hands on my shoulders. "Allie will take care of you, okay, sis? There's nothing to be afraid of now."

I nod, though I still feel uneasy.

"This way," Allie says. We walk past dozens of tents, which I assume hold at least a handful of men apiece. Clearly they've continued to bring in more forces as things have gotten worse. I had no idea there were this many under Major Norton's command, and it makes me feel small and silly with my little band of friends.

Once we get past the tents, there's a big clearing. In the center is a metal structure that is squat and round, like an armored turtle buried in the sand. Armed guards surround it, and as far as I can see there's only one small door on it, directly in front of us.

This must be the entrance to the excavated factory.

I hold my breath as Allie shows the guards her badge. They part, but she still has to put her palm to a scanner. Then she sticks her face up against a machine to scan her retina. Finally, a mechanical voice says, "Name, please."

"Allison Porter." The door opens after a *whiff* and a *clank*. "Welcome to the Radison Manufacturing Company, everyone, birthplace of Radiasure."

The stairs seem to go on forever. Sickly yellow lights guide our way—they're just enough to make sure we don't kill ourselves falling down the endless steps. The air smells like the desert after a storm, when the ground is fleetingly damp before the sun comes out again.

"You know what would be nice right now?" Carlos' voice sounds too loud in the cavernous dark space. "An elevator."

Allie smirks. "There will probably be one in the future, but it wasn't exactly the first priority when there was so much more to restore down here."

"Just how big is this place?" Brady asks. There's an enthusiasm in his words I didn't expect. Then I realize he might be as excited by the idea of a cure as I am—he'd never have to worry about hurting someone by accident again.

"I'm not sure," Allie says. "They're still digging. The Major seems to have a good idea of what this place is like, though— maybe he'll explain it to you now that you're here. I'm sure curious about it."

"He hasn't told you?" I have to admit I'm surprised.

She seems annoyed, but pushes it aside. "I'm not privy to all top secret information. Just the things that involve my experiments."

"Huh," is all Seth says. I glance at him, sure he's thinking a lot more than that. He hasn't said anything since we left the office, and I can't tell whether he's happy to be here or not.

Finally the lights below are close enough that I realize we're looking at the floor of a giant hallway. The tiles are midnight blue, as are the walls. Thick cables run along the baseboards, a smaller chord diverging from the bulk to a light every twenty yards or so.

"We've just barely gotten this place in workable order," Allie explains. "The rooms were mostly intact, but all the wiring and plumbing has been damaged by age or the blast that destroyed the above-ground portion of the factory. That's why we couldn't initially set up my lab here."

We make a left when the hallway forks, and after another right turn the place is suddenly alive with workers. Some are cleaning, while others seem to be rigging more wires and pipes. The distinct sound of machinery can be heard, so I figure if we keep going we'll find the place where they're still excavating.

But what's most interesting is that there are doors along the hallway. They are numbered crudely with spray paint. Offices? Testing rooms? Workers' quarters? I don't know what they used to be, but for some reason they make this place more real. People used to work here, making this drug that changed the world. Did they know what they were doing? Were they proud or ashamed? Or maybe it was just a job like any other.

Seth grabs my arm out of nowhere, stopping me as our group goes forward. His lips brush against my ear as he says, "Fiona, there are people in those rooms."

I force myself to remain calm despite Seth's clear worries. This is where I'll be when I take the first dose of Allie's cure. "That makes sense."

"That's all you have to say?"

"What do you want me to say? That I'm backing out?" I

pull away from him. "If you're still so upset about it, why are you even here?"

He purses his lips, glaring at me so hard I have to look away. "Because I don't have a choice. What, did you think I'm here as a show of support?"

"No." *But I hoped.* I walk quickly to catch up with the group.

Allie opens a door with the number twelve painted on it. "This will be your room during testing, Fiona. Since the equipment is still being unloaded, you'll have to wait here until then."

"Okay." I walk forward as confidently as I can, but then stop at the door. "Um, Allie?"

"Yes?"

"Would it be okay if I could wait until my mom and Miles get here? I don't want them to miss it. You know, if it happens."

Allie purses her lips, seeming reluctant. "We really need to start all the testing at the same time, but hopefully we'll have word from them before that. Don't worry too much—I've projected that at this stage of development, the cure, if it works, should last several days."

"Oh." My heart soars at the thought. I didn't dare hope it would last that long. "Okay then."

I head into the room, which is sparse to say the least. There is only a bed and a chair, plus a small nightstand stacked with medical stuff. The wall to the right is a mirror, ceiling to floor. I worry it's one of those observation windows where you can see through on the other side, but I'm still glad for it. I want to see everything I can if this works.

As I sit on the bed, Seth, Brady, and The Pack come in. Their expressions vary from Hector's mildly concerned to Seth's angry to Carlos' scared.

Seth takes the one chair, and they all sit on the floor like this is some weird story time. I figure I do owe them an explanation, but so much has happened that I'm not even sure where to begin.

"So, first question." To my surprise, it's Brady who starts. He knows the most of everyone, and yet he looks seriously upset. "Why didn't you tell me we could volunteer to take the drug?"

Seth explodes from his chair. "You are *not* taking it! Do you hear me? This is an illegal experiment on *human specimens*. Am I the only one who sees how insane that is?"

"Jeez, so I need your parental consent now?" Brady glares at his brother, then turns to me. "Is this why you guys have been fighting more than usual?"

I look at my bracelets. "Yes."

"What if you die?" Bea's voice is shaky. "Look at this place, Fiona. This isn't a hospital—it's barely a bunker."

"Hospitals haven't given me much when it comes to answers about myself. I could find them here." I sigh, feeling like I'm about to get ganged up on. It was bad enough when it was just Seth who knew I'd be part of the experiments.

"Or you could get seriously messed up," Hector says.

"You're letting them turn you into a lab rat," Carlos says.

"If you haven't noticed, *everyone's* messed up." I fold my arms, wishing I could kick them out. I don't need this lecture again. "I'm not ignoring the risks. I know I could die; I know it could do permanent damage; I know it might not work at all. But what you guys don't understand is that it's worth it

255

to me. What I could get in return—being visible—it means everything to me. If that makes me a lab rat, then so be it."

This clearly doesn't register for anyone but Brady, who is nodding while everyone else shakes their head. "I get it, Fi. I'd volunteer right now."

Seth points his finger at his brother. "Don't you dare. If you care about me at all, Brady, you won't make me deal with that on top of possibly losing the only girl I've ever cared about."

I shrink at the words. The guilt is heavy—it gets heavier every day—but as much as I care about Seth, I can't sacrifice this chance for him.

Brady shakes his head. "You guys don't understand how life-changing this could be for me or Fiona, do you?"

"Please don't," Bea says quietly as she leans on Brady's arm. "Just…please. I'd rather deal with your ability our whole lives than lose you."

This seems to suck the words right out of Brady, but Seth fills the silence. "Ditto. You guys forget we like you just the way you are. We can deal with the hard parts just fine."

I glare at Seth, wanting so badly to say he doesn't have to deal with my invisibility at all—I'm the one who still can't see herself, who has to deal with it every time I look in a mirror. It's so unfair for him to even use that argument. "Well, I'm tired. If you don't mind I'd like to sleep before I become a lab rat. And when this works I'll use it to stop The Phantom and anyone else who threatens you. Then you can thank me for taking the hit."

I grab the blankets and cover myself in them. They're stiff and smell like bleach. I wait for someone to say something back, but instead I hear the door open and footsteps as they leave. When it slams behind them, I pull the blankets down, expecting to be alone.

But Seth is still there.

"They just care about you," he says.

"I know." I wish I could make it better. I know I'm being selfish. But I can't stop myself. "Thanks for staying."

"This could be the last time I see you alive. I have to stay." His eyes water, but he stops it before he cries. "You better live. Or I'll never forgive you."

"I will." I say it for him, though we both know very well that once I take this drug, I won't have any say in the outcome.

Chapter 37

A couple hours pass before anyone comes. There's no word on my family—my phone seems to be useless down here as well, which makes me worry the mic on my glasses doesn't work either. I'm not sure where The Pack has gone, but I'm almost relieved they're not here to see what might happen to me. If it does work, I want to be the first one to see myself. If it doesn't…well, it'll only hurt them more.

Allie comes in with a nurse at her side, her smile tentative as she hands me a clipboard. "Fiona, I'm sorry we haven't heard from your family yet, but we've waited as long as we can under the circumstances. We need to move forward with the testing. If you could fill out the information you know, that'd be great. After that your nurse will take what vitals she can from you."

"Okay." I look over the first page of the form, though I feel sick knowing my mom and Miles aren't here for this. They were so excited when they heard about it over the mic. I could use their support about now.

As I start filling out my medical information, the door opens again. I hope it's The Pack at least, but it's Major Norton.

"Allie, you and the nurse can prep the other patients while I talk with them."

Allie looks like she wants to protest, but she does as she's told. Major Norton waits a few moments before he speaks again. "I wanted to thank you for your information on The Phantom—I'm sure you went to a lot of risk to get it. Honestly, I owe you for that, so I'll tell you about the factory."

Seth perks up a little. "Really?"

The Major nods. "It's quite simple, really, but I would like to keep my connections to this factory top secret, do you understand? I don't want my superiors to pull me off this due to conflict of interest."

Seth raises an eyebrow. "Sure. I just want to know if my family had anything to do with this place."

"Your great grandfather did." The Major puts his hand into his crisp jacket and pulls out a picture. Seth and I crowd around the photo—it's an old black and white image of five men standing in front of a building I assume is the old Radiasure factory. Even I can see the family resemblance between Seth and the guy on the far right. "Greg Mitchell was the head contractor."

Seth sits back, and I think I see horror in his eyes. "So part of this is my family's fault?"

"I don't know what to tell you." Major Norton points to the guy in the middle wearing a white coat much like Allie's. "*My* grandfather, Patrick Norton, was one of the scientists who created Radiasure, so I'm not one to say you shouldn't feel guilty. It's the whole reason I'm here."

It takes me a minute to realize my jaw's dropped. When I put myself together, I manage to say, "When did you find out?

I thought all that was buried by the government. You know, to protect them from being hunted down."

"I found out about five years ago, when I was promoted to Major. I'd always believed that destroying the remaining Radiasure stores would help bring the world back into order, so I went digging for information. It was difficult, but I figured it out thanks to my ability and asking the right people the right questions." He sighs, and there's a weight to it I never noticed before. "Eventually, I was able to track down the creators, but I never expected to be related to one of them. I always knew my grandfather lived in a remote part of China, though I would have never guessed *why*."

I put my hand to my mouth. China? My dad's plans to get the real formula. The guy they murdered. "They finally found him."

Major Norton nods. "Before I could get there."

"He still had the papers?" Seth seems angry. "Why didn't he destroy them?"

"I don't have details; I just know he's dead and the formula is out there. They could have had a mind-reader or a brainwasher on the job for all I know." The Major pauses, as if he needs a second to compose himself. I can't stop thinking about the brainwasher Dad had me and mom kidnap from Val Sutton— was that why? She would have been able to persuade him to tell. "The point is, I had to act fast if I wanted to stop the syndicates from making the drug again."

"So you're here to make up for what your family did?" I ask.

"I don't think anyone can make up for what Radiasure has done to the world," the Major replies. "But I still want to right as many wrongs as I can. That's why I found Allie and the factory plans from Mitchell Construction and an endless list of rumored Radiasure caches. I think once we have a cure—once people see that there's a way to make the world different—things will change."

Seth and I remain silent. I can't tell how my boyfriend feels about the information, but I have to admit it totally alters my opinion of Major Norton. While I'm not happy with how he's treated me in the past, it makes more sense now. My dad killed his grandfather. Of course I'd be a huge suspect.

"One question," Seth says. "How'd you get the factory plans?"

This seems to surprise the Major. "I bought them from your father a few years ago. The military could have copies somewhere, but I don't have the clear—"

"So he knows about this place, the layout, everything. He's always known," Seth says flatly. "Well, shit."

"Shit?"

I wince, realizing just how bad this could be for us. "Seth's dad has been working for Juan, as far as we can tell."

Major Norton lets out a string of cuss words as he heads for the door. "I'm sorry I have to leave like this, but this is a serious security issue. Can't trust anyone these days to…"

His voice trails off as he leaves, and then the door slams shut. It's so quiet I wonder if these rooms are soundproof—I can't hear any workers, now that I think about it.

"I guess he's not so bad after all," I say.

Seth rolls his eyes. "I bet his grandfather had good intentions when he created Radiasure, too. Sounds like the apple doesn't fall far from the tree."

Then what does that say about you? I want to say that so

bad, but I bite my tongue and continue filling out my forms. I'm tired of fighting with him. Especially now that it's pretty much the same argument over and over. All I want is for him to hold me and tell me he still cares in spite of everything.

Allie comes in with the nurse again, who takes my blood pressure and temperature and weight. After that it gets more difficult because they want a blood sample. The nurse runs her fingers over my arm, her lips pursed. She looks to Allie. "I don't think I can do this. Even if I find the vein, I won't know when the vial is filled."

Allie frowns. "What if we do a finger prick?"

"How will we know how much we have without contaminating the sample?"

"Fine, I guess we'll have to be satisfied with this." Allie looks to me, feigning a smile. "Maybe after today you won't have this problem again."

"Weird." I can't keep the grin from spreading across my face.

"Have you finished the forms?"

"Yup." I hand them to her.

Allie pulls a small bottle from her pocket, opens it, and taps one glowing red pill into her palm. I stare at it, this whole thing becoming frighteningly real as she holds it out for me. It's so tiny, seemingly harmless, but it makes my heart race. "Alright, this is it. You're the last one to take it—we'll be observing you over the next several days to see if it has any effect. Please be as detailed as possible in telling us how you feel after taking it."

"Okay." I take the pill from her, and the nurse hands me a glass of water.

"Fiona." Seth's voice cracks on my name, and when my eyes

meet his I can tell how scared he is. "Are you sure you have to do this?"

I look at the cure in my hand. Seth can see I'm holding it, but to me all I see is the red, glowing pill hovering in the air.

It's all I can see.

Maybe I'll lose everything because I want to see more than that, but the answer is still the same and it puts me at ease. "I'm sure."

I pop the pill in my mouth, take a swig of water, and swallow.

Chapter 38

Twenty minutes later, and I still don't feel anything. Worse than that, I don't *see* anything. I keep staring at the mirror, hoping that I'll be more than a teal dress and white capri leggings. Maybe I'll fade in like a ghost becoming solid. Or will it happen all at once? It would be weird if my insides showed up before my skin...

Oh hell, I don't care how it happens so long as it does.

"Doesn't look like it's doing anything," Seth says, and I swear he sounds happy about it.

"Shut up."

He smirks. "If you stare any harder that mirror might break."

I set my glare on him instead. "Don't talk like that—what if they can hear you?"

"There's no one on the other side. No bugs." He shrugs. "Besides, what does it matter anymore? If everyone can see you, I won't have to be worried about pretending I can't. That'd be nice. We could just be *normal* and utterly boring and not special. That's what you want, right?"

His voice has an edge to it that makes it clear he hates everything about this. Something clicks. "Wait. Are you...*mad* that I want other people to see me and not just you?"

No answer. But I don't need one because that says it all.

"Do you know how incredibly possessive that sounds?" I stand up, suddenly too frustrated to be still. "It must be so easy to have an invisible girlfriend. No one will steal me away. No one can tell me I'm pretty but you. I have to rely on you completely to know what I look like!"

He folds his arms. "That is *not* what I meant—I was trying to say I *like* that you're special, and I just wish you could accept it instead of trying to change yourself. You're perfect just how you are."

"I'm not trying to change anything! I'm just trying to *see* myself. This isn't plastic surgery."

"It's much more dangerous." He looks away, and it feels like he's holding back. "When you could just *trust* me. Do you know how insulting it is that you can't take my word for it when it comes to your appearance?"

These words sting more than any before them. This is what has really been bothering him all along. "Do you know how insulting it is that just because I want more you think I don't trust you?" I ask.

"Why am I not enough?"

"What?"

He stands, his chest heaving as he tries to contain his emotions. "Before all this happened, I thought we were…things were good, Fi. It wasn't perfect, but the second you heard about this drug it was like everything I ever told you didn't matter anymore. Now you're acting like I've never tried to understand when that's *all* I've tried to do. Hell, I'm the only person still here!"

My lips quiver as the truth fills me with shame. He's right, but I don't want him to be or to admit he is.

Seth stares at his feet. "I wish you'd stop pushing me away."

"And I wish you'd stop lecturing me! Especially when you're the one who has it easy in this relationship—it *does* look normal to you. You don't have to deal with my invisibility at all! It's all on me, and then you tell me I should get over it." I lie on the bed and cover my head with the pillow, embarrassed.

The bed creaks, and I can tell he's sat next to me. There's a long pause before he replies, "Fiona, are you saying you're *jealous* that I can see you?"

"All the time." Tears spill out against my will. It sounds so ridiculous put in those terms, but it's true. "It's not fair."

He puts his hand on my hip and gently squeezes. "Why haven't you ever told me this?"

"Because it's stupid. I knew you'd say that, too. I'm supposed to be happy about it, feel lucky, and so often I just wish I was you. Sometimes it's downright infuriating that you know what I look like naked and I don't."

He lets out a low chuckle, mocking me just like I thought he would. "You're right. It's not fair. At all."

I freeze, not sure I heard that right. Pulling the pillow from my head, I look at him. His eyes meet mine, and they're softer than I've seen them in weeks. "What?"

"There's nothing fair about it." He lies down next to me, our noses almost touching. "You know what else isn't fair? That Brady has to be afraid of hurting Bea when all he wants is to hold her. It's not fair that Hector's ears hurt constantly, or that Graham never has to go through an airport security line. Also, it's not fair that your mom can unlock any door she wants, or that my dad can apparently fight like Bruce Lee. *Nothing's* fair about life, but would it be any different without mutations?"

I frown. "It'd at least be a little more even."

"Would it?" He pushes my hair behind my ear. "Good people would still be poor. Horrible people would still find power. And it would still be almost impossible to find the right time to tell your crazy girlfriend how much you love her."

My eyes bug out. Suddenly all the weird, awkward moments between us the past several weeks make much more sense. "That is horrible timing. Like, seriously random, Seth."

He smiles. "Hey, I figure I better let you know in case that drug does something terrible to you. So it's out—I love you."

My stomach fills with butterflies. What was a huge fight now makes complete sense. I thought he considered me stupid for what I was doing, when all he was worried about was losing the girl he loves. Me. He loves me. Though I assumed he loved me, I had no idea hearing the words out loud would mean so much. But they change everything, like a lens bringing the world into focus.

"I love you, too."

He kisses me, and everything else is forgotten. I pull him on top of me, my insecurities nowhere in sight. I thought I needed to see myself to feel okay with this, but what I really needed was to know where we stood. Now that I know he's that committed to me, I feel free. My head spins as I get maybe a little too lost in him, considering we're in an underground bunker.

Then what felt like butterflies in my stomach changes to a sharp stabbing sensation. I gasp, and Seth pulls back.

"Did I…?" His face goes pale as he takes me in, and the stabbing spreads so quickly that I can't find the ability to scream.

"S-Seth…w-what's…hurts…"

He's off the bed without a reply. I think I hear the door slam, but the pain has consumed every inch of my body. It feels like I'm burning from the inside out on top of swallowing hundreds of tiny razors.

Looks like the red pill has decided to do something after all.

My body shakes violently, and I pray I don't throw up. I'm really starting to regret my choice when I hear Seth's voice again. "Hurry and help her!"

"I can try." I think it's the nurse speaking, but I can't move my head enough to see. "Except I can't give her an IV, and I'm not sure her stomach will handle pain pills. The other patients are experiencing acute pain as well—none of them have passed through it yet."

"I don't care about the details!" Seth yells. "Just help her!"

The nurse tries to give me pills, but putting them in my mouth triggers my gag reflex and I lose it. Seth grabs the pink bin just in time to catch it. As I heave, I'm vaguely aware of the fact that my puke glistens.

I've never seen that before.

"It'll be okay," Seth says as he helps me lie back.

"Mm." My vision is blurry and dim. It might be playing tricks with me, but I swear that the last thing I see before I pass out is spindly red veins in the shape of a hand.

My hand.

Chapter 39

When I open my eyes, Seth sits at my bedside. His eyes fill with relief, and I get the sense that I was out for a lot longer than it feels. "It's good you're awake, because you promised not to die."

"How long...?" That's when I notice there's something weird in my vision, and it stays in the same place no matter which way I move my head. I have to cross my eyes to look at it, and that's when I realize the thing is a nose and that it probably belongs to me. I raise my hand, and for the first time in my life there are fingers and palm, forearm and elbow.

"You're not dreaming," Seth says.

"Are you sure?" Because I can see my skin, and it's tanner than I expected. My nails are seriously stubby, but there are the freckles Seth described. They make me smile.

He nods. "More like you were having a nightmare. You were in so much pain they finally knocked you out with something. The drug took a couple hours to fully work, and Allie was so excited I wanted to punch her."

I sit up, though I don't immediately turn to the mirror. Instead I look at the door, reveling in the fact that there's more than clothing in my peripheral vision. "Where is she?"

"I told her you'd want to be alone when you saw yourself for the first time, and that I'd call her when you wanted." He takes my hand, and when I look at it on mine my heart leaps for joy it's so beautiful. "Should I go now?"

Nodding, I say, "You know me too well. Thanks, Seth."

"Of course." He kisses my cheek, blocking my view of the mirror. "Just so you know, Allie said the other patients are seeing less effectiveness already. You might not have much time."

"Okay." I gulp, knowing the people I most want to show could be impossible to reach. "Any word on my family?"

He shakes his head. "I'll be right outside if you need me."

Seth leaves then, and it's just me and the mirror. My heart pounds with excitement. This still feels like a dream, and for a moment I'm afraid I'll wake up the second I try to look. So I pull off my blankets, and there are my legs and feet jutting out of the white leggings. The hair on my calves isn't nearly as bad as I imagined, just a light blond that hardly stands out. Bending over to touch my toes, I run my fingers over them in awe. They are real. I'm real.

I choke back tears. It's a miracle. Even if it won't last long. I want to kiss Allie for this chance.

Taking a deep breath, I decide it's time for the mirror. I turn quickly, and for the first time my own eyes are staring right back at me. I can't move as I take myself in. It's like meeting someone I'm sure I should know, but I can't quite remember them.

I'm shocked that the first things I see are the people who made me—Mom and Dad. Mom's wild hair. Dad's sharp jawline.

Mom's eyes. Dad's cheek bones. For a moment it's jarring to think I look like the guy who hurt us so much, but then I start to see how much Miles and I resemble each other. If I was visible all the time, there'd be no mistaking us as siblings. That makes everything better.

As I stand up from the bed to get a closer look, everything about how I move is familiar and yet not. My walk seems more awkward than I pictured. I don't stand very straight. I feel... bigger and taller now that my clothes cover skin.

"This is so weird," I say to myself, just to see how my mouth moves. My eyebrows rise in surprise because my lips look so strange in use, and then my expression shocks me even more. My face does all sorts of things I could never picture. I glare and smile, purse my lips and roll my eyes. I frown, thinking about how often I do these things and how much they give my feelings away. No wonder Seth can read me so well.

I look down to my dress, realizing this could be my only chance to see my whole body before the drug wears off. My face goes red at the thought, which is yet another thing I can't believe I'm seeing.

Though I'm not sure I'm ready for the full view, I still pull my dress over my head. Then I slip out of my leggings and unsnap my bra. Finally, I pull off my underwear and force myself to look again. My skin is much lighter under my clothes, and it's beyond strange to see my belly button. My legs are toned from all the running. But I swear my butt is twice the size I thought, while my boobs aren't nearly as impressive as I imagined.

I guess I don't look awful, but I have to admit I feel like Seth has been generous with the compliments. Tilting my head, I try to see what's so great about me naked. I don't get it. "This is what he gets excited about?"

The more I look in the mirror, the more uncomfortable I get. I can't help thinking how much more dingy my hair is than the "golden" he told me. And my nose is weird, always in my view. Does that mean it's too big? Are my eyes too close together? My teeth are a little crooked. The hair under my arms is also starting to look gross.

Truth is, as excited as I am to see myself, I'm not nearly as pretty as Seth claims.

I can't help thinking of the drawings I've made him do, how I never liked what he created. Maybe I kept expecting to see a model appear on the page, not a normal girl who just happens to be invisible. But I am normal. Just like I wanted to be.

It makes me feel more inferior than I expected.

Feeling too exposed, I scramble for my clothes, for safety. How in the world do people look at themselves? That isn't fun. As I put on my clothes, I keep watching myself in the mirror. Clothes make it a little better, something familiar to go with the face I should know but don't. I cover my mouth, the reality of it crashing down on me.

This isn't me—this face has never been part of my identity.

Now that it is I don't know how to feel about it. I don't like it as much as I thought I would, that's for sure. Freaking out, I begin to pace the room. It's just like when Seth revealed he could see me; I can't hide and I want to. How do people live constantly exposed to the world's eyes?

There's a knock at the door, and Seth's muffled voice comes through. "Fiona?"

I don't answer, embarrassed now that I know *exactly* what he's seen all these times.

"Are you okay?"

"No." I'm not sure he can hear me because it's a whisper, but the door opens anyway. He must have been watching. I cover my face—why would he want to watch me when I look so weird? Suddenly it seems crazy that he said he loved me at all. He comes in, and the first thing out of my mouth is, "You lied."

He gives me a confused look. "What?"

"I look weird!" Curling in on myself, my eyes find the floor. But my feet stare back at me and so I close my eyes. "That's why you hated drawing me, because you didn't want me to find out."

He laughs. And not just a little, but a big booming laugh. "You're kidding, right?"

I don't answer.

"C'mere." Seth puts his hands on my shoulders and pushes me back to the mirror. I don't want to see that stranger again, not right now. "Fi, just look. You wanted to see us together, didn't you?"

My head snaps up at his words, and this time the mirror doesn't seem so scary because he's there with me.

He smiles wide, pulling at my hair. "Golden highlights." Then he touches my nose. "Cute little button." He brushes his fingers against my arm. "And freckles. When did I ever lie?"

I bite my lip.

Seth grabs his ears. "You don't think I know these stick out a little too much?" He points to his arm. "Or that I'm pretty much a scarecrow? Or that my freckles aren't actually

273

as attractive as you claim?"

"They are, too."

"Maybe." He turns me so that we're facing each other. "Fiona, I didn't want you to do this because I knew you'd react like this. It doesn't matter if you can see yourself or not—you've never been able to accept yourself as you are. That's not something you can fix by changing the outside. It comes from inside."

I look at myself in the mirror again, knowing he's right. It's not my reflection's fault that I'm disappointed. That's completely on me. "I'm trying, but I don't know how."

"You'll figure it out. But in the meantime…" He puts his arm around me and pulls me right up against him. "Don't we look good together?"

Though I roll my eyes, I agree with him. It's surprising how, despite our imperfections, we seem to be perfectly matched. When he's next to me, it's easier to be comfortable with myself. I hope there comes a day when I can stand confident on my own, but it's good to know Seth's here for me until I do. "Do you have your phone? We should take a picture while we can."

His smile gets bigger as he pulls it from his pocket. "That's better."

Seth takes a few pictures of me on my own, and I marvel that I'm there in them. I'll be able to see these even when I disappear again—maybe that will keep me from thinking this was just a dream. Then he takes a bunch of us together, and as I flip through them I can't help but grin. "We really do fit together."

"Told you." Seth motions toward the door. "You seem to be feeling better. Do you want me to get anyone?"

My heart skips at the thought. Seth is one thing, but what would everyone else think? "It's kind of now or never, isn't it?"

He nods. "Any requests for firsts?"

If there's no word on my family, then I figure Graham's still out trying to find them. That means… "If The Pack wants to see me, I wouldn't mind. But they seemed kind of mad."

He nods. "They've probably cooled down. It was a lot to take in all at once, with the cure and you and the factory."

"True."

"I'll be right back."

"Okay." I take a deep breath in an attempt to calm my nerves.

Bea comes in first, and instead of shock there's only a huge smile. Brady's smile is smaller, but he oozes happiness. Hector's reaction is a nod of approval. To my surprise, Carlos is the one who frowns. After the non-stop attempts at hitting on me, I figured I'd at least get a catcall.

Bea comes over and punches me. "You're lucky it worked, because I was gonna kill you otherwise."

"Why do people keep threatening to kill me?" I rub my shoulder, while I try not to feel self-conscious under everyone's gaze.

Bea smirks as she looks right into my eyes. "You really are pretty, Fi."

"Eh," Carlos says. "I liked it better when you were invisible."

Seth glares at him. "Excuse me?"

"She looks fine." Carlos waves his hand at me, more disinterested than I thought possible. "But this takes out all the mystery. Not exciting anymore."

"Gee, thanks." I fold my arms, feeling weird, though I should be happy that Carlos will probably never hit on me again. So this is how it feels to be judged on your appearance.

Hector smacks the back of his brother's head. "Shut up, man. Who wants to hear that?"

"I'm just being honest!"

Brady shakes his head. "Only further proof that Carlos is a dumbass. He's just saying that because now he's positive you're out of his league."

I look away, embarrassed. I've wanted people to see me my whole life, but now that it's here I can't believe how much I *don't* want to talk about my appearance. Seriously, how long can a conversation about what I look like go? Time for a subject change.

"Forget about me—just think what this could do for you, Brady." I smile as I look between him and Bea. "No more worrying about hurting anyone."

His face goes beet red. "I can't even picture it."

Seth points at his brother. "It's not happening until this drug is stable. Fiona went through hell before it worked. Allie said all the patients did. Speaking of, she'll be wanting to get your vitals. I'll send the nurse to get her."

"Okay." I suck in a breath, not particularly excited because she'll want to poke at me. I've never pictured what it would look like to see a needle in my skin. It makes me queasy. Better distract myself. "Let's hurry and take pictures, guys. This is kind of a big deal."

"Hell yes it is!" Bea hops over, and Seth takes our picture. Then Hector, Carlos, and Brady join in. They all take turns taking pictures, and I tell myself it's okay to smile because these might be the only images I'll get for awhile.

Allie and the nurse come in, and they tell everyone but Seth they need to leave until they're finished. "Sorry," Allie says to me. "The other patients are already experiencing decreased effectiveness. I want you to enjoy your friends, but I need these tests, too."

"I understand." I gulp as the nurse pulls out a needle.

"Fi, look at me," Seth says. "It won't be as bad that way."

"Do I look that scared?" I ask, though I do what he says. The nurse rubs something wet in the crook of my elbow, and then there's an uncomfortable prick that makes me cringe.

He smirks. "You've gone pretty white."

"How are you feeling?" Allie says as the nurse keeps fiddling with my arm. How many vials of blood does she need?

"Fine." I glance at my reflection. I *am* pale. Funny. "Still getting used to my face, and I feel exposed. But I'm not in pain, and I don't really feel sick. A little hungry, though."

She smiles. "We'll get you something to eat from the mess hall on the surface."

I nod. "So, was it a good first test?"

Allie's face turns more serious. "The pain levels were much more than anticipated, and some of the other patients are still feeling ill despite their mutations having gone away. So though the drug *did* do its job, the side effects are still light years from ideal. And the fading is much faster than I anticipated. Hopefully in the next round I can make it last longer."

Finally the nurse finishes, and directs me to hold the cotton swab to my skin. "You can't expect perfection on the first test," I say to Allie. "This was incredible for the time you've had with the element."

Allie offers a tiny smile. "Thanks. Oh, I wanted to ask you about possibly getting more merinite—I don't have much left from the first sample we took."

"That's fine. Just take Graham with you when he gets back? No one else."

"Of course." She picks up a vial of my blood, seeming in awe that she can see it. "This is quite exciting, to have the privilege of seeing you like this."

A sudden wave of gratitude hits for what Allie's given me. "Can I get a picture with you? For memory's sake."

"No!" Allie blurts out.

Seth gives her a surprised look. "Why not?"

Allie waves it off, seeming embarrassed. "I just don't like my picture taken. And besides, this is supposed to be top secret."

I frown. "I just wanted a picture with the person who made this possible."

"I'm sorry." She stares at the ground. "You were the one who made it possible though. I couldn't have done it without the merinite, and that's all thanks to you."

"Oh well…" My voice trails off as I catch sight of myself in the mirror again. There's no mistaking that there's something less solid about the way I look. "I guess it's starting to wear off."

Allie looks up, panic on her face. "Oh no! We need to test these samples now."

"On it!" The nurse is already halfway to the door, Allie right on her heels.

Seth doesn't say anything as he watches me fade. Now that I'm going, I'm not sure how to feel. Part of me is relieved, but then the other half can't stop staring at my reflection in the mirror. I need to memorize it. I don't have enough time to do that. I go from slightly hazy to ghostly to barely there in less than half an hour. Then I'm back to a teal dress with white leggings.

Seth takes my hand. "Are you sad?"

"I don't know." I can't take my eyes off the mirror, surprised by the confidence I feel now that I'm back in my own invisible skin. "Maybe I will be later, but right now I'm glad to be back to my—"

The door bursts open, and Graham flies in. His eyes are wide and he pants. "We're in trouble, Fi. Big trouble."

"What?" If Graham is saying that, then it must be horrible. "Where's Mom and Miles? Did you go out to get them?"

"We were too late." He cringes as he holds out his phone. There's a picture, and it's terrifying. Above Mom's bed, there's a message written in what I'm sure is blood: *I have her. You know what I want in return. —The Phantom*

Chapter 40

I find the bed just before my legs give out. This can't be happening. The Phantom kidnapped my mom, and I have no doubt that blood on the wall is hers. She's hurt, captured, alone. And I'm here seeing myself. "What are we gonna do, Graham? What about Miles and Lee Seol?"

"Missing. We have no proof The Phantom took the Navarros or Miles and Lee Seol, but that doesn't mean he didn't." Instead of floating, he actually sits on the bed next to me. "Madison is a war zone, sis. Major Norton is working on a plan to take back the town, but Juan's men are already approaching the factory."

I put my hand to my mouth. I feel so helpless and entirely at fault. "I wish I'd told everyone to leave town."

"No one knew they'd move so fast."

Pursing my lips, I think of Seth's dad. He figured out Lee Seol's meet-up with the Spudlings…we should have told the Army that day. But instead I gave The Phantom time to plan. "We have to get Mom back."

Graham nods. "But she's probably at their base under SuperMart. It'll be hard to get in there."

"Lee Seol can."

"We just have to *find*…" Seth begins to say, but then grabs his head. He crumples onto the bed, and it looks like he's biting back screams.

Graham stares at him. "What's wrong?"

"I don't know." I put my hand on Seth's shoulder, knowing exactly what's happening to him. This vision glitch looks much worse than usual by the way his face contorts with pain—way too reminiscent of the first time it happened. "Seth? What do you need?"

He just moans back.

"Should I get a nurse?" Graham asks.

"No!" I yell, and my brother stares at me like I'm insane. How am I supposed to cover this up surrounded by people who can't find out? "It's just…"

The doorknob turns, and my worst fear is Allie walking through. It would be slightly less bad if it were The Pack, though they've been so suspicious lately as it is. But the person who appears is one I didn't expect at all. It's Tagawa, in combat uniform, complete with rifle in hand. As if his bony spikes weren't intimidating enough. "The Major asked me to come get you and your friends—you're needed up top."

"Oh?" I look to Seth, who doesn't seem in any condition to move. "Can we wait a little bit? He has a pretty bad headache."

Tagawa looks as intolerant as ever. "It can't wait. Juan's guys are closing in."

Graham eyes him suspiciously. "Then we're safer down here."

"We need you guys to fight—is that a problem?" Tagawa spits. "Least you could do when we're trying to rescue your family."

I sigh. "Seth, I'm gonna help you move, okay?"

Seth holds his shaking hand out to me, and I take that as good enough. I have no idea how we'll get up there without people suspecting there's something seriously wrong with him, but Tagawa makes it seem like we don't have much choice. Seth clings to me as we head out the door, and I hope this episode passes before he faints.

"Whoa," Hector says when he sees us. "What happened?"

Brady seems to be searching for some kind of excuse as he takes his brother from me. "He's been so stressed his migraines are getting out of control."

"Let's go." Tagawa motions for us to follow him.

"No…" Seth whispers.

I stop, looking to Seth. "No?"

If it weren't for Brady, I'm sure he wouldn't be standing. "Stay. Here."

"Stay?" Hector sounds loud against Seth's whisper. "Why?"

"We gotta go!" Tagawa yells. "If pansy boy can't walk just carry him."

"Can't he stay here and rest?" I ask, getting annoyed with this guy who has no idea what my boyfriend is going through. "He can't fight anyway."

He shakes his head. "My orders were to bring everyone."

"Don't listen to him," Seth says with a little more *oomph*. "He's lying. It makes no sense for us to go up there. Think about it."

I stare at Seth, trying to figure out what he really means. Does he see something suspicious? Hector puts his hands on his hips, seeming to take his best friend very seriously. "What makes you think he's lying?"

Seth cringes, and I have no idea how he'll answer. "Because…he…there's a jaguar tattoo on his chest."

"What?" Tagawa laughs. "Is this guy crazy?"

"I'm not." Seth stands a little taller, and I hope that means he's feeling better. "I can see it."

The Pack looks like they're about to go into shock. I'm not sure if they believe him or not, but I know he's telling the truth. Which means Tagawa is the spy. No wonder The Phantom seemed to know what was going on with the Army. I step forward, my fists balled. "That's why you didn't 'wake up' when The Phantom was beating me up that night. You knew he was coming—you probably even helped him avoid security!"

Tagawa looks at me in mock shock. "You seriously believe that shit he's talking?"

I look back at Seth, who seems weak after the pain his body just put him through. When his eyes meet mine, I know he's saying it's okay to tell the truth. "I know he's right because he can see me—and he can see right through your shirt and pretty much anything else."

Gasps from The Pack. Hector grabs Seth. "Is it true? You can see Fiona?"

Seth nods. "I'm not a math savant. I have X-ray vision."

No one has time to react, because at those words Tagawa takes off running. Clearly he knows he's been caught.

"Get him!" Graham yells, shooting off down the hall.

Everyone but me and Seth sprint after him, and without Brady's help Seth can't seem to do much more than sit on the floor. He puts his hands to his head and sighs, "Well, that's not how I planned to tell them."

"Horribly good timing though." I sit next to him, trying not to smile. There's a loud thud from around the corner, which I picture is Tagawa taking a blow from Brady. The guys cheer their victory. "I guess that means we need to take the traitor to Major Norton. Think you can make it?"

"Yeah." Seth pulls himself up, and we head for the surface.

When we tell Major Norton about Tagawa, he blows a gasket. Then he tears into an interrogation of the traitor, which reveals that he was planning to deliver us to The Phantom's men just outside the factory. The Major pounds on the desk. "You better tell the truth if you want to live—was it you who took down the power on the fence?"

Tagawa looks to the side. "Yes."

"Damnit." The Major yells orders into his comm unit, then turns to us. "I guess I should thank you for catching him before he took us down entirely. Maybe now we can make some headway."

"How bad is it out there?" I ask.

His hesitation says everything. "At this rate, it'll be a few days before we can reach The Phantom's base."

"That's not fast enough," I say. "If we don't give him the merinite, he won't keep my mom alive that long."

Graham nods. "We have a day. Tops. At least that was standard in our syndicate."

Major Norton folds his arms, thinking. "We'd hoped Allie would have a better working cure that would help us take down The Phantom—he'll be almost impossible to capture even if we do take back the city. His ability is too powerful.

But we need to get your mother now."

"You'll have to let Fi go out there solo, sir. She's got a good team," Graham says with more confidence than I have currently. "I'll help Allie get more merinite, and hopefully we'll have something to permanently stop The Phantom soon."

"Seems like that's the best we can do." The Major looks to me. "Juan's forces are fewer on the east side—you'll have the best chance sneaking out that way."

I stand tall, focused only on saving my mother. "We better get going then."

We head off into the desert at a quick jog. The sun is already low in the sky, meaning we don't have nearly as much time as I want. And I have no plan. "So," Carlos says after we get past the danger zone, "where exactly are we going? And how are we supposed to break into The Phantom's base?"

"We have to find Lee Seol and Miles." I pull out my phone, hoping for the best. If they're alive, Lee Seol will see this somehow. I text to Miles' number: *Please tell me you're alive.*

When my phone buzzes almost immediately, I don't think I've been so relieved. It's from Lee Seol: *At waterfall. Hurry.*

"They're alive?" Bea asks hopefully.

"Yeah, at the waterfall. Let's pick up the pace." I have to hope that Lee Seol has some crucial information that will make this a hell of a lot easier, because right now it seems impossible.

"So…" Hector says, about halfway there. "You have X-ray vision, huh?"

Seth cringes. "Sorry I didn't tell you sooner. When I was a kid I was afraid you guys wouldn't talk to me anymore if you knew I'd seen through your clothes, even though I couldn't

285

control it. Then it just…I could never find the right time."

"Sure explains a lot," Carlos says. "Especially with Fi."

"You're not mad?" Seth asks.

Hector shakes his head. "Always had a feeling you were hiding something—figured you'd tell me when you were ready. Just didn't think it'd be like *that*."

"Seth has horrible timing," I say.

"I really do." He hangs his head, and everyone smiles.

When it gets too dark to see well, Carlos takes the lead and we follow in a tight line behind him. As we descend down the cliff side, I try to scan the area but mostly it's too dark. I can make out the water, the stars glinting off the surface. The bigger shadows are trees that I hope no enemies are hiding in.

"See anything bad, Carlos?" I whisper.

"Nope." His eyes roam over the small valley. "But that doesn't mean there's no one here to ambush us."

"Shh, let me listen," Hector says, and I think we all hold our breath. He points toward the water. "Someone's breathing over there."

"Hope it's them," Carlos says as he follows Hector's direction.

It better be, because we've already used too much time getting here. If we're supposed to infiltrate The Phantom's base by tomorrow, we need to be working towards that now. As we approach the waterfall, I can feel the water splash at my feet. Hector pauses, and then whispers, "There's rustling… like clothes, I think. It's hard to tell with the wat—"

Before he finishes, a figure emerges from behind the rocks and tackles Bea. Brady goes into attack mode, but stops short when the person says, "*Mija!* Are you okay? We've been so worried."

"Rosa!" I exclaim just as three more figures appear.

"If we get out of this alive, you three are grounded until graduation," Alejandro says. "You should have told us you were involved—I shouldn't have heard it from Fiona's brother."

"Sorry," Bea says.

"Now, now, best intentions were had." There's a click and then light—Miles looks relieved as he holds the flashlight to his face. "Glad you're safe, Fi."

"Took you long enough," Lee Seol grumbles as she messes with her super phone.

"I was kinda busy." I head to Miles and pull him into a hug. "Really wish you could have been there for it."

He tenses at the words. "I take it the drug worked? We lost sound on your mic when you went underground."

"Yeah, it worked for a little bit," I whisper, the image of myself in the mirror already seeming like a dream.

Miles nods as he pulls back, and his eyes look haunted. "It happened so fast, Fi. Me and Lee Seol were in the living room working on the cracked network. Mom was sleeping since she had a late shift yesterday. And then we heard her scream. By the time we got up there, the blood was on the wall and they were gone. The Phantom must have taken Radiasure so he could pull Mom through with him."

I gulp, unable to say anything at the account.

"Bastard," Lee Seol says. "I had no idea wall walking wouldn't set off alarms, but apparently he can go right through lasers no problem. He must have been planning this for awhile, because he didn't appear on any of the cameras I put around the house. He knew the blind spots."

Seth swears. "We need to do something *now*. Do we even know how to get into The Phantom's base?"

"It's underground," Lee Seol says. "I've been able to get a basic layout of the place, but Crisis put extra security on the passwords to open the doors. He's trying to get me out of their system, but I'm hanging on. Those doors won't open without the right code."

Brady flexes his muscles. "What if I punch my way in?"

Lee Seol shakes her head and pulls out what I think is a folding screen. She opens it until it's about the size of a piece of paper, and then an image lights up on it. It's a blueprint. She points to a bunch of round things by what looks to be a huge door. "See these? They're bombs. Rigged to go off at the slightest attempt to use force. So unless you are also indestructible, I wouldn't recommend punching."

"Shit," Carlos says, and then Rosa smacks him. He gives her an incredulous look. "What am I supposed to say, Ma? There is a *fortress* under our SuperMart—look at that thing!"

Hector lets out a long sigh. "And we thought we were so safe here."

"There's no such thing as safe," Alejandro says as he sits down on a nearby rock. He looks up at us, his face set in determination. "You only have one choice, but from what Miles told me you might not like it."

"What's that?" Seth asks.

"What could possibly be so bad at this point?" I say. "I'm up for anything if it means stopping that psycho."

Alejandro scratches the back of his head. "Well, you're gonna have to talk to your dad, Seth. There's no doubt John has the codes."

The shock on everyone's faces is unanimous as Brady says, "You *knew*?"

Alejandro nods, and suddenly Bea's dad will never look the same to me again.

Chapter 41

"No," Seth says before Alejandro can get another word out. "I saw what he does—I'm not talking to him ever again. I don't care if he has what we need."

I want to argue with my boyfriend, since my mom's life is on the line. But I can't blame him for feeling that way. "He said if we interfered again he wouldn't hesitate to hurt us."

"He's a traitor," Brady growls.

Hector holds up his hands. "Hold on now—what are you talking about? I thought your dad didn't do anything but alcohol and drugs."

Alejandro lets out a long, tired sigh. "That's his way of coping with what he's had to do all these years, *mijo*. Just after his wife died, Juan was already threatening us. Everyone knew what Brady was, and Juan wanted to indoctrinate him early. They were coming for us, too. We didn't have a lot—you think they left us alone just for the money? No, John was part of the deal. He agreed to work for Juan as long as he could remain undercover."

While it all makes sense, it's hard to take. "So he really does work *for* Juan?" I ask.

"Yes, unwillingly." Alejandro looks sad and tired, but also relieved, like having the secret out is a weight off his chest. "It was either him or our kids. How could I tell him not to do it? So I said I'd take care of you guys like my own, make sure the construction company was run well. It was the least I could do when he was sacrificing his soul for us."

Seth balls his fists, looking away. "Don't make it sound like he's noble. You think I'm happy to know my dad became a murderer for me?"

"I'm not *asking* you to think of him as noble," Alejandro says. "I'm just telling you this because you need his help and I believe he *will* help you. He only gives Juan the bare minimum. Because he's undercover, he gets all the information first and then filters what he wants to Juan."

I can't help thinking of all the holes in The Phantom's information—how he knew I was here and yet not that Seth can see me, how he seems to know someone is hacking but not that Spud is *here*, how he knows we have the merinite but not that it's in a cave. As much as I don't want to admit it, I say, "That does make sense. He must have a lot of stuff on us—and it's obvious Juan *doesn't* have all that information."

Seth purses his lips, and my guess is he doesn't have an argument for that.

"If this code is half as jacked as the last one," Lee Seol grumbles, her eyes glued to her super phone, "then asking him is our best shot."

I want to demand that we go with this plan, but when I look at Seth and Brady I can't. They are so pissed about this—and their feelings do matter to me even if my mom is at stake here.

Taking a deep breath, I say, "What do you think? Should we?"

Seth raises an eyebrow, and then looks to Brady. "How do you feel, bro?"

Brady frowns. "As much as I don't want to talk to him, we can't let Fiona's mom die."

Seth nods. "I'll do the talking then. You can stay outside."

"Sounds good," Brady says.

"Okay, enough shitting around. Go kick some ass." Lee Seol comes up to me, the big-screen map in front of her. "Get a good look at this layout, Fi. It's not a huge place, but that doesn't mean it'll be easy to find her."

"Everyone, study this before we go. Lee Seol, you think you'll be able to keep in contact with us from here?"

"Should be fine, since I have their network when you go underground. And I got fifteen hours of battery—you better be done by then."

"Call Seth if I don't answer. I'll probably have to go invisible at some point." Though the thought of having to be naked after I've seen what I really look like? I shudder.

"Yup. I'm watching Graham, too," Lee Seol says. "So do your job and leave the worrying to me."

Miles gives me a pat on the back. "Get going."

The second we hit the edges of Madison, it's clear this won't be easy. The streets are crawling with Juan's guys, and this time they aren't pretending to mind their own business. They're armed, and their eyes scan everything in search of intruders. Luckily, we have just the thing to throw them off.

Bea cups her hands around her mouth, looking positively

excited that she gets to use her skills to their fullest tonight. Taking a deep breath, she sends some kind of sound out there. About six seconds later, a loud crash startles the patrollers, and they head into the darker depths of the nearby park.

"Better book it!" Bea takes off at a run, and we follow because she's the only one who knows the sound's direction.

We do this about five times—with a variety of sounds and three close calls—before we make it to Seth's house. I should be worried about Mr. Mitchell, but all I can see is the damage to the Navarros' place. The windows are smashed, and the door is torn off its hinges. There are horrible Spanish words spray-painted all over the stucco walls, and all I can think is thank goodness Miles got Rosa and Alejandro out before they joined Mom.

Seth's house looks remarkably untouched in comparison, which now makes sickening sense. He glares at the lit window as he says, "You guys watch the perimeter—me and Fiona will go in."

"Sounds good," Hector replies. "Bea will yell if I hear anything out here."

"Okay." Seth takes my hand, and we walk up the path to his front door. Remembering the last time we faced his dad, my heart pounds as he pulls out his keys.

The house is quiet, save the humming of the refrigerator. We take cautious steps as we head for the kitchen. That's when I hear the *clink* of glass on the counter. As we round the corner, Seth's dad comes into view. He's slumped over a bottle of hard liquor and a shot glass. Barely glancing at us, he says, "Don't think I can't take you out just because I'm drunk."

293

Seth's glare is cold. "Nice to see you, too."

His dad points at Seth, his finger not swaying the littlest bit. Though judging by how little is left in the bottle, he must be hammered. "Don't get smart with me, son. Because I've just about had it with all the trouble you and your little girlfriend have caused me—do you know how hard it is to cover your ass?"

Seth rolls his eyes. "Whatever. If you actually wanted to help, you would have told us what was up from the beginning."

"And be executed?" Seth's dad pours himself another shot and downs it. "Life's shit, but it's better than being dead."

Seth balls his fists. If I don't intervene, we'll get nothing from this except broken bones. So I grab Seth's arm and pull him back. "No offense, Mr. Mitchell, but I'm not here to talk life choices—you have to know The Phantom has my mother, and I need her back. Alejandro said you might have the codes to break into his base."

"Oh?" Seth's dad smirks. "So you're here to convince me to hand them over?"

"Yes."

He laughs as he pours yet another drink. "Did you not hear what I said? I prefer not dying. Who do you think he'll assume gave you the codes?"

"There wouldn't be any proof."

"Proof." Swig of liquor. "You're a syndicate baby, dear Fiona, you know very well that proof is for courtrooms—and when was the last time any of these people saw one of those? I'd be dead just for being a suspect."

I purse my lips, knowing he has me there.

"If you only care about yourself," Seth's voice is quiet, but still strong, "then why haven't you told them all the stuff you *really* know? Should we tell The Phantom you forgot to mention the cave?"

Mr. Mitchell pauses. "You'd never give away that information."

"But why didn't you, Dad?" The pain on Seth's face kills me. I can tell he wants his dad to say it's because he cares. Maybe that's all he's ever wanted to hear from his father.

His dad's eyes show no emotion when he replies, "Some information is worth more money than I get paid."

"Liar," I say before I can think better of it. "Tell yourself whatever you want—it's obvious you're protecting us. If you really wanted power and security in the syndicate, you'd rat us out because Juan would trust you forever if you sold out your own family."

Mr. Mitchell raises an eyebrow. "Who says I haven't?"

"What?" Seth says just as a piercing sound comes from outside. If it weren't for the walls I'm sure my ears would be shot.

"Bea!" This could mean only one thing, and as I stare at Seth's dad I can't believe the smile he wears. "You knew we'd come here!"

"Of course you would. Crisis said your little Spud hadn't gotten into the passwords yet. Alejandro got out." He runs his finger around the lip of the shot glass. "It was only a matter of time. I waited up for you and everything."

Seth swears. "Let's get outta here. We'll have to find another way."

I nod, though I'm pretty sure his father has sentenced my mom to death. We head for the front door, but Mr. Mitchell lands in front of us, silent as a jaguar.

"Move!" Seth yells at him.

"Make me."

Though I'm sure Seth knows he can't beat his dad, he still throws a punch. Mr. Mitchell grabs his arm, pulls him closer, and then puts a hand around his neck. I jump in, trying to pry his fingers off, but he pushes me to the floor. As I watch Seth fight to get free, I feel helpless. Even if I strip down and try to surprise him, he could hurt Seth before I attack.

"I can crush his windpipe," Mr. Mitchell says like it's not his son he could murder. "So how about you tell your friends out there to surrender before that happens?"

He has me. And he knows it.

Pulling myself off the floor, I blink back tears. I look at my boyfriend's pleading eyes, but I can't do what he wants. I love him too much. "I'm sorry, Seth, I can't let you get hurt."

"That's a good girl." Seth's dad nods toward the front door. "Now call off the attack."

I head to the door, and they follow right behind me. Outside I'm met with a surprising amount of chaos. A half dozen of Juan's men are down, clutching their heads from whatever Bea did to them. There is shrapnel everywhere, which doesn't make sense until I realize Brady probably tried to destroy the guns instead of the people. That boy, good hearted even now. How did he come from such a twisted father?

The remaining thugs give Bea and Brady a wide berth while holding their hands to their ears. If it weren't for Mr. Mitchell, we probably would have won this fight.

"Fiona! We're kicking—" Carlos calls when he sees us on the porch, but then he realizes Seth's dad has him by the throat

296

and horror takes over.

Mr. Mitchell pulls a gun from his pocket and points it at me. This all feels way too familiar. "Tell them to come peacefully."

I gulp, wishing I could say anything else. "It's over, guys."

Chapter 42

After they cuff us, Juan's men shove all of us but Seth in the back of an armored truck. I assume Seth gets to stay with his dad, so we know not to fight back if we want him to be alive when we get there.

Though there are no windows, I can only assume we're headed for SuperMart and the secret underground base. The longer we drive, the louder the gunfire gets. I wish I could see what the hell is going on out there, because it sounds like we're driving right through the middle of a battle.

"What are we gonna do now?" Carlos' voice is panicky.

Hector shrugs. "This is where we wanted to go anyway, isn't it?"

"But not as prisoners!" Bea says.

I wonder if Hector might be on to something. Mr. Mitchell couldn't give us the code without being suspected of helping us. But capturing us is a different story—he looks like he's doing his job. I hold on to this tiny shred of hope. Maybe, just maybe, we'll find a way to escape.

Then I think of what Seth would say to my theories—he'd tell me not to hold my breath when it comes to trusting his dad. And he's probably right.

"I can feel you thinking," Brady says to me. "What is it?"

"Nothing."

My stomach drops, which is the only way I can tell we're going down. I imagine it's some kind of steep ramp going under SuperMart. The truck skids to a stop, and our captors open the back door. Seth stands there with his dad, looking more furious than ever.

"This way," Mr. Mitchell says as he points his gun at us. The other men seem to have gotten new rifles as well. "I wouldn't try anything if you want to live."

I tip my chin up. "Wasn't planning on it. Right now at least."

The smallest wisp of a smirk crosses his face, and I want to hope that means something good. We follow him to a fortified door I assume is the one on Lee Seol's blueprints. Mr. Mitchell puts his hand to a security pad, and then it asks him to enter an I.D. code. He pushes Seth through first and the rest of us follow.

That would have been impossible to get through, I think as we walk down a stark hallway lined with doors. It looks more like a hospital than a den of criminals. Not that *all* dens are dirty, but this one seems overly clean. And then it clicks.

It's a lab. Duh.

We round a few corners, and I try to keep track in my mind how the layout matches up with what we saw on the screen. It doesn't work well. The only thing I know is who we're headed for, and I'm not sure I'm ready for him. When Mr. Mitchell finally opens a door, I see The Phantom sitting at a folding table. His long hair is pulled back from his face, and he smiles as his thugs force us to sit in front of him. "Welcome."

"Where's my mother, asshole?" I know I should mind my words, but seeing him safe in his hole makes my blood burn.

He glares at me, but says nothing. Instead, he grabs a remote and points it at the TV on the nearest wall. When the image appears, my heart about stops.

It's Mom.

She's in a bed, weeping, and her arms are chained down so she can't use her telekinesis. I can't stop staring at the bandage over her forehead, which has dark spots of blood. Just how hard did he hit her? Must have been enough to knock her out so she couldn't fight back.

"I would not throw insults if I were you," The Phantom says. "Since I'm already this close to killing her. Must be hard to care about people."

"Let her go," I growl.

"I'd be glad to." He holds out his hand. "Just give me the merinite first."

In that moment, I wish I had it. Because I don't know how else I'll convince him and why does it matter now that Allie can reverse mutations? "I don't have it."

"You're more foolish than I thought," The Phantom snarls. "Did you honestly think you could save her—save this town—with your little band of greenie vigilantes?"

I don't answer. In the silence my phone buzzes in my pocket, but I can't exactly pick it up since I'm cuffed.

He stands, pounding the desk. "This is *Juan's* town. It always has been. Are you so delusional you think you can take something from our syndicate? Let me make this clear—you've been *allowed* to live here by the grace of Juan. Not because we didn't notice. Not because you've fooled us. And if you want to keep living here, you better start paying your dues."

His words smack me across the face. How could I forget this world? How could I think getting free of Dad meant I could remain syndicate free forever? There's no such thing as syndicate free, even when you think you are. The Pack is living proof of that.

I look down, a sense of defeat washing over me.

"It's *not* Juan's town," Bea says in the silence. Everyone turns to look at her. "Does he live here? No. We do."

This seems to spark something in Carlos. "Yeah! I don't see his name on the sign. It's just Madison. Not Madison: Property of Juan Torres."

"Has he purchased the property deeds?" Hector adds. "Are any of his claims legal?"

The Phantom waves his hand, and each of them gets hit with the back of a gun. "You should not talk, otherwise I'll have them pull the trigger next."

The Pack tries to stay strong, but that threat makes an impact. We're all one wrong move away from dead, whether or not what they said was true. The idea of The Pack dying...

My phone buzzes yet again, and I worry it's something vital from Lee Seol. I wish I could grab it. The only thing I can do is buy some time and hope for an opening to answer.

"Just stop, okay?" I say, grasping for something that might distract The Phantom from his goals. "Look, I don't have the element, which means I can't give it to you even if I wanted to. I know Juan's probably breathing down your neck about that, but can't we strike some other deal?"

His eyes narrow. "Like what?"

I glance at Mr. Mitchell, who is as emotionless as ever. Despite that, I know why he did what he did. He's just like Graham—happy to do the dirty work if that means the people he cares about are safe.

"Me." It's a lie, but maybe he'll go for it.

"Excuse me?" The Phantom says at the same time Seth yells, "No!"

"You heard me. I'll give you my dad's secrets, even do work for you. Just let my mom and everyone else go."

He snorts. "You think that's enough? Not even close."

"What about me, too?" Brady asks, and I try not to curse.

Seth's eyes about pop from his head. "What is *wrong* with you guys? Stop offering yourselves up like martyrs!"

The Phantom shakes his head. "It's sad that you think this would be enough to tempt me. The only thing you can do to fix this is to hand over the merinite—then we *might* let you live here in peace for awhile. Why is that so hard? You gave it to the Army. Surely you know they're just another syndicate."

I purse my lips, searching for anything else. My phone *rings* this time, though I know it shouldn't be able to turn off vibrate on its own. The whole room stares at me as the pop tune repeats. "Sorry?"

The Phantom seems more curious than angry. "Your phone should be disabled down here."

"What?" There's too much worry in my voice. He definitely picks up on it.

"Who is able to call you down—?"

"Fiona! Where the hell are you?" A muffled voice comes

302

from my pocket, but I can tell it's Lee Seol. "We have a HUGE problem! You have to abort your mission now."

"Get the phone," The Phantom commands. A guard pulls it from my dress pocket and hands it to him. "Who's this? How did you make this phone work?"

"Psh, you hired the wrong hacker, bitch," Lee Seol says. "Is Fiona there?"

"I'm here!" I call. "But I'm kind of a prisoner right now."

"*Kind of?*" The Phantom says incredulously.

"It doesn't matter, since whoever has you might want to hear this too." Lee Seol clears her throat. "We just got a distress call from Graham. His so-called girlfriend knocked him out at a certain location, took the merinite, and ran."

"What?" I stand, only to be shoved down by my guard. "Why?"

"I don't know, but I did a statewide sweep of my networks to see if anything weird came up." There's a long pause. "It's bad, Fi. Someone sent an old-school coded radio message to your dad's headquarters in Vegas, and I think it's Allie."

My eyes go wide, unable to wrap my head around it. "No. What did it say?"

Lee Seol sighs. "*Have cure. On my way.*"

I slump into my seat, unable to say anything but, "Shit."

Chapter 43

Everyone's talking at once, and I think they're demanding answers from me or Lee Seol but I can't process anything except Allie is very likely taking the cure to *my dad*. So he did have a girl here; she was just so deep in none of us saw it coming. And she used us, her ex-syndicate members, so well.

Seth's words about how a cure could be used just as badly as Radiasure swirl in my head. Dad could neutralize anyone who stood in his way *and* produce his own Radiasure. He'd be unstoppable.

What have I done?

This is all my fault. I knew what could happen, but I cared more about what I wanted than what it could do to everyone else.

"Cure? What do you mean by that?" The Phantom demands as I sit there in a daze. "And are you saying the Army's scientist is really with the O'Connells?"

Lee Seol groans. "Look, dude, I don't work for you. I'm trying to talk to Fiona, and you're hearing this because it can't wait. Once Allie's over the Nevada border we're *all* screwed. So if you know what's best for you let the girl talk—otherwise I'm sure Juan'll have your heart on a platter this time tomorrow."

The Phantom grimaces, but then looks to the guards. "Uncuff them."

They do as he says, and then he begrudgingly hands the phone over to me. It still takes me a second to find my voice. "H-how did she lie? The Major trusted her completely—and he's a flipping lie detector."

"My guess is it's her ability. She probably lied about chemistry being her strength," Lee Seol says, and I can't help but eye Seth. Are all savants covering up something else? "We're on our way to get Graham, who's too injured to fly. Allie took the Army truck they drove out to haul the merinite, so you'll have to find a way to intercept her—I'm sending you and Seth my estimates on her route and speed, the make of the truck, etc. Just...stop her. At all costs."

"Okay, thanks," I sigh, the fatigue of late nights finally catching up with me. "No wonder she was happy to keep the merinite location from the Army. So much for blondes being stupid."

"What? Allie's not blond!" Carlos says out of nowhere. "She's got dark brown hair."

I blink a few times, confused. "No, she doesn't."

"You couldn't mistake it for blond. Like ever," Bea says.

Brady and Hector nod in agreement, but when I look to Seth it's clear he's with me in the blond camp. I gasp when I remember he said he saw through her hair dye. Did he? Or was it something else? "Hey, can you ask Miles what color Allie's hair is? And if she and Graham have any pictures together?"

"Okay..." Lee Seol humors me. "He says it's brown and Allie doesn't like having her picture taken. Do you think...?"

"She's a hypnotist," I say over her. That explains how she

305

could get past Major Norton. I've heard of hypnotists so powerful they can convince a person they're dying, and then they really do. "She must do it through eye contact, but she could never see mine."

Seth's ability must have blocked it—he saw right through her power quite literally. And did her power aggravate his glitching vision more? No wonder he was so suspicious when everyone else seemed to love her. My heart sinks when I realize I have no such excuse. I fell for her claims and promises all on my own, because she had something I desperately wanted.

"That makes sense, because her face doesn't register in my system. She must look different to people every time she changes location," Lee Seol says.

"We better get on this." I grip the phone tightly, a surge of vengeance washing through me. My dad's been playing us this whole time. I could scream at the insanity of it all. "Call if you get anything else."

"Yes, ma'am." She hangs up.

I turn to The Phantom, who is much less threatening as he takes in this information. Maybe I'm seeing things, but I think this expression might be fear. "Juan will kill me for this. He'll kill us all. You know that, right?"

"I do." As much as I'd rather not, I have to seize this opportunity. For all I know, the Army might not believe Allie's a criminal—who knows how long she's been changing their perception? At least with Juan's men I know they're trained to hate my dad's syndicate. "So why don't you let my mom go, and then I'll give you my info on Allie? We can catch her before she gets to Nevada if we hurry."

His pale lips crease into a thin line.

"C'mon. This is mutually beneficial. Everything else is meaningless until she's gone." I hold my breath, hoping he'll cave. We need his vehicles, because heaven knows Sexy Blue can't drive fast enough.

"Get the bullet car ready," The Phantom says to his men as he walks towards the wall to his right. He's halfway through and still talking. "We're leaving now."

I hold my breath the entire time it takes him to come back with my mom. When she appears in the hallway, I rush over and wrap myself around her. "Mom! I'm so sorry. It's all my fault."

She sobs into my hair. "I'm just glad you're alive."

I shake my head, unable to find the right words to express how much regret I feel. Eyeing The Phantom, I ask him, "Can you get her back home?"

He doesn't seem happy about the request. "I have a car that should be able to make it, if you trust me to do that."

"I don't really, but I don't want her here." I hold her tighter, wishing I didn't have to leave her when she must be in so much pain and shock. "Hector, Carlos—would you mind watching out for her while we hunt down Allie?"

Hector nods. "We won't be of much use to you anyway."

"Psh, I don't wanna miss the fun." Carlos frowns. "But I guess this is important."

"Thanks." I guide Mom over to them, and Hector takes her from me. "You know who to call when you get there, right?"

"Duh," Carlos says.

A few men come back in to tell The Phantom that his "bullet car" is ready to go. Then we rush back down the halls as Seth looks over Lee Seol's estimates. I don't bother, since it's math and despite my boyfriend's best efforts I'm still barely passing. It's creepy how he's smiling over all the calculations.

"You know how you always say those word problems with the trains are useless?" Seth says. "I'm using that principle right now."

I roll my eyes. "Shut up and use it then."

"Fine."

When we get to the massive garage, there's a vehicle there that looks quite literally like a bullet, with its cone-like front and sleek silver color. The back is much wider, and I guess it's some kind of jet engine. "Is that a rocket or a car?"

The Phantom smirks. "Both. If Allie's on the road, she can't run from this. There's only room for six. If you want all your people, John's coming, too."

"You bet I am," Mr. Mitchell says.

I don't like this idea, but there's no time to argue. "If that makes you feel better."

Seth curses loudly at his phone. "How fast can this thing go?"

"Over three hundred miles an hour, if need be," The Phantom says. "Why?"

"Because she's mostly likely halfway to the Nevada border. Going even double her speed we wouldn't catch up." Seth taps at his screen a few times. "But if it's really three hundred miles, we should be able to find her before she meets up with any O'Connell forces that might be waiting for her."

"Let's go then." Mr. Mitchell is already opening the driver's side door like he's used this bullet car before.

When I get in, I'm met with an interior that looks more

like a space shuttle than a car. The seats are huge and heavily padded. There are also straps that make regular seatbelts look like decorative ribbons. I barely get myself buckled in before Mr. Mitchell starts the roaring engine. As the hole to the surface opens up, Seth says, "You're looking for a medium-sized, white truck with a large tank for holding liquid."

"Like a gas truck," Seth's dad says simply.

"Yup."

I can't help thinking how easy it is to set aside differences when everyone's lives are on the line.

Mr. Mitchell slowly drives the bullet car up the ramp and onto the main surface road. Now that there are windows, I can't help but stare at the scene before us. The Army has tanks everywhere, men on the ground fighting The Phantom's thugs. Gunfire is constant, but there are also shows of mutation power. A flare of fire or a body contorting in strange ways to avoid getting hit. People being knocked off their feet by seemingly nothing. Floating objects hurled back and forth.

Madison has been destroyed. At least from the burning buildings and crumbled structures I can see. The sight is more painful than I expect. This place—where I found myself and my friends and my life—is on the verge of destruction. I can't stand it. And yet there's nothing I can do but go after the girl who could ruin the rest of the world.

"Hold on," Mr. Mitchell says as we swerve onto Main Street.

The engines sound like they're charging up, and before I can blink we're thrust forward so fast it takes the breath from me.

Chapter 44

It's a good thing there aren't many cars driving the freeway in the middle of the night, because there's not much Mr. Mitchell can do besides honk his horn continually to warn people we're coming. I know planes travel quicker than this, but it's shocking how fast three hundred miles an hour is on the ground. Everything outside is an inky blur with hardly a flash of light to interrupt.

"How are we supposed to spot the truck in this thing?" I ask.

The Phantom points to a screen in the dashboard. "There's an extended vision camera and scanner. We'll see it."

I nod, satisfied. I'm impressed with The Phantom's technology—it's much better than he ever let on. He made it look like he'd just brought a brute squad, but clearly it's so much more. Of course, I should expect this from a syndicate second-in-command, but I guess all those years of Dad saying Juan was an idiot influenced my perception.

Pretty sure Juan's not even close to stupid.

I don't know how long we've been traveling, but both Mr. Mitchell and The Phantom perk up as something flashes on the screen. Even from my seat I can see this vehicle looks more like what Allie might be driving. The Phantom leans over to Seth's dad and says, "Don't kill her on sight. I want to see this cure."

"Yes, sir."

Raising an eyebrow, I turn to Seth. Sure enough, he's looking right back at me. I don't want to say anything out loud, but The Phantom's interest in the cure is bad. All that matters right now is stopping Allie, and yet what happens after is what scares me most.

"Better watch our backs." Bea's voice fills my ears, and I turn. She and Brady hold hands across the small aisle. Her eyes almost meet mine. "This might get dirty for real."

She's right. I don't want to, but I prepare for what we might have to do to survive. Even if that's killing.

"That's it," The Phantom says. "It has to be."

Mr. Mitchell begins to slow the bullet car, and my body presses against the seatbelt straps. Though it feels like we're going much slower, we still pass cars in a blink. The reflection of a white truck shines in our headlights, and my adrenaline goes into overdrive.

Seth's dad turns the wheel and slams on the brake. We swerve around the truck and stop horizontal to the highway. The truck's lights blare into my window, and I worry Allie will slam right into us out of revenge. But just before she hits, the car stops and she's out at a breakneck pace.

I slam my palm on the button to release my straps, shoving the door open as fast as I can. But I'm immediately met with the ping of a bullet against metal. I jump back in, but leave the door where it is.

"You better leave!" Allie screams. She sounds nothing like

311

the sweet girl she pretended to be. "I have backup coming!"

"We gotta move," The Phantom says quietly as he looks my way. "This one's you and me, Fiona."

"Yup." I start undressing, despite the utter embarrassment I feel in front of Seth.

The Phantom smirks. "You get the gun. I'll distract her."

"Got it." With the last of my clothes off, I opt to open Seth's door next.

Sure enough, Allie shoots again. "Stay where you are!"

I go back to my door, while The Phantom slips out in his incorporeal form. Peeking my head out to see how she acts, I'm glad I waited because she fires two quick shots—both of which fly right through The Phantom.

Allie seems to be shaken by this, but she stands her ground. "I don't know how you found out, but you're already too late. Make sure to tell Juan that, before he kills you."

As quietly as I can, I step out of the car and slowly make my way toward her. The Phantom smiles cruelly. "As you can see, I'm pretty hard to kill."

"Oh really?" Allie laughs. "Keep telling yourself that."

"Tell me about this cure you've supposedly made," The Phantom replies. I'm closing in on her, the gun just yards from my fingertips.

Allie stares him down, and I wonder if she's trying to hypnotize him. More than that, I wonder if it'll work when he's incorporeal. "There's no 'supposed' about it," she answers. "The first test worked, and the rest will only make it stronger. Then the O'Connells will be in charge of the whole world, and Jonas will never leave my side."

It makes me sick to hear her say my father's name, to know she's so addicted to his scent that she believes she's in love with him.

"Prove it." The Phantom comes a little closer, putting Allie on edge.

Allie seems to like this answer. "You want to try one?"

"Maybe." He looks away, and I get a sense that he might actually want to. "I get tired of being hungry and thirsty all the time. It'd be nice to be normal." My eyes widen at the admission. I don't know if it's real or if he's being hypnotized, but either way he's wavering. I have to act fast.

"Here." She reaches into her dress pocket—I assume to get the pills—and that's when I grab the gun. Her eyes go wide, and her grip tightens around it. "Get off!"

I shove her arm toward the ground, trying to block her fingers from the trigger. She fights back, but I'm stronger. I can get this gun from her. I know it; she knows it. All it comes down to is when.

Allie tries to trip me, but she can't see my legs. "Ugh! Stop!"

"Give me the gun!" I step on her foot, and she lets out a shriek. "You tricked my brother! You made me help my stupid father again! You think I'll let you get away with that?"

She manages to elbow me in the side, and I falter to the point that she almost gets control again. I don't know where my backup is, but I sure could use some soon if she keeps being so stubborn.

"Your brother was the easiest mark ever," she says. "He *wanted* to believe me. Maybe it runs in the family."

My anger flares at her words. She'll so regret saying that. I throw my head into hers, and it knocks her to the ground. The gun is mine, and I throw it as far away as I possibly can. Allie searches for me, fear suddenly replacing all her confidence. "No hypnotizing me. What will you do?" I ask.

She glares in my general direction. "You're such a waste of talent."

"Feeling's mutual." The betrayal hits anew. I thought she was such a good person. She had all these noble goals and the talent to reach them. "Was any of it real? Or did you even have a sister that died?"

Her lips purse. "That was real."

"How could a hypnotist like you fall for my dad?" I say, though I know it doesn't quite work like that. His smell would get her before she ever looked at his eyes.

"He let me study Radiasure. He believed in me when no one else did."

"So that wasn't the Major…" I can see my dad taking Allie in as a young girl, secretly "mentoring" her just in case she proved useful. In fact, she's probably why he discovered the real Radiasure formula first—he knew to look because of her.

"Where's the drug?" Mr. Mitchell yells, and that's when I realize everyone else has gotten out of the car. They stand behind me, ready to attack. Maybe that's why she hasn't tried to fight back. "You're stalling with your little stories, but I'm not stupid enough to fall for that."

I frown, realizing he's implying that I am. "It's in her pocket."

Allie's glare is furious. "You're such a flip-flopping traitor, you know that? Why are you helping them? I'm the one who helped you!"

My voice is caught in my throat. It *does* feel wrong to side with Juan's syndicate on this, but her side's not any better. When I think about all that's happened, I *have* taken whatever side helped me most. Does that make me as bad as her?

"More like you used her," Seth answers. "You only helped her because it meant helping yourself! Fiona had the merinite—you had to play nice with her family. You're the traitor."

Allie looks at the ground. "I did what I had to do."

I stand a little taller. Maybe we are the same, but that might not be a bad thing. "It's too bad we want different things. That drug is *not* going to a syndicate—I don't care what good it can do if you're giving it to my father."

"Enough of this crap," Mr. Mitchell springs forward like a cat. He stands over her with the gun pointed at her head. "Hand over the pills, or I'll shoot you and then take them."

Allie doesn't move, doesn't speak. I feel sick because Seth's dad will do it. And though she messed with Graham's head and deceived the Major and tried to steal the merinite, I still don't want to see her die. "Allie, please hand it over. It's not worth your life, is it? You can't do anything when you're dead."

"Shut the hell up," she says, though she digs into her pocket and pulls out a small plastic bottle. It glows red in the darkness.

The Phantom strides forward. "Give it to me!"

She smiles wide, and then she throws it over their heads. "Go and get it."

"No!" Mr. Mitchell looks back just long enough for Allie to kick him in the balls, and he crumples to the ground.

She dives for his gun, but The Phantom is there first.

Bang.

His shot hits Allie in the head. She's gone. Bea whimpers, covering her eyes at the same time Brady shields her from the gory scene. I stand there frozen, not ready to accept that she's dead. Just like that. The Phantom didn't even think twice about it.

"Make sure they don't move," he says as he hands the gun back to Mr. Mitchell. "I'll get the drug, and we go. The O'Connells' backup can take care of the body."

"Yes, sir." Seth's dad turns to us, holding up the firearm.

The Phantom heads for the glowing speck of red in the dark desert. All my warning bells go off as I watch him. If he gets that bottle, it's just as bad as Allie having it. She's already done the hard labor—all Juan has to do is work on it some more to make the cure better.

I want to run over there and get it first.

There's no guarantee Mr. Mitchell won't notice my footsteps as I sprint.

But I take off anyway.

Chapter 45

Everything is chaos in my ears. Mr. Mitchell yells something, but then Bea's voice screeches over that and there's punching. Loud punching. Is it Brady? There are gunshots, but I don't look back. I keep my eyes on the red pills, on The Phantom's dark silhouette ahead of me.

I'm faster. I gain on him, but this only makes me nervous because I don't have time to hide my footprints on the dusty, dry ground. They will give me away, and I'm not sure how to fight someone I can't touch.

Taking several steps at a diagonal, I decide it'd be better *not* to be close when I pass him. I pump my legs as hard as I can, the fact that I'm naked barely registering against my goal. The Phantom hears my footsteps, and his face fills with rage as he searches in vain for my body.

"Don't you dare!" he yells into the night.

The pills are feet away, and I crouch down to grab them. When I turn, I'm shocked to see he's right there—he doesn't hesitate to slam into me. He feels perfectly solid as we hit the ground.

"Give me the pills!" His hands reach for them, but I move them just in time.

I push and struggle against him, hating that he's so close when I have no clothes on. That discomfort is distracting me more than I want to admit, but I try to focus on keeping the pills from him.

The Phantom finds my neck and squeezes. "I can kill you, too. You know I will."

My first instinct is to pry his hands off, but then the pills would be within reach and he knows it. My lungs burn, and I kick wildly as I try to throw him off. I get weaker as my body begs for air.

"I've strangled people before," he says with a disturbing note of enjoyment. "I know it doesn't take long."

I can't reply. My vision is getting hazy.

"Fiona! Throw them over here!" Seth screams. Hope blossoms in me. I don't know exactly where he is, but it sounds like he's to my right. So I chuck the bottle as hard as I can.

The Phantom jumps up, his only focus the cure and the power that comes with it. I gasp for air, attempting to pull myself up to see what's happening. It's dark, but there's enough light from the cars to see that Seth has the bottle and Bea and Brady stand in front of him as protection.

Mr. Mitchell has his gun trained on them, while the Phantom stands there huffing and puffing. Seth opens the bottle, pouring the pills into his hand. "Hell, I'll swallow them all myself."

My jaw drops, knowing just how painful that would be. Possibly painful enough to cause death.

"You're bluffing," his dad says.

"I will do it." He looks at the pills. "There's only five."

"Seth! Don't!" I pull myself up, but my legs are too shaky

to run. "You could die!"

He shoots me a look, and I think it might be a little bit vengeful. "It's not fun when the people you care about sacrifice themselves, is it?"

"Yeah, yeah." His dad is the one who answers this. "You've made your point. Put the pills away now. You know I can shoot you before you swallow those. Stalling will get you nowhere."

"Just shoot him," The Phantom says. "We're wasting time."

I can't quite tell in the darkness, but I think Mr. Mitchell hesitates.

The Phantom turns to him. "Can you not shoot him because he's your son? Then give me the gun."

Seth's dad slumps. "I…can't do it."

"Tsk, here." The Phantom walks over, and I can't believe what's happening. Bea lets out a loud scream in an attempt to stop them, but they fight through the pain. Brady lunges forward. Seth moves the handful of pills toward his mouth.

And I'm too far away to stop any of it.

I should have never thrown that bottle.

The Phantom puts his hand on the gun, and I think that's me screaming but I'm not sure. Then there's a loud bang, and I freeze because surely it's too soon. The Phantom barely touched the firearm. He couldn't have shot at Seth yet.

But then The Phantom's knees buckle, and Mr. Mitchell catches him before he hits the ground. It takes a second for my brain to realize what happened.

Seth's dad shot The Phantom.

"You…" Blood sputters from his mouth as Mr. Mitchell gently lays him in the dirt.

"Sorry," Seth's dad says with a smile that says anything but apologetic. "Had to make sure you were solid when I pulled the trigger."

"How...c-could...?" The Phantom goes limp.

I stand there, dumbfounded. When Seth's dad faces his sons, I have no clue what to expect. From the looks of it, neither do they. He scratches his head and says, "C'mon, you really think I'm heartless enough to let you guys get hurt? I've done a lot of horrible things, but I'm not that far gone."

"W-why?" Seth finally gets out. "You waited so long. You sold us out and everything."

His dad holds his hands out to the empty desert. "No syndicate witnesses out here. All I have to say is that the girl killed him and then I killed her. Everyone thinks I'm still loyal."

Brady frowns. "What about us? Won't they expect you to take us back?"

"Maybe." Mr. Mitchell stoops down and pulls something off The Phantom's hand. My guess is it's a ring. "But they won't question me if I tell them I got the command ring from The Phantom before he died. Looks like I just got a promotion. Lucky me."

My jaw drops. "You planned this, didn't you? Your goal was to get second-in-command out of this somehow."

He turns in my direction, his smile shrewd. "No better way to protect the ones you love than to be in power, right, Fiona? Yes, I've been working my way up so I could have enough sway to keep Juan's eyes out of Madison. Did I know it'd happen this soon? Not exactly. But opportunity knocked."

"So..." Seth looks extremely uncomfortable, and I can't begin to imagine how he feels about this. "What now?"

His dad shrugs. "I take the bullet car, you take the truck, and we haul ass back to Madison. After that? I pull Juan's men out, and you decide what you want to do with those pills. Because as far as I'm concerned, what Allie had was all a bluff—the wrong stuff. Damned Phantom was following a dry creek."

Seth nods slowly. "And what about you?"

"What about me?" He looks confused for a second, but then seems to understand. "I imagine you won't be seeing much of me anymore, though I don't think you'll mind that, will you?"

Seth and Brady look at their feet, seeming resistant to admit the truth.

"Take care of yourselves. Don't get into any more trouble." Mr. Mitchell turns his back to them at this point, heading for the car. He throws my clothes out and shoots off before we've made it to the road.

No one speaks as I get dressed. Or as we drive the dark road back to Madison. Or as we veer off towards the cave to dump the stolen merinite back where it belongs. It's only as we pull up in front of my house, which looks just the same as ever, that Bea says, "Did that really happen?"

"I think so," Brady answers.

"Let's get inside." Seth heads for my home. The second we step inside, we're met with a crowd of worried faces. The Navarros, my mom, Miles, Lee Seol, Graham. They practically tackle us in relief, asking questions much faster than any of us can answer them.

"She's *dead*?" Graham cries when we get to Allie.

My heart breaks for him. Maybe she didn't make the best

choices, but who does these days? I'm not proud of mine lately. "I'm so sorry, Graham. The Phantom just…"

He covers his ears, and his feet hit the ground. "No."

"I know, hon." Mom is right there with him, comforting, though she's been through a lot today. It looks like Rosa has already healed Mom's wound. I kneel next to them, adding my hug to Mom's.

Then Miles comes, patting Graham on the back. "It's a lot to take in."

"Yeah…" Seth winces. "I don't mean to intrude on the grief, but there's still more to tell you."

We talk until there are no more words to say and daylight brightens the windows. No one seems to care about that—we all agree it's time to sleep, since it looks like everything has settled as much as it ever will.

Seth follows me up to my room, and when he shuts the door I already know what he'll say. "What should we do with these?"

He pulls out the bottle of pills, which we somehow neglected to mention. I stare at them, my heart twisting with conflicting emotions. I want to keep them so badly, but I shouldn't. It would be hypocritical, wouldn't it? And yet to have just a few more opportunities to see myself…

I gulp. "I don't know, Seth. I can't pretend I don't want them."

"I know." He comes closer, taking my hand and pressing the bottle into my palm. "I think we can all agree the caves have to go, but I don't think I have a right to tell you what to do with these. Not now that they'll probably be the last of their kind."

Curling my fingers around the bottle, I take a deep breath. "I need to think about it. My brain is fried."

322

"Mine too." He wraps his arms around me, and for a second everything snaps back to normality. It feels weird, but also amazing. I can only hope there's more of this to come, but who knows for how long? "Sleep well, okay? Call me when you wake up."

He starts to pull away, but I grab him back. "Stay."

"Are you sure I won't get in trouble for that?"

"Not today." I bury my head in his chest and take a deep breath, though we're both grimy. After almost losing him however many times today, I don't care what he smells like. "I can't be alone after that. The more I think about what happened…it's scaring me worse now."

Seth runs his hand over my hair. "Okay, I'll stay then. Don't have to twist my arm."

I look into his eyes, the ones that have always seen me better than I see myself. He kisses me, and I wonder if I'm better off believing his vision of me than my own. But still, I keep those pills under my pillow the whole night.

Chapter 46

Major Norton comes by a couple days later. He's in shock about Allie, but he doesn't seem as bad as Graham. My brother is a husk of a person, losing the girl he loved, knowing it was all a lie to her. I wish I knew what to do for him. All I can manage is trying to convince him to eat.

"It seems Juan's men have completely pulled out of the area," the Major says as he sips at some coffee I made. "My guess is you know why."

"I do." Yesterday Seth found the deed to his house signed over to him and Brady, as well as Mitchell Construction. Turns out their dad had been hoarding a lot more money than they could ever dream of. "But I'm afraid I can't tell you about it. I hope that's okay."

He nods slowly. "There are some things that should be kept buried."

"Like the factory?" I ask tentatively.

"It seems that's the best I can do." Major Norton lets out a heavy sigh, and I wonder if he might be the most "heroic" of us all. He at least had the best motives, I'm sure. "I wished for so much more, but it's clear now that time can't be reversed."

A lump forms in my throat, because as I've thought over what to do I've come to the same conclusion. "Maybe there's another way to make the world better? If anyone could find it—I think it'd be you."

He smiles. "I don't know about that, but I won't stop trying."

"Me either."

"Good." He stands, looking proper in his dress uniform. The Army is having a ceremony for those lost in the fight two days ago. "I better go. Will you be attending?"

"Yes, of course," I say as I follow him to the door. "How could we not honor the people who tried to keep our little town safe?"

"Thank you." He salutes my family, who are all crammed in the living room. He particularly zones in on Graham. "I know it might be difficult, son, but if you ever wanted to serve in my unit I'd be happy to have you."

Graham doesn't answer. I'm not sure he even heard the offer.

Mom frowns. "Maybe I'll talk with him later, you know, when he's had time to heal some."

The Major nods. "I'm sorry for not getting you out sooner, Lauren. We should've taken greater precautions."

Mom bites her lip. "It's okay. My family was there for me."

"They certainly were." He tips his hat, and he leaves without asking about Miles or Lee Seol. I'm grateful for that.

"I hate the Army," Lee Seol states once he's gone. "But that dude isn't so bad. I'd *almost* consider doing a job for him."

Miles raises an eyebrow. "That's high praise, coming from you."

She elbows him. "It is."

I sit in the recliner, so I can see my whole family there at once. Even though we're a little bit broken, knowing they're safe means everything to me. I'm glad I have them to lean on when things get hard. And now that I've seen myself I can't deny how much I belong to them. My face said it all.

Smiling, I finally know what I want to do.

After the ceremony, Seth, Brady and I go for a run in the desert. The path has been battered, and yet the familiarity of this place can never be taken from me. Because it's my home, no matter who else thinks they can claim it. We stop in front of the cave, take it in.

Seth looks at me, seeming a little nervous. "Are you sure?"

"You could think about it more," Brady says.

"I don't need to think about it more." I walk forward and put my hand to the giant boulder blocking the cave.

"But what if you change your mind?" Seth asks. "You do that sometimes."

I shoot him a glare. "That's why we *need* to do it, right?"

They're both silent, staring at their shoes. I get the sense that, even after all that's happened, a big part of them doesn't want to give up this place.

I don't want to, either. Not really. But sometimes you need to give up things—good things—for the better stuff ahead. "I thought that seeing my reflection would fix everything bad I felt about myself, and it didn't. I thought a cure would fix the world, but it won't. I thought we could keep this place without suffering the consequences, but we can't. I think I'm gonna try accepting life the way it is. Maybe then I'll be happy with all the really amazing things."

Brady lets out a sad sigh. "I guess you're right, but it still sucks that I have to bury it."

"Yeah." I lean on the boulder and pull the pill bottle from my pocket. I've kept it with me every second since Seth handed it to me, but now I think I'm ready. I pop open the cap and pull out one. "I decided I need my family to see me. They deserve that much after all this."

"Fair enough." Seth leans next to me. "What about the rest?"

"I don't want them anymore." I smile, never thinking it was possible to feel this way. "It might sound crazy, but I *like* being invisible. I don't want to be something I'm not anymore."

Seth smiles to his ears. "You have no idea how glad I am to hear that."

"I kinda like hearing it, too." But I also know I might never have come to that conclusion if I hadn't seen myself. It was a stupid thing to chase, and yet I'm sure I had to do it. With that in mind, I hold out the bottle to Brady. "Here, the rest are yours."

His blue eyes widen with surprise. "What?"

"I know you need them." I grab his hand and place the pills in his palm. "Maybe they'll help you figure out how to be okay with yourself, too. You've been trying so hard, but it feels impossible, right?"

Brady wipes at his eyes. "Thanks, Fi."

"Of course." I pat his arm. "But you still have to destroy this place first."

He lets out a short laugh. "Okay, okay. Meet me at home?"

"Sounds good." Seth grabs my hand, and we take off.

We run like that for a long time, listening to the mountain

crumble behind us and watching the horizon open up in front of us. I can't help feeling like we're leaving all our troubles behind, and everything ahead is full of miraculous possibilities.

Acknowledgments

First and foremost, I have to thank Sara O'Connor and the Hot Key Books team for asking me to write more about Fiona and The Pack. Without their desire for a sequel to *Transparent*, this book truly would never have been written. Thank you, everyone, for your support and love for this world I created—it means so much more than I can express.

Secondly, thanks goes to my extraordinary agent, Ginger Clark, who believed I could write this book in six small months and reassured me all along the way. I feel so fortunate to have you on my side! I couldn't ask for a better publishing ally.

Blindsided wouldn't have happened without the tireless encouragement of my two friends and crit partners, Kiersten White and Kasie West, who read this novel as I wrote it, one challenging chapter at a time. Thank you so much for always being there for me, both as writers and friends.

Also, thanks to Michelle Argyle, Jenn Johansson, Renee Collins, Sara Raasch, Stephanie Perkins, Sara Larson, and Candice Kennington for being the best writer friends a girl could ask for. You guys are my Pack, and just like Fiona I'd be lost without you punks.

I have to give a big shout out to Kayla Olsen, who critiqued *Blindsided* in record time, and gave me key feedback to make the book a lot less embarrassing to send off to my editor. And of course thanks goes to Jenny Jacoby, my editor, for making my book so much better with her editing skills. Thanks so much for helping me look smarter than I am.

Last but not least, I owe so much to my family. To my husband, Nick, thank you for supporting me through the crazy drafting and editing, for watching our kids as I ran off to the library so many times, and for being patient with my crazy schedule. You are the best husband of 2013! To my wonderful mother, Kim, and my sweet mother-in-law, Barbara, thank you for taking your big share of hanging out with my kids as well—your support means everything to me. And to my little sister McKenna, thanks for being my biggest fan and always reminding me why I write in the first place. Love you all!